"I kill them because they're trying to kill me. That's all there is to it."

"Allow me to send you to the afterlife!"

PRINCESS OF WHITE LIGHTNING

Isana Gayhone

MERCENARY

Zig Crane

"All I care about is if you're willing to pay me what the job's worth."

"Please protect my companions."

MASTER SWORDSMAN

Alan Clows

"You shithead...!"

THIRD-CLASS ADVENTURER

Elcia Armet

WITCH
AND
MERCENARY

CHARACTERS

WITCH

Siasha

"It's been so long since I last talked to someone that I got carried away. Please forget every-thing I said."

WITCH AND MERCENARY

CONTENTS

Witch and Mercenary

Majo to Yohei Vol. 1
©Chohokiteki Kaeru (Original Story)
©Kanase Bench (Illustration)
This edition originally published in Japan in 2023 by
MICRO MAGAZINE, INC., Tokyo.
English translation rights arranged with
MICRO MAGAZINE, INC., Tokyo.

Seven Seas press and purchase enquiries can be sent to
Marketing Manager Lauren Hill at press@gomanga.com.
Information regarding the distribution and purchase of
digital editions is available from Digital Manager CK Russell
at digital@gomanga.com.

Follow Seven Seas Entertainment online at
sevenseasentertainment.com.

TRANSLATION: L. Kino
ADAPTATION: Regina Geronimo
COVER DESIGN: Nicky Lim
INTERIOR LAYOUT & DESIGN: Clay Gardner
COPY EDITOR: Jade Gardner
PROOFREADER: Amanda Eyer
EDITOR: Laurel Ashgrove
PREPRESS TECHNICIAN: Melanie Ujimori, Jules Valera
MANAGING EDITOR: Alyssa Scavetta
EDITOR-IN-CHIEF: Julie Davis
PUBLISHER: Lianne Sentar
VICE PRESIDENT: Adam Arnold
PRESIDENT: Jason DeAngelis

ISBN: 979-8-89160-302-8
Printed in Canada
First Printing: October 2024
10 9 8 7 6 5 4 3 2 1

Witch and Mercenary

NOVEL

1

WRITTEN BY

Chohokiteki Kaeru

ILLUSTRATED BY

Kanase Bench

Airship

Seven Seas Entertainment

PROLOGUE

"THEY'VE SURE GATHERED QUITE THE FORCE," a young man murmured under his breath as if he could hardly believe the number of troops milling about the encampment. Mercenaries, the lord's personal soldiers, and even militia were preparing to head out.

Another man standing nearby cleaning his sword chuckled as he overheard him. "Of course they have. You can never be too prepared, eh? It's a witch we're hunting, after all."

Witches.

They were said to wield unknown arts called "magic" that could manipulate even the weather. It was said that long ago, a witch destroyed a country that provoked her wrath overnight. Another created a flood that swept a village away just for fun. Those were but two of the countless rumors illustrating how dangerous they were.

It had been many years since the creatures known as "monstrosities" roamed the continent, and so people from other countries were seen as the biggest threat as of late. But the one mysterious entity that still remained in these lands was the witch—the epitome of terror and dread.

"Was it really necessary to go so far just to win an inheritance dispute?"

"That's not for us to judge when we volunteered for the job."

"Touché."

The driving force behind the mission was the succession issue faced by the lord of these lands. He had two sons—twins. Both were equally skilled and possessed the same stubbornness that prevented them from reaching a compromise.

They quarreled incessantly over who should succeed their father, constantly trying to outdo each other and earn brownie points. It seemed the elder of the two had finally taken it upon himself to distinguish himself by hunting one of the witches of legend.

Apparently, he had determined that he would need the aid of more than just his private soldiers. As a result, he threw money around to attract men ready to fight, resulting in today's massive gathering.

"I'll do anything as long as the coin is good..." the young man said to himself as he crossed his arms. "Still, this is my first time going after a witch."

He looked to be in his midtwenties, with short, cropped gray hair and a large frame rippled with muscles. His face, covered in scars, gave him an intimidating presence that left no doubt as to what his profession was.

This young man was Zig Crane, a mercenary.

"Magic, huh? I suppose I could turn to fairy tales for tips on how to deal with it."

Zig tried to imagine battling this unknown enemy, racking his brain for ideas on how to handle the situation. Some of the idle chatter he heard at taverns mentioned how witches could conjure balls of fire without using any tools or call forth the wind, but he remained dubious that these kinds of feats were even possible.

"Regardless, witches *do* exist. Putting aside whether magic is real or not, it'd be wise to assume they're capable of all the tricks the gossip suggests."

Zig had his doubts when it came to magic, but he accepted that the threat witches posed was very real. There were too many stories about the damage they caused to dismiss them all as fairy tales, and many major powers were eager to subjugate them. In the past, several other forces had been sent after the very witch they were tasked with hunting today, but they all ended in failure. This mission was clearly far beyond the scope of any lone individual.

Because of this, Zig originally believed witches weren't a singular entity, that perhaps they were representing some sort of group. *Maybe they're part of a state-sponsored coalition, or perhaps a crime syndicate...*

But whatever the case, the pay wasn't anything to scoff at, and the request was a legitimate one that came through the guild. The hefty commission showed how hazardous this mission was, but taking on dangerous tasks was the very nature of this line of work, no different from his previous jobs.

I can't let my guard down, but there's nothing to be afraid of either.

That was all Zig was thinking as he waited until the time of departure, blissfully unaware that this misconception would greatly influence his future.

The subjugation force departed about thirty minutes after the leaders of the various mercenary bands and troops of regular soldiers wrapped up their deliberations. With a group of a hundred mercenaries and a hundred soldiers, there was no missing the squadron as they marched through a thick forest filled with tall trees.

Their lack of preparation combined with the many outsiders within their ranks would make them incredibly vulnerable to surprise attacks, but armed forces biological weapons wouldn't stand a chance.

They had the advantage of greater numbers.

There was no way they could lose.

There wasn't a man among them who thought otherwise.

That is, until they saw *it*.

The first signs of an abnormality appeared early in the afternoon. Some of the soldiers sent to scout ahead returned with reports of a house.

"I haven't heard any word of someone living out here. It's highly likely this is the enemy's base."

The captain of the squadron was skeptical that it was truly a witch they were seeking. Not one person from any of the other subjugation forces ever returned. Even if it was a witch they were up against, would it really be possible for her to dispose of so many men by herself without leaving even a single survivor? No matter how powerful an enemy was, surely there was a limit to how much they could do all on their own.

He surmised that their best chance of success would be to catch their target unawares and surround her. He already had several scouts deployed around the troops' periphery. In addition, he ordered holes to be dug at various points along this cordon and deployed mercenaries to wait inside them—they were going to act as a living shield.

He felt a bit of remorse after giving the command, but the men were being paid handsomely for the job.

After advancing into the forest a little longer, they reached a clearing.

"That must be the house the scouts reported," the captain said. "Something about it seems off, though."

It was slightly larger than the average private residence, but even from a distance, it didn't appear to be made of wood or stone. If he had to make a guess, it looked like it was constructed from earth.

It wasn't that you couldn't make a home from such a material, but why choose *earth* of all things in an area where lumber was so bountiful? His mind was still trying to wrap around this incongruity as he began to give his men orders.

"Everyone, be on your guard. First squad, surround the house and sweep through the interior. Second squad, you're on support. All other squads should patrol the—"

His words were cut short, gaining a barrage of questioning looks from his subordinates. They soon realized why.

A woman had appeared in front of the house from seemingly out of nowhere.

She appeared to be in her early twenties, with ink-black hair that flowed down to her waist and eyes so vividly blue they looked like the seas pulling him into their depths. The contrast was emphasized by her skin, so pale it was as if she were bathed in moonlight.

She was a woman of unparalleled beauty, but there was only one emotion that rose in the hearts of every soldier that laid eyes on her: fear.

This was the witch.

"...Prepare yourselves for battle, men!" the captain yelled. "The enemy is the witch straight ahead. Ready your shields! Archers, prepare to fire!" He shot off a flurry of instructions, leaning on his years of experience to beat back the overwhelming feeling of dread.

This was much, much worse than he expected.

Out of all the enemies he encountered in the past, this one was far and away the most dangerous. He felt like punching himself for taking the situation so lightly. After a beat of hesitation, the soldiers scrambled to follow his instructions.

It was at that moment that the witch cast her hands in their direction.

She appeared to be saying something, but she was too far away for them to be able to make out the words. While she mumbled, the soldiers finished their battle preparations.

The vanguard crouched down with their shields lined up before them while archers notched their arrows in the rear.

"Ready... Fi—"

The captain was about to give the order when a strange smell filled the air—a pungent odor that he'd never smelled before.

"What is that?" someone asked.

But as soon he spoke, the earth bared its fangs.

Goosebumps rippled across their skin as the pungent odor spread through the ranks. The soldiers began to murmur among themselves as they noticed the change in the atmosphere.

Zig sprang into action. His instincts screamed that if he remained where he was...he would certainly die.

He leapt onto one of the nearby pack horses, using it as a springboard to grab a branch from one of the tall trees flanking the squadron.

Even though he didn't weigh as much as a heavily armored knight, one would think it impossible for someone with the amount of equipment he was carrying to make such deft movements. However, years of training and mercenary work had made his body resilient and capable of these feats.

The moment he grasped the branch, cracking noises reverberated from the earth as conical spikes, about the height of an average human, shot out from the ground. They jutted up one after another, impaling anyone they encountered. In the blink of an eye, many of the soldiers were dead.

They hadn't expected an attack like this, let alone the direction it would be coming from. It sent the squadron into a state of panic.

"Come on... This has to be some sort of joke, right?!"

Chills ran down Zig's spine as he looked in horror at the scene playing out beneath him. If he had been a second slower in making his move, he would've been yet another soul among the dead.

"Damn it. What in the hell is going on?"

He climbed to the top of the tree, scanning around to see what had caused such horrible devastation. That was when he noticed the witch directly facing the troop of frontline soldiers.

"No way... So it really *was* a witch?" Even if he wanted to, there was no denying it. There was no other explanation other than it was the witch's doing.

In the intense chaos, some of the troops began to flee.

They're gonna run away? Zig shook his head disapprovingly.

Half of the commission had been paid up front; they had all accepted the job knowing the dangers involved. Working as a freelance mercenary, the issue of breaking trust wasn't that big of a deal to Zig, but choosing the easy way out once he'd made up his mind wasn't his style. He was the type who stuck to his guns.

Still...

"I just have to pray the guy who hired me isn't one of those corpses..." Zig sighed as he leapt from the tree he was using as scaffolding.

The witch's attack caused a great deal of damage, but not enough to completely decimate the entire squad. The earthen spikes weren't strong enough to penetrate through heavy armor, and some of the soldiers in light armor were lucky enough to avoid them.

The witch gently stomped the ground.

"Don't worry about her. Attack!"

A volley of arrows was released at the captain's order. However, something rose from the ground, blocking the seemingly countless projectiles.

Whatever it was that protected the witch took the shape of a large shield. Two of these earthen creations were large enough to fully cover a person, and she had three of them. They floated around her, slowly revolving in the air.

An armored knight raised his spear and rushed in for an attack. The witch turned to face him, and the shields moved when she raised her hand. The knight thrust his spear into the middle of one with all his might. The strike caused some cracks, but the bulwark held. The second shield rammed him from the side, his position preventing him from dodging. The blow dented his armor and forced him to release the spear. As he fell to the ground, the third shield crushed him from above.

The other men froze at the sound, which was much like a large piece of fruit being squashed.

The first shield began to mend itself, and the soldiers stepped back in stunned silence.

"You monster..." The captain winced in agony as beads of cold sweat ran down his body.

The witch recited something unintelligible and clapped her hands.

The ground began to shake as a rumbling filled the air.

"Wh-what's going on?!"

A pile of earth and clay gathered before the witch. The rumbling ceased as she waved her hand, transforming it into a humanoid shape twice the size of an adult man. Its body was stout and slightly hunched forward. It had no face, and it reminded the men of the golems from fairy tales.

The witch pointed toward her attackers. The figure turned in the direction she indicated and began to walk forward.

"Here it comes! No cowering! Prepare to engage!"

As the troops regrouped in order to intercept the clay figure, the witch continued to cast spells that would strike down the invaders once and for all.

A shadow suddenly appeared.

Zig dashed out from behind the soldiers, dodging the clay figure's side attack and leaping into the air, using its body as a foothold. Taking advantage of the momentum, he brought his sword crashing down.

"Nghhh!"

The witch hastily manipulated the shields, stacking two of them on top of each other to block the blow. The force of Zig's attack almost cut through the middle of the second shield.

He clicked his tongue in annoyance. "I didn't expect this to be so tough."

The witch looked slightly shocked as she quickly moved the third shield, but Zig kicked it away while pulling out his sword.

The shield swung at him but missed due to the distance he managed to create between them.

Zig and the witch stood about ten paces apart. They exchanged no words, but it was the first time since the battle began that the witch had shown any sign of alarm.

She stared at the man before her gaze shifted to the weapon he carried. She'd never seen anything like it before. The handle was at the center, with longswords extending from either end.

A twinblade.

A weapon scarcely used in battle due to its structure, it was difficult to employ in military formations since the whole body was required to wield it. If the user's competency wasn't up to snuff, the weapon would handle them more than they could handle it. Just one look at the sword was enough to tell it was heavy—it was no wonder that the slashing attack from earlier was so powerful.

The witch was aware of the danger she was facing, but...the twinblade's weight made it difficult for the man to maneuver within a small radius. Because of the distance between them, she could do as she pleased. She decided to improvise and use her magic to take him out from long range.

A moment later, the ground exploded.

Zig closed the gap with such quick steps that he appeared to be an illusion. The range she thought she had wasn't nearly enough. Her breath caught in her throat as he swung the twinblade in her direction.

Immediately, the witch changed the spell she was casting and moved the shields to protect her. The attack sliced through the second shield, which was still repairing itself. Without even needing another swing, the blade on the opposite end of Zig's sword repelled the first shield and sent it flying. The third shield, however, was able to block the weapon as it swung back around.

With his twinblade and the earthen shield locked in a dead heat, Zig saw the witch's face for the first time. He looked into those blue eyes, trying to understand the emotion dwelling deep within them.

The witch glared at him and sent a stone projectile flying straight for him, but he raised his gauntlet, deflecting it. His speed took her aback, but the third shield had given her enough time to cast another spell.

A new shield emerged from the ground beneath Zig. He leapt back, avoiding it as more spikes burst from earth—he was simply too fast for them to find their mark.

The witch was puzzled. How was he anticipating her magic? This man didn't look like he could use it himself. Was he using some technique to detect whenever her spells activated?

If that were the case...

Zig kept a close eye on his opponent while he caught his breath. Battling a witch was an unexpected challenge, but he was putting up a better fight than he'd expected.

The fact that she wasn't very adept at close-range combat was a big factor, though not surprising. Her long-distance attacks were so powerful that it made sense she didn't have much experience fighting in melee. Her magic was potent, but their skirmish was like a person struggling to crush a winged insect. Although she could handle many attackers at once, duels didn't seem to be her forte.

And then there was *that*.

"Whoa."

He dodged to one side and again distanced himself as he caught a whiff of the pungent odor. He didn't understand why, but there was always that particular smell before she released her magic.

Offensive spells gave off that stench, defensive ones smelled a bit like iron.

Thinking back, he remembered the same irritating scent wafting around them right before the witch's initial attack. It had been much stronger then. Perhaps the strength of the odor changed depending on the scale at which she was casting magic.

However, the witch didn't seem to be aware of that tell. Each time he detected and avoided an attack, she looked utterly perplexed. He was grateful she hadn't figured it out yet—all he had for protection was a breastplate, thick greaves for his legs, and gauntlets on his arms. They were enough to ward off sword attacks, but he wouldn't last long if he took a direct hit from the witch.

Fortunately, she seemed to feel threatened by his assault as well. It would be impossible to destroy all her shields, but if he could somehow slip through and land a blow, he had a chance. He braced himself, not wanting to miss even the smallest chance of an opening.

The witch started to move. Which was it going to be this time? Offense or defense?

Zig readied himself but was immediately hit with such a suffocating odor that it made him grimace. She was attacking...and it was going to be stronger than anything she'd cast so far.

He fell back to shake off the chills that were running down his spine.

Spikes once again erupted from the ground, though they didn't seem to be focused on him. One after another, their positions appeared random, scattering all over the battlefield. The barrage didn't seem to discriminate between the regular soldiers and the clay figure that were still locked in combat.

Being skewered meant instant death. Even if one of the troops managed to evade a spike, losing their footing would also seal their fate. Zig desperately tried to dodge them. Though he was getting sliced and diced as they grazed him, he didn't have time to worry about his injuries.

The onslaught continued even when the witch lost sight of him, only ceasing when the ground was so littered with spikes that they were the only things she could see.

Her breathing was labored as she scanned the vicinity.

The clay figure was destroyed beyond recognition. Rivers of blood gushed out from countless impaled soldiers, mixing with the dirt and turning it into sludge.

There were no signs of movement anywhere.

Confirming that she was successful in exterminating the invaders, the witch heaved a sigh of relief, her body weary after casting so many spells in succession. She couldn't recall the last time she'd felt so worried for her life.

She had just turned and started walking away to rest when a loud roar echoed out. Whirling back around, she saw something leaping through the wall of spikes.

Zig appeared once more, cutting his way through the dusty clouds. The witch's eyes widened in astonishment. He was covered with wounds and his protective gear was in tatters, but his fighting spirit was very much intact.

"Gwaaaaah!" He brandished his twinblade and let out a piercing battle cry.

She immediately tried to create some protective shields, but her movements were sluggish. The strain of pushing herself so hard earlier was likely taking its toll.

He instantly cut through two of the shields while she was still forming them, but she was somehow able to protect herself with the remaining one. However, it was unable to stop his momentum and the blow knocked the shield away. The witch tumbled to the ground, and the shield—which she'd lost control of—turned back into a lump of dirt.

Getting back on her feet, she was met with a blade thrust right in front of her face. She stared at Zig, who was panting heavily. After a long pause she finally said, "I didn't think *anyone* would be able to avoid all that."

It was the first time he heard her speak and he wasn't expecting her voice to sound that way. She seemed composed despite the circumstances, and yet...her tone was no different from any other young woman.

But...she was a witch.

"Are you going to kill me?"

He slightly grazed the witch's throat with his blade, leaving her question unanswered. "Why are you killing people?"

The witch smiled. "What a meaningless thing to ask. Must I have a reason to kill?"

"Answer the question." He pushed the blade slightly further into her throat.

"I kill them because they're trying to kill me," she said. "That's all there is to it. I don't really care whether humans live or die. There, are you satisfied?"

"I guess."

The witch shrugged. "You could spare a little sympathy for me, you know. Relatively speaking, I'm the victim here. Although...I did kill a lot of them."

"I'm a mercenary. You could be a pleasure-seeking killer or a benevolent member of the clergy, but once I've agreed to and accepted a request, all I can do is kill you."

The witch looked utterly crestfallen at his response. "Seriously? In that case, there was no point in asking that question."

"That's not true."

"How do you figure? Whatever. Please just get it over with." The witch squeezed her eyes shut and stuck out her neck.

It was so easy to just end it. Zig silently stared at her throat. *Just how many people have I killed up till now?* He had no right to condemn her—he'd sent so many souls to their graves himself. It was only thanks to making a living from snuffing out countless lives that he survived this long.

She was no different from him.

He just wanted to live—that was the only reason he killed. It was for that reason Zig silently sheathed his blade, turned, and began to walk away.

The witch, growing impatient waiting for the end to come, opened her eyes. "What are you doing?"

Zig sat down on a nearby earthen spike that had broken apart and started to tend to his wounds.

"Can't you tell?" he said. "I'm trying to do some first aid."

"I can see that much. But...umm...do I have to wait until you're done...?"

"Is there something you need? It's fine, just spit it out." He paused for a moment. "Actually, this is perfect. Come help me out."

"Excuse me?" the witch said in bewilderment. Still, she approached to help.

Zig was carefully cleaning out his injuries and wrapping them with bandages. She crouched before him and gently touched his wounded hand.

A vaguely sweet scent filled the air as a faint glow covered her fingertips. Moving her hand so the light brushed against the gash, Zig watched the skin begin to slowly knit back together.

"That sure is a handy trick," he commented.

"Uh, thanks," she said. "So...are you at least going to tell me why? Why you haven't killed me, that is. I doubt you're a bleeding-heart kind of guy."

"Look."

Her eyes followed where he was pointing. On the edge of an area that had a cluster of spikes like the top of a pincushion, she could make out the remains of some regal-looking armor. The set was so mangled that it was impossible to discern who was wearing it, but it seemed to be more decorative than practical. It was likely the corpse of someone of high status.

"What am I looking at?"

"The man who hired me. He's the son of the lord of these lands."

"Oh, my condolences, I guess." Her tone was laced with uncertainty. What was he getting at? "Even though I'm the one who killed him."

"I'm not getting paid if my client is dead, right? I don't work for free."

"Come on, that can't be true! Won't his father reward you handsomely if you come back with a witch's head as your trophy?"

Zig sighed in dismay, realizing that a witch would be unfamiliar with how human politics worked.

"Picture this," he said. "Your precious son gathered a bunch of troops and went off to subjugate a witch, but the only one who made it home alive is some random mercenary. Just this guy...and your son and the rest of his squadron are all dead. There's no proof. No one saw anything, but somehow, he has the witch's head. If he comes back saying, 'I was the only survivor, but I killed the witch, so can I get my money now?' what do you think is going to happen?"

She looked thoughtful. "In the best-case scenario, he'd be hanged. If he's not so lucky, he'd be tortured, and his body would be put on display at the prison gate after being dragged around the town."

"Exactly." Zig took on work that required him to kill in order to live. If it wasn't possible for him to get paid, then there was no longer a job to do. Killing the witch would only be for his personal satisfaction.

Thus, he wasn't going to.

"...So that's how it is?" The witch dropped her gaze to the ground, brow furrowed, like she was considering his words. Zig, oblivious to her ruminating, finished tending his wounds and began to examine his equipment.

His armor was tattered and falling apart. The cost of the repairs alone meant that this entire endeavor had been a complete waste of time. He almost wanted to cry as he crunched the numbers in his head, trying to see if his income could cover his various expenses.

To add insult to injury, he knew he needed to avoid taking any jobs in this region for some time. He doubted anyone would remember the face of a random mercenary who'd joined the eradication force, but it didn't hurt to be cautious.

"And you're okay with all this?"

Zig completed his preparations and was still considering what his next move should be when the witch's voice brought him back to reality.

"Does it really matter?" he asked. "When I take on a job, I do as I'm asked. I won't betray my client, but I'm not so righteous as to go back and make a report that's going to get me killed. The squadron was annihilated—this witch hunt was a failure."

"No, it was a success," she protested. "The witch was defeated by the valiant sacrifice of the soldiers and would never show her face in these parts again."

And we all lived happily ever after, right?

The witch prattled on like she was spinning her own fairy tale. As he once again started thinking of what he should do next, something she said caught his attention.

"Wait, what are you talking about?" Zig asked.

Her gaze took in his confusion. "I want to hire you as my bodyguard."

"Are you serious?!" he blurted out before he could stop himself.

"Of course!" she replied proudly.

"Why?"

He couldn't read her intentions. The witch, meanwhile, could see the bewilderment written all over his face. Her eyes remained downcast, but her lips curled into the smallest of smiles.

"I'm tired," she said softly. "I'm tired of being pursued time and time again. Tired of having to keep changing where I live. I'm always being hunted, and I've had it."

Her face wore a look of resignation, as if she was weary of life itself. She looked like a young woman, but in that moment, he could see all the years she lived weighing heavily on her.

Zig remained silent. Once again, those eyes of bright cobalt rose to meet his.

"I want you to take me to a place where no one will come after me."

Though the request was ambiguous, and she didn't seem to have a plan, her tone was laced with earnest sincerity.

Zig examined her face, recognizing the expression on it.

She had the look of someone who had nothing left. Someone who was standing at the edge of a cliff and on the verge of ending it all.

Standing back and watching it happen would be no skin off his back, and he was well aware of the effort required to keep her from teetering over.

All the more reason to refuse.

"Sorry, but I'm not interested in your sob story."

She looked like she wanted to protest but stopped short, swallowing the words as she cast her eyes down.

"All right. Sorry for asking something like this out of nowhere."

She looked up again, a lonely smile playing across her lips. With a laugh, she said, "It's been so long since I last talked to someone that I got carried away. Please forget everything I said."

Her laughter rang hollow. When she realized the feigned mirth wasn't fooling anyone, she hung her head again.

"I'm a mercenary," Zig said.

"I know."

"I'll take any job if it pays enough. I'm the type who's even willing to kill other people. That's why..." He glanced at the witch. Her eyes were still locked on the ground. "...All I care about is if you're willing to pay me what the job's worth."

The witch gasped, looking up to meet Zig's stare.

That's right. I'm a mercenary. I'll take on any job, no matter how troublesome, as long as I get paid.

He was a seasoned professional. He wasn't his younger self anymore—the novice that would have wholeheartedly chosen to stand back and watch her fall.

"Can you pay?"

"Y-yes! I can pay! I can pay you!"

The witch looked flustered as she fished around in her clothes. After a while, she seemed to find what she was looking for and presented Zig with a gem. "This should work as an advance payment, right?"

The jewel sitting in her palm was a deep shade of crimson and about the size of a child's fist. Its gleam was captivating, a sight to behold as he studied it.

"Hmm."

"What do you think?" the witch said proudly. "Magnificent, isn't it?"

"I don't know..." he said slowly.

"What...?"

"If I had a talent for evaluating jewels, do you think I'd be working as a mercenary?"

"I suppose you have a point, but..." She seemed disgruntled—that gem probably meant a lot to her.

"Is it really that good?" Zig asked skeptically. "How much do you think I could get for it?"

"I dunno."

He looked exasperated. "You're killing me here."

"Why would a witch know anything about human exchange rates?"

"You've got a point. Still, this could be an issue."

The gem would probably fetch a considerable sum, but when taking all the future expenses into consideration, he couldn't say for sure if it would be enough. As he puzzled over whether he could make ends meet, he remembered something she mentioned earlier.

"You called this an advance payment, right? Do you have more gems?"

She nodded. "Yes. I have three more that are about the same size. Is that not enough?"

"That's not what I'm saying. We can talk about my commission later in more detail." He began to mumble to himself. "Three more, huh? That should work..."

She gave him a questioning look, so he continued his explanation.

"I'm going to be blunt here. There isn't a place on this continent where a witch won't be pursued."

Her face immediately darkened. Since all the other aspects of mysticism on the continent had vanished, witches were the only feared entity remaining. Everywhere they went, they were faced with hostility.

Each nation actively sent out witch-hunting expeditions to save face and show the other countries that they weren't afraid of these creatures of folklore. There were cases when deceased people were posthumously declared witches to boost morale, while others were falsely accused and persecuted for witchcraft. And that was just the tip of the iceberg.

"This continent's been embroiled in disputes for ages," Zig said. "Whether it be skin color, language gaps, or cultural differences... the people here are desperate to snuff out anything that's remotely different from them."

"It's so foolish," the witch said as she stared into the distance. "No matter how much time passes, they never change."

She had lived for so many years... It was likely she was a long-time witness to the disgraces of humanity.

Zig smiled self-deprecatingly. "I guess that makes guys like me, who are able to put food on the table thanks to those conflicts, the equivalent of parasites."

"Oh! No, that's not what I—"

"It's fine. I knew what I was getting into when I signed up for this line of work. Let's get back on topic. What it comes down to is there's nowhere in these lands where an extraordinary entity like a witch is going to be welcomed."

"You can't mean to suggest..." The witch gasped as realization dawned on her.

"That's right. You'll need to go to the unknown continent."

There was one other continent that the people of this continent had been aware of for some time now, but the currents were rough and being unable to read the tides meant that it was initially unreachable. However, a survey of the tidal currents had recently been completed, and boats that could withstand the rough conditions had been designed and manufactured. Following the mass production of these boats, there were plans to start dispatching full-scale research groups.

"What about all the talk that you can't traverse the waters with today's ship-building technology?" she asked.

"How long ago did you hear this 'talk'?"

"Oh? I wonder how many years it's been. One, two, three, four..."

Zig sighed as he watched the witch start to count on her fingers. *I never realized a difference in life span caused such a discrepancy in one's sense of time...*

It's been some twenty-odd years since he heard the bold proclamations of, *"Passage to the unknown continent will be possible in the near future!"* as a young boy.

Just how old is this witch? Zig wondered before going back to discussing the plan. "Investigation teams are leaving for the unknown continent soon. We'll infiltrate one of them."

"Is that even possible?"

"It'll cost money, but the chance isn't zero."

The investigation teams were usually made up of many foreigners as state-sponsored expeditions were difficult to conduct due to the lingering possibility of invasion from another country. Instead, merchants from various countries would work together to open a new sales channel, pooling their resources to reduce the involved risks.

Each nation planned to take advantage of this concept by sending their own personnel to join the investigation team. Not only would they be able to keep an eye on enemy movements, but they could also determine what sort of profits they might gain from the unknown continent.

Since all parties involved were keeping tabs on each other, no one could afford to devote too much manpower to the project, but they couldn't ignore the far-off land brimming with possibilities either.

"It should be pure chaos at the moment, so there's no better chance to sneak in than now."

The witch silently processed all the information he had given her. *His proposal does make sense, but there's no guarantee witches won't be persecuted on the unknown continent as well. No one even knows what's over there in the first place! It's highly possible that I could be in greater peril than being hunted here.*

Still...

"Jumping headlong into the unknown doesn't sound so bad if there's a chance I won't be scorned or pursued," she said with a slightly cocky smile, her resigned attitude from earlier completely gone. "Are you okay with that, though? It may not be easy for you to return if you accompany me all the way over there."

"That's fine," he replied. "It's part of the job. Besides, I've gotten tired of seeing the same battlefield scenery over and over again."

Zig had no hesitation when it came to killing people. He survived so long by being a soldier for hire, he didn't know any other way to make a living. But that didn't mean he enjoyed it.

"Well, I look forward to being in your care...umm..."

That's right. He hadn't given her his name.

He smiled wryly as he extended a hand. "I'm Zig. Zig Crane."

The witch seemed taken aback by the gesture, her eyes wide as she gazed at his outstretched hand. After a moment's hesitation, she gingerly reached out and gripped it tightly, as if she were trying to reassure herself.

"It's nice to meet you, Zig." A smile broke out on her face as she felt the warmth radiating from his hand. "My name is Siasha. Just Siasha."

Witch and Mercenary

CHAPTER 1

JOURNEY TO THE UNKNOWN CONTINENT

AFTER ABOUT TWO DAYS OF TRAVEL BY HORSE-DRAWN carriage, they arrived in Estina. It was a coastal nation with thriving trade and fishing industries. And, thanks to the multitude of ships constantly coming and going, it was where they'd try their luck at infiltrating the investigation team.

"That's...*incredible.*"

Siasha gasped in astonishment at a sturdy-looking ship that loomed over all the others in the port.

"That's the main ship for the investigation team, the one for all the VIPs. What we're trying to board is that foreign vessel over there." Zig pointed at a ship that was about half the size of the one next to it.

The witch's eyes narrowed at the sight.

"Are you disappointed we have to take the small one?" he asked.

"What do you think I am, a child?" she retorted. "That's not it..." As she shook her head in disgust, her tone became wistful. "I was just wondering why humans spend all their energy on fighting when they have such amazing technology."

"Because it's easier to take someone else's success than to succeed on your own. A lot of conflicts start for that reason alone."

"What a harsh and petty world we live in."

"Some people have an insatiable desire to innovate, others have an insatiable desire for depravity."

"So, those driven by greed are revolutionizing the world, despite going about it in completely different directions."

"You've pretty much hit the nail on the head," Zig said. "Anyway, let's head into town and get a room. We can start preparing for our journey after that."

"All right," Siasha agreed.

Rations, camping supplies... The list of things they needed to buy seemed endless. Since Zig's protective gear was completely in tatters, it needed replacing as well. To make matters worse, the influx of people arriving in the city for duties related to the investigation team made securing a room even more difficult. The only opening they could find was at an upper-class establishment, and thanks to all the commotion, the rates were higher than usual.

"S-seriously?" Zig stammered. "One hundred and thirty thousand for a double room per night?!"

"Calm down, Zig. Keep your cool."

Siasha tried to placate Zig after the huge blow to his wallet left him trembling, but she couldn't help but giggle. The man who came at her wildly flourishing his sword without even a hint of fear was shaking in his boots like a new recruit!

It took a little while for him to recover from the shock, but once he had his bearings back, Zig started to go over what items they would need.

"So that's all of it?" Siasha asked. "Okay, let's go shopping."

"Not yet," he said. "We've got to exchange those gems for cash. We don't have any money."

"Oh...right."

With the gems being their only chance of recouping what they'd spent on the room, the pair headed out to look for a jeweler. Since many merchants frequented the city, they were soon able to find a relatively large establishment.

As Siasha was about to enter, Zig stepped back.

"What are you doing?" she asked.

"You're going to be the one to exchange the gems," he said.

"What? But I've never done anything like that before!"

"Think about how it'll look if a mercenary randomly shows up with a bunch of gems. I'll probably be arrested on the spot for suspected theft." He tried to look reassuring. "You'll be okay. A large establishment like this isn't going to be too ruthless since it might mar their dignity and reputation. Besides, they're not going to just be looking at the gems; they'll take the client into account too."

"The...client?"

"The way someone behaves reveals their status and prestige. Clients that possess those qualities get better treatment...apparently."

"Hey!" she said in indignation. "You're going to spring that unsettling information on me at the last minute?!"

"It's just something I heard from a merchant I shared drinks with once. Well, I don't think it's too off the mark...probably." He pushed Siasha, who was still squealing her displeasure, into the shop.

All eyes were on them the moment they stepped into the quiet interior. The merchants passed over Zig, thinking he was just Siasha's bodyguard. Instead, their attention locked onto the beautiful black-haired witch.

The barrage of stares made her flinch.

"Think of them as your enemies," Zig whispered. "Treat them like you would as a witch. Just don't overdo it, okay?"

"All right." Siasha squeezed her eyes shut and took a deep breath before slowly opening them.

Suddenly, her demeanor was completely different, a shift so dramatic that it felt like the temperature inside the shop dropped. All the staff and even the other customers were transfixed on Siasha as she smiled captivatingly.

It may not have been deadly, but no one could deny the witch's overwhelming presence.

"May I help you with something, Miss?"

Snapping back from the shock and remembering that they were proud professionals who needed to conduct themselves as such, one of the shop's clerks approached her.

"I have some items I'd like to sell." Siasha produced the gems, impressed by the clerk's quick recovery.

"An appraisal, is it?" they asked politely. "Please allow me to take the items."

The clerk placed the gems on a tray and headed toward the back of the shop. Though their face didn't betray any emotion, they were surprised at the size and luster of the jewels. After some time, they returned to where Zig and Siasha were waiting.

"They're all in excellent condition, so we would be willing to purchase the lot. How does three million orth sound?"

That sum was well beyond what Zig expected they would offer, though he tried to hide his amazement.

"That's fine." Siasha, having no awareness of the market rate, accepted without hesitation.

Her ignorance was becoming an advantage. Her demeanor, fine features, and cavalier attitude toward money told everyone in the shop one thing: She was, without a doubt, someone of high status.

After completing the transaction, they left the shop.

Siasha stretched out her arms and sighed. "Phew, that made my shoulders so tense. How did I do?"

"Very well." Zig was sporting a large grin at their unexpected luck. "I figured those gems were quality items, but I never imagined they'd fetch *that* price."

The steep price he'd paid at the inn was a drop in the bucket compared to three million orth! Despite all the expenses that lay ahead, that amount was a very tidy sum. And they even still had one of the gems, just in case they needed it later.

"How much money is it, exactly?" she asked.

"Let's see..." He tried to mentally work out the numbers. "If a regular soldier worked around the clock for a year without taking time to even eat or drink, they would probably make about this amount. If you wanted to save up while living in moderation, it would take maybe four to five years."

"Wow, that's great!" Siasha grinned and clapped excitedly. "So, will this do as an advance payment?"

"What are you talking about? This amount is enough to pay for an escort with all the bells and whistles attached and then some."

"No, no. This can just be the advance payment."

"...Pardon?"

Zig's good mood was suddenly overcast with dark clouds of doubt. Being offered *too good* of a commission automatically triggered his danger senses, especially in his line of work.

"Just what are you expecting of me?" he asked.

"I was thinking I'd keep you on as my bodyguard and advisor once we reach the other continent."

"Your advisor?"

Siasha scanned the vicinity as they walked. "I've been thinking about it ever since we got here, but I know far too little about living in society. I don't know what sort of food that stall is selling, for instance, or even how to go up and buy it." She pointed at a stall selling chicken skewers. "I want to try that."

Zig approached the elderly vendor. "We'll take two, Gramps. Plus whatever drinks you happen to have on hand."

"Coming right up!"

The stall owner got their orders ready in a flash, and they continued to walk as Zig started to eat his portion. He took a big bite out of his skewer, showing Siasha—who looked confused on how to eat her own—what to do.

She followed his example, albeit a little more daintily. A smile spread across her face as she savored the taste of the chicken before continuing to speak.

"Basically, I'd like you to teach me various things until I've acquired enough common sense."

"You do know the place we're going is just as unfamiliar to me, right?" he said.

"Still, I'm sure you have a leg up on me," she insisted.

"Probably, but wouldn't it be easier to hire a local guide once you get there?"

"It's a matter of trust."

Siasha took a sip of her fruit water, the tart liquid making for a perfect palate cleanser.

"Trust, huh... What have I done to earn yours so much?"

"At the very least, I know you're a man who loves money enough that he's willing to offer his services to a witch. As long as you see me as a worthy meal ticket, I'm confident you won't betray me."

"Interesting logic," he said with a nod. "But you're right, I do love money."

Siasha nodded approvingly and held out the money bag. "I'll pay your commission in installments. This amount will be for your advance payment and to cover all the necessary expenses, okay?"

"Sounds good." Zig took the hefty bag from her.

"I'll make sure you get your money's worth," she assured him.

"I'd expect nothing less."

The sun was setting by the time they finished buying the rest of the items they needed and found a blacksmith they could pay to repair Zig's equipment.

"Shall we get dinner soon?" Siasha asked as their bellies began to rumble. The only thing they had eaten for lunch was the chicken skewers.

"Actually," Zig said, "we've got one more thing to do that involves meeting someone at a restaurant. Once that business is concluded, we can eat."

They soon arrived at a large restaurant with elegant seating and sophisticated decor. The atmosphere oozed with luxury.

"I'm surprised you're familiar with such a high-class establishment." Siasha's eyes were wide as she glanced around.

"This place is for doing business. There are private rooms on the upper floor that can be used for having conversations you don't want others to hear."

He gave one of the employees his name and told them he was meeting someone. The employee bade them to follow and led them to a room located at the end of the second floor.

A diminutive man sat inside, already waiting for them. He looked respectable, but even his well-groomed appearance couldn't hide the shifty air about him.

"Well met, Zig," the man said. "I see you're still alive, somehow."

"And you haven't changed one bit."

The two men didn't seem to waste time exchanging pleasantries and verbal punches. The mercenary took his seat, and the witch sat beside him.

"This is Cossack. He's an informant," Zig explained to Siasha.

She smiled and gave the man a little bow. "It's nice to meet you, sir."

"Charmed, I'm sure," Cossack replied. "Hey, Zig, what's the deal with this looker? Is she your woman?"

"No way." The mercenary shook his head. "She's my client."

"Figured as much. You never were the womanizing type."

"It's a waste of money."

"See, this is what I'm talking about." Cossack shot Siasha a dismayed look.

An ambivalent smile played across the witch's lips; she wasn't quite sure how to respond. Not paying her any heed, Zig started to broach the topic of work.

"About *that* request I made," he said. "Does it seem like it's viable?"

"Oh, that. It is...but it's going to cost you."

"That's not a problem."

Cossack instantly bristled. "You're seriously going? No offense to the lady here, but there are plenty of groups that would hire you with all the perks. I can even introduce you to a few if you want."

"Big groups aren't for me," Zig said firmly without hesitation.

Cossack didn't seem disappointed, likely expecting that response from the beginning. He took out two bangles and handed them over. Just one touch made it clear that they were unique, their design different from any mass-produced item.

"Well, whatever," the informant said. "You've made your decision. The ship's departing in five days. You'll be able to pass as a young researcher and her bodyguard. Consider these as your tickets; make sure you're wearing them on your left arm on the day of departure."

"Thanks."

Zig was looking over the bangle when Cossack asked him another question.

"There're a few mercenaries going along as part of the vanguard unit that's heading over in advance. If you run into them, do you think you could pass along the word to come and see me as soon as they're back from the job?"

"Are they people I know?" Zig asked.

"You'll know if you see them."

"Sure, if I happen to run into anyone."

Cossack nodded, finding the response acceptable. Once Zig and Siasha put their bangles away, the informant called over one of the restaurant's employees.

"We're done with business now," he said. "It's been a while, so let's share a drink. Can you hold your liquor, little lady?"

"As much as anyone, I suppose."

The table was soon crammed with various dishes, with even more on the way.

"Are you going to be able to eat all of this?" Siasha asked, gaping at the sheer volume of food.

"Hm?" Zig glanced at her. "This isn't even that much."

"I'm sure you've witnessed his ridiculous brute strength, little lady," Cossack said. "He consumes just about as much as you'd expect to maintain it."

"Oh, I get it now," she said. "So that's why he can keep his physique even after eating this much?"

The realization seemed to placate Siasha as she watched Zig eat his fill. The contrast of the small and dainty bites she was taking next to him scarfing down the food made Cossack chuckle. As they ate, the two men spent time catching up and making small talk.

Suddenly, Cossack, who was only eating to accompany all the drinks he was knocking back, sighed.

"It's not like you to sigh," Zig remarked.

"I heard a rumor about you not that long ago."

"Oh, yeah? What was it?" The mercenary washed down his meal with booze and leaned back to take a short breather from feasting.

"The rumor implied you might be dead."

"Heh." Zig let out a chuckle. "I haven't heard that one before." *But I have a good idea where it came from.* He feigned ignorance, leaning forward to appear interested in what Cossack had to say.

"Not too long ago," the informant continued, "there was a big fuss in the neighboring country about one of the lord's sons orchestrating a witch hunt. He decided his personal troops weren't enough, so he sent out a call for mercenaries. Apparently, you were one of them."

"You know your stuff. I wouldn't expect any less of an informant."

"With that conspicuous weapon of yours, even an amateur would be able to suss it out. Anyway, the mission was a success, but it came at a considerable cost. The bodies were so mangled that not a single one could be identified.

"Apparently, it was a grizzly sight. The lord's first son and all of his troops were annihilated, and there were no other survivors beyond a few mercenaries that managed to run away. Two fairly well-known groups were completely wiped out in the battle." Cossack looked thoughtful. "Still, it must've been a brilliant battle if they were able to take down the Silent Witch."

"The Silent Witch?" Zig repeated. He gave Siasha a sideways glance, but her face revealed nothing.

"Don't tell me you took on the job without any prior knowledge?" Cossack looked shocked but continued to explain.

"Now, this doesn't go for all witches, but they're usually a combative bunch. If someone encroaches into their territory, they'll attack and try to eliminate them. They'll fight back vigorously to completely eradicate their enemy.

"But this witch is different. She'll try to scare people off if they come into her territory, but she doesn't usually hurt them. Even after being the target of countless witch hunts in the past, she never tried to seek revenge. That's how she got the name—"

"The Silent Witch," Zig finished.

"They say she resided more to the east in the past. Even though she's apparently one of the most powerful witches out there, she won't attack unless the other party initiates, so they didn't consider her to be very dangerous. Ever since the current lord took the throne, it was forbidden to go after her. However..."

Cossack's voice took on a slightly darker tone.

"His idiot son took it on himself to score some points with his daddy. His folly was successful, but the witch's body was never found. The father should be on the receiving end of some punitive action from the upper echelons by now."

Even if he brought it on himself by not keeping his son in check, Zig couldn't help but feel a little sorry for the lord.

Being dealt a punishment from the bigwigs after one of your sons went and got himself killed seems like rubbing salt in the wound.

"Getting back on track," the informant said, "what I want to know is how the hell you managed to come out alive after getting mixed up in all that."

"You said it yourself," Zig said. "No one survived except the mercenaries that ran away."

Cossack snorted as he downed his drink. "Horseshit! Even if you were up against a witch, you expect me to believe you wouldn't have the balls to stay and fight?" He was most likely drunk, but his keen senses as an informant didn't seem to dull. "There's something you're not telling me."

Zig's deadpan expression didn't waver, making it impossible to glean any more information from him. "I don't know what you're talking about."

Cossack shifted his gaze to Siasha. When she noticed him staring, she looked up from her post-meal tea and smiled at him, head slightly to the side. It didn't seem like she was hiding anything either, despite being under his scrutinizing stare. That she was unperturbed was in itself suspicious, and he gave her an even closer look. Even if she was a normal person with nothing to hide, his shrewd appraisal should elicit some sort of reaction. A sheltered little girl wouldn't have the mettle to keep her composure.

Siasha returned Cossack's gaze as she continued to smile at him. It almost felt like those eyes staring back at him were penetrating his very soul. It was incredibly disturbing, and he felt chills running through his body as his danger senses went haywire. The informant experienced many perilous situations in his life, and this felt just like those times...

...No, the danger he was sensing was greater than anything he'd ever encountered before.

From what he could tell from her mannerisms, she seemed like she was swift on her feet, but this girl was an amateur, right? She didn't look like she particularly had any combat experience.

Am I getting spooked by a mere wench?

He remembered the words he said earlier—the witch's body had never been found.

"No. It couldn't be—"

He was cut off by a splashing sound. The wooden cup he was holding was now sporting a hole, with booze leaking out. At the bottom was a silver coin—someone had thrown it with enough force to turn it into a projectile. If the coin had hit him anywhere else...the resulting wound could have been fatal.

Zig slowly looked up, his tone casual. "Let's just keep it at that, shall we?" He reclined into his chair, showing that he was unarmed. "Depending on what happens, I may have to kill you."

At those words, everything clicked into place. Despite not feeling even a hint of malice from the mercenary until that moment, Cossack's blood ran cold.

"Have you lost your mind?" His voice was raspy.

Zig smiled. "How many times have you questioned my sanity by now?"

"Probably every time you've decided to do something overly reckless, but this is different."

"My answer hasn't changed. I'll do anything, as long as I get paid."

"Apparently!" Cossack spat out as he slumped back in his seat with a loud thud. He tried to pour himself another drink before realizing it was impossible due to the hole in his cup. Clicking his tongue in annoyance, he settled for drinking straight from the bottle. By the time he finished downing the whole thing, the previous tension was gone from his face.

"About my fee, it'll be two million orth. All inclusive."

"Are you sure about that?" Zig pressed.

"It's your damn life! Do with it what you please."

It was the same line he used every time he questioned Zig's sanity.

Zig smiled and gave a little bow. "Thanks, I'm in your debt. And since that's already the case, would it be too much trouble to ask you to keep spreading the rumor that I'm dead?"

"Oh, sure, sure. Consider it included in my commission."

"Much appreciated."

"You owe me one."

"I know." Zig placed the bag of gold coins on the table and stood up. "Always a pleasure doing business with you. Later."

Siasha bowed in gratitude before getting up to follow the mercenary.

"Just one more thing," Cossack interjected. "...Did you win?"

Zig paused, his hand wrapped around the doorknob.

"I'm here, aren't I?"

He didn't look back as he left the room.

Five days later, it was time for the ship to depart. It was almost disappointing how easy it was for them to board—they even spent time worrying over escape routes and creating alternative plans in case they were caught!

Despite the initial anxieties, they felt relieved it was all for naught.

The ship was making excellent progress, though the currents were rough. It was as if it was always facing a headwind. They enjoyed only a few reprieves of calm waters.

Regular vessels were ill-suited for traversing these tides, which was why they were on this specialized craft. At least...that was what Zig could gather on their journey so far.

"And...there's basically no information about the unknown continent itself," he continued.

"Huh? What's that supposed to mean?"

It was their second day at sea, and they were lounging in their cabin. Zig was briefing Siasha on the information he'd gleaned, the two of them trying to piece together a vague picture of what their future held.

Siasha seemed puzzled by what she was hearing. "Shouldn't the vanguard unit have arrived by now? Why wouldn't they have sent any word?"

"It sounds like they still haven't been able to get in touch with the ship that went ahead."

According to the plan, one ship was going ahead of the main force to go ashore and find a place to set up camp.

"Maybe some of the local wildlife devoured their messenger pigeons," Zig surmised.

They were hoping to obtain as much information as possible since they were headed to an unknown land where anything could happen, but there didn't seem to be much news from the other passengers.

"We can't help it if there's no information available," Siasha said. "But...there *is* something I've been wanting to ask you, Zig."

Her eyes shone with curiosity as she gazed at him from her position sprawled out on the bed.

"You were able to read my spells before I cast them when we were battling, right? Was there some sort of principle behind it?"

Zig sighed, "Oh, that..."

"I won't force you to talk about it if you don't want to. I understand that a warrior wouldn't be eager to reveal their cards."

After a few moments contemplating, he spoke.

"That's not the problem. To be honest, I don't really understand it myself. Would it make sense if I told you they had a smell?"

Zig didn't know the reason for the smell, but perhaps the witch would have a clue?

"A smell, you say?" she asked slowly.

"Right. It was downright putrid before you cast anything offensive, and when you used magic to heal my wounds, it gave off a sweet scent."

Siasha furrowed her brow and groaned. "Hmm... Was there anything else that stood out?"

"Anything else?" He tried to recall that battle. "Oh, right. That attack of yours that practically turned the ground into a pincushion had a way stronger smell than the other ones."

"This is just a guess," Siasha speculated, "but mana can't be used as is."

"What's...*mana*?"

"Oh, that's where I have to start from?" Siasha's tone began to sound authoritative, almost like a teacher. "Basically, it's the fuel used to cast magic."

Zig listened as she launched into an impromptu lesson. She looked like she was having fun—perhaps she enjoyed explaining things?

"Invoking magic requires several processes. The first process is drawing forth mana." Siasha raised one finger before continuing. "Imagine using a bucket to scoop up water from a lake. The second process is manipulating it."

"What do you mean?" he asked.

"Mana is manipulated depending on the purpose of the spell. You know, using it offensively or defensively... But once it's given a purpose, that's the only thing you can use it for. For example, you can't use offensive mana for a defensive spell. The third process is giving the manipulated mana a form. In other words, the casting itself. There are various ways of doing this, like making symbolic gestures or incantations."

Zig kept listening as he tried to absorb all the information.

"Those are the processes that are involved in invoking magic. I think what you smelled was a reaction from the mana when it was going through the manipulation stage."

"You *think*?" he said. "Which means..."

Siasha looked slightly vexed as her legs dangled off the bed. "Right. I don't know for sure."

Zig watched her pale limbs swing back and forth. "Why not?"

"Being around mana is as natural as breathing to me. It's been a part of my life ever since I was born. I can only make speculations because it's not something I'm consciously aware of. I think it also probably functions differently than smelling something like you normally would."

Zig once again thought back on their battle. "You may have a point. It felt like I was sensing those smells with my mind instead of my nose."

If he had been using his normal sense of smell to detect those odors, it likely would have taken longer for him to realize that she was about to cast magic. Depending on the direction of the wind, he may not have been able to pick up anything at all.

"Hmm..." he mused. "That probably means it wasn't just me. The others should've sensed those smells too."

"I think they did," she replied. "I do recall the troops stirring before I let my magic loose. I just thought they started to realize their lives were in danger, though."

"Why wouldn't they try to avoid it then?" Zig realized the answer as soon as he posed the question. "It would be difficult to make that association right away."

"Exactly. Most of them were dead before they had the chance to connect the dots. And even if they did, it's not like they could've easily dodged an attack of that scale."

"That makes sense. Can I ask you something?"

Siasha got up from her bed and went to sit across from Zig. "What is it? What do you want to know?"

"Why are you in such a good mood?" She was in such high spirits that he couldn't help but ask.

"This is the first time anyone's ever asked me about myself." She smiled bashfully. "It just made me happy for some reason."

Zig felt the corners of his own mouth starting to turn upward at the sight. He put his hand up, trying to hide his expression and appear nonchalant.

"You didn't create fireballs or call forth a flood, though. Why is that?"

One of the witches of rumor was said to have flooded a village before turning anything that managed to survive into a sea of fire. Siasha gave him a wry smile and waved her hand in front of her face.

"That story's been blown out of proportion," she said. "No single witch has that much power. The type of spells we lean toward using depends on our attribute."

"What's an...attribute?" It was another word he had never heard before.

"There's an affinity between each kind of spell and the individual's mana. For example, I'm good at manipulating earth and rocks. It's not that I can't use other materials, but it takes a lot of energy, and the results aren't as effective, so I usually don't.

"However," she continued, "depending on certain conditions, we can accomplish great feats. A witch with a water affinity could probably change the flow of a river to flood a nearby town, just like I could probably cause a landslide to bury a mountainside village."

If that's the case, I guess all the hullabaloo over witches makes sense, Zig thought.

"What about healing magic?" he asked. "What affinity is that?"

"Well, when you're manipulating a body... A human affinity, maybe? Mana is intrinsically part of the physical being, so I think it's something anyone could use. I learned just recently that the composition of witches and humans is surprisingly similar."

"You better not experiment on me," Zig warned.

So magic wasn't just some omnipotent force that one could use to do anything, but abilities with principles behind them. Zig was never one for book learning, but having his curiosity about the unknown satisfied gave him a pleasant feeling.

"That was very interesting," he said. "Thanks for sharing your knowledge with me."

"Not at all!" Siasha said cheerfully. "I'm happy I was able to solve a few riddles myself."

The ship drew ever closer to their destination as the pair continued to discuss—or rather, Siasha continued teaching Zig—about magic.

It was the morning of the twentieth day aboard the ship. The ship's lookout rubbed his tired eyes and peered out into the horizon. He could just make out something in the daybreak haze…

He bolted from his spot to spread the news.

The entire ship was soon in an uproar; yelling voices filled the air as the crew ran to and fro. They had finally made it to the unknown continent!

"So, this is the other continent?" Siasha asked as she squinted into the distance. Nothing looked out of the ordinary except for some mist. "It doesn't look like there are any signs of human life."

She searched high and low through the telescope she'd borrowed from one of the sailors, but all she could see was a single ship. It was most likely the one that the main party sent ahead a while back.

The ship's captain was barking orders at the scurrying crew. From what she could hear, they would be pulling ashore soon. However, only the passengers of two ships would be permitted to alight; the others would remain at sea a slight distance away.

These ships happened to be the ones carrying all the mercenaries and other outsiders. It made sense that these groups would go first—they had to make sure everything was safe. Though they were an eclectic bunch, they were still a force to be reckoned with.

"So we basically have to be scouts?" Siasha asked.

"We'll need to be on high alert," Zig said. "Since no one from the vanguard unit came to meet us, it means there was likely some kind of trouble."

There wasn't a single person remaining on the vanguard ship. Putting aside the fact that they never received contact of any kind, it was very strange that no one was aboard.

The mercenaries and outsiders were ordered to split up into squads of about ten people and explore the vicinity. They disembarked, leaving only a skeleton crew behind. As the squads surveyed the area, some began to talk amongst themselves.

"The ground feels soft here, huh?"

"And yet the terrain is so rough. Isn't it usually smoother? Plus, there's so little grass."

Wetlands in their home continent were usually more even and covered with grass and moss. However, this one was rocky in certain areas, which made it difficult to get a good foothold.

"Maybe the plant ecosystem is different over here."

Zig broke away from his group when they reached the shore and found a small hill he could climb to scan the horizon. He spotted what seemed to be a village far off in the distance.

"It looks to be about half a day's walk away," he murmured to himself.

Feeling relief that there were signs of human civilization, he tried to refine his estimations, stopping short when he felt the ground tremble.

"Was that an earthquake?!"

But there was nothing more beyond the slight tremor. Zig began to head back to his squad, when something caught his eye.

"What's this?"

He squatted down, noticing something shining on the ground. Picking the item up and examining it closely, he found that it was a gold insignia—the type usually worn by soldiers or large bands of mercenaries.

He recognized the design: a pair of hawk wings. Perhaps it came from one of the mercenaries Cossack told him about, the group that was part of the vanguard unit.

"Hmm..." Zig narrowed his eyes. Pocketing the insignia, he headed back down the hill.

Siasha was sitting on the ground a good distance from the rest of their group. As Zig approached, he could see a look of concern on her face as she rested a hand against the earth like she was checking on something.

"What's the matter?" he asked.

"Something's off," she said softly. "Unless the earth is dry, cracks in the soil repair themselves pretty quickly. It's not natural for them to last such a long time in a place where the ground is so wet."

"Maybe they were made recently?" Zig suggested. "Like there was an earthquake or something?"

"No...I don't think that was the cause. If there was an earthquake strong enough to crack the ground, the shoreline would've been even more roughed up, don't you agree?"

That's true, Zig thought. *I don't recall seeing any signs of damage caused by an earthquake when we disembarked.*

The earth slightly trembled again.

"Hm, is that an earthquake?" someone from their group asked.

Zig was beginning to feel uneasy. There was something *very wrong* about this place.

"You two over there!" the captain of their group yelled over to them. "Go back to the main force and report on these findings."

Zig was too deep in thought to give a response.

What exactly happened to the vanguard unit? It wasn't a huge issue that they weren't around, but there must've been a reason they moved out. Their group was also pretty decently sized, but they didn't even leave any traces...not even a footprint.

The ground began to shake again, this time stronger than before. He hadn't paid much attention to the cracks in the earth when Siasha pointed them out, but this time, he gave them another look.

What he saw within seemed to be squirming.

"Look out below!"

At the captain's order, Siasha began to move. Zig quickly scooped her into his arms and jumped to the side. A long object burst out directly from where she had been standing, fracturing the ground in the process.

Zig put Siasha back down and immediately spun around, unsheathing his twinblade and slicing toward their attacker. Whatever it was felt squishy. It tumbled to the ground, cleanly split in half.

"What the hell is this?!" he exclaimed.

It appeared to be about ten feet long and about as thick as an adult torso. It had no eyes and was dappled with pink and red—like the color and texture of muscles stripped of skin. Numerous fangs lined its circular maw, looking more like thorns than teeth.

If he had to guess, those were used for stabbing prey and holding it in place as opposed to ripping it apart. The joints in its jaw looked flexible, like it could extend or unhinge the entire thing in a flash.

This creature fed by swallowing its food whole. By completely engulfing its victims and marring the ground with its movements, it could erase any traces of humans in the area.

"I think we found our culprit," Zig said.

"Thanks for saving me," Siasha groaned. "But what is that thing? It's gross..."

Zig looked around. Judging from the creature's size, it was large enough to consume one grown man. He didn't know how many people belonged to the vanguard unit, but there were perhaps a dozen—or a couple dozen in the worst-case scenario—of these creatures roaming around.

"That's some nerve, attacking *me* of all people from the ground..."

Siasha's tone told him she was beyond offended that her attacker came from the very element she manipulated. A pungent odor started to drift through the air as she moved her hands.

"Don't do it," Zig warned. "There're too many people around. Don't forget why you came here in the first place."

"Ugh! But..."

"Just cast something defensive that's hard to detect. I'm here to protect you, remember?"

"...Fine."

Siasha dispelled the magic she was preparing and started to cast a different spell.

"I directed my mana beneath the ground," she said. "I can detect where they are for you."

"That's a big help."

Suddenly, he heard panicked shouts coming from their group's direction. He and Siasha began running toward them, with Zig taking care to stay close to her.

What they saw when they arrived looked like a scene straight out of hell. The troops scrambled around in a panic as monsters burst up from the ground to swallow them whole before they could fight back.

One man attempting to run away was launched into the air as several of the creatures tried to ambush him at once. Up he sailed... straight into a waiting maw. He desperately tried to break free of the sharp teeth digging into his legs.

"L-let go of me! Le—"

Another monster clamped its jaws around his head, cutting off his screams. His arms and legs went limp as the creatures tried to pull him into the ground like a grotesque display of tug-of-war.

The spine-chilling sight sent the other members of the group scattering in all directions.

"Calm down!" the captain shouted. "Don't split up! We'll get the main force to—"

"They're done for," Zig cut in.

Zig realized there was nothing he could do to help as he watched the carnage unfolding before him. He was about to move away before the monsters turned their attention to him and Siasha when she motioned for him to stop.

"Be quiet. Stay right where you are."

What she was thinking, he didn't know, but he immediately clenched his mouth shut and stood rooted to the spot. The monsters whipped their heads around as if they were searching for something.

He could feel the sweat running down his back as they turned his direction. However, to his surprise, they started to sink back into the ground. The earth shook again, tremors growing weaker as they seemed to head for the ones who'd managed to escape.

Zig remained frozen in place for what seemed like forever. Once all signs of the monsters' presence completely disappeared, Siasha gave a sigh of relief and finally relaxed.

"You can move now," she said softly. "Oh, but try not to make any loud sounds. Use soft voices."

"I see." He kept his voice low. "So, the noise attracts them."

"Right. I thought it might be heat at first, but they all clustered around the captain and the people running away."

The monsters didn't have eyes. Dwelling underground meant that sight probably wasn't necessary. Instead, they seemed to rely on sound to track their prey. They perhaps usually lay in wait beneath the earth, emerging only when unlucky creatures wandered into their territory.

"So those are the kind of creatures that live on this continent," Zig murmured. "Doesn't seem like it's a matter of the ecosystem being different..."

Siasha giggled, almost as if she felt the creatures were someone else's concern. "Sheesh, we've sure come to a messed-up place."

Zig looked up as it struck him that it was going to be much more difficult to keep her safe than he'd initially thought. At least the sky here was also blue.

"Okay, let's make our way back to the ship," he suggested after taking a moment to recover. "They won't be able to come after us in the water."

He was met with silence.

Zig was ready to move, but Siasha remained quiet and still. He gave her a dubious glance. She was staring blankly toward the ocean, her eyes completely devoid of emotion. Something about their emptiness made his skin crawl. Whatever she was watching... he knew it wasn't going to be pleasant.

Somehow able to overpower all his instincts screaming *Don't look,* Zig slowly turned around.

A horned whale, around 165 feet long, was piercing through the massive ship carrying most of the investigation team's forces. It had rammed the vessel so hard its body was protruding about halfway out of the water.

The ship began to sink, broken cleanly in two after the attack. Those closest to it were not spared—the force of the impact capsized some vessels and pulled the others beneath the waves. The ships farther away seemed unharmed at first glance, but if Zig squinted, he could see something clinging to their sides.

The forms looked humanoid, but they definitely weren't human. Their bodies were covered in scales, and they had webbing on their hands and feet. Their faces were filled with malicious intent, and there were so many of them flooding onto the decks that they were impossible to count.

By the shore, the worm-like monsters were attacking a different squad, while the scaled creatures stormed the boat that had brought them to shore.

All Zig and Siasha could do was silently watch the scene play out in front of them.

"Well, then..." he finally said.

"Yeah..."

Both of them turned on their heels at the same time.

"Shall we?" Zig asked.

"Sounds good."

Their adventure had only just begun.

It took around two days for them to reach the village Zig had seen from the hill. They didn't know what happened to the others who made it to shore. There could possibly be some survivors, but they had no desire to find out or offer any help.

Their initial plan upon boarding the ship was to make themselves scarce in the chaos of arriving at the unknown continent, so they had brought along a decent number of rations. However, they soon realized they had no way of replenishing their stock—

they didn't have any of the local currency on them and needed to find a way to procure food.

"This will be our first time interacting with the locals," Zig advised. "This looks like a normal village, but be on your guard... just in case."

"Okay," Siasha said. "What are we going to do if we can't communicate with them?"

"Pray. Also, I can speak three of the primary languages, but don't get your hopes up too much."

"That sounds more promising than finding a god willing to hear the prayers of a witch... I didn't take you for the scholastic type, though."

"My line of work means going to a lot of different countries and talking to a lot of different people. I'm no grammar expert, but I suppose you could say I'm conversational."

I've found an enemy.

How much does the job pay?

I'm hungry.

They were all just phrases that got his point across but were surprisingly handy in a pinch.

After mentally readying himself, Zig entered the village. Siasha stayed close, looking around them.

There were people working in the fields. Most of them had brown or dirty-blond hair and didn't look particularly extraordinary.

"Excuse me, do you have a moment?" He called out to a middle-aged woman. Her skin was a deep tan, likely from years of doing farm work in the sun. She broke out into a grin when she saw his face.

"What's this?" she exclaimed. "I don't think I've seen the likes of you around these parts before, young man. Are you a traveler?"

She understood him! Zig felt a surge of triumph when he realized she spoke the common tongue he usually used.

"Is there somewhere we can get food here?" he asked. "And also a place to rest?"

"Do you have money?" the woman asked.

"No. The ship we came here on was wrecked. Would trading items work?"

"A ship, you say? Don't tell me you traveled here from across the sea?"

"That we did."

The woman gave a sigh of exasperation. "Do you have a death wish? You must be out of your minds to want to traverse the Infernal Sea!"

"The Infernal Sea?"

"You don't even know about that? You really must've come from a far-off place..."

The people living here probably didn't realize that Zig's homeland considered this place to be the *unknown* continent. He couldn't tell if it was due to rural ignorance or if they just weren't aware that the other continent existed.

"To be honest, I've never seen the sea for myself," the woman continued, "but there aren't many that leave for it who make it back alive. The whole area is teeming with monstrosities."

Monstrosity.

That was a word he never expected to encounter here, of all places. The grotesque monsters that only appeared in fairy tales were alive and well in these lands.

He thought back to the worm-like creatures they encountered a couple of days ago. If he had to give them a name, monstrosity seemed quite fitting. He would have never believed such things existed if he hadn't seen them with his own eyes.

The woman was still speaking. "Sounds like luck was on your side. Oh, you wanted food, right? The crops are good this year, so pretty much everyone should have items available for trade—including myself, if you wish."

"That would be great," Zig said. He always kept a stock of small gemstones on hand for times like these.

It wasn't uncommon for rural villages that were far from major cities to not have a type of currency. Sometimes it proved too difficult to exchange for or obtain foreign ones. After searching for a commodity that had value regardless of the country and was also easy to keep on hand, he settled on small gemstones. Any mercenary worth his salt would typically do the same.

Zig bowed his head as a sign of gratitude as the woman eagerly accepted the trade—stating that her daughter would love the gemstones.

"Are there any larger settlements around here?" he asked.

"If you exit this village and keep heading to the east," she replied, "you'll reach a town called Halian in about five days. It's the biggest one in these parts. I'm guessing you're handy with that sword on your back? You might be able to make it as an adventurer."

"An adventurer?" He had never heard of that profession before. *How does one make a living out of going on adventures?*

The thought piqued his curiosity, but he knew he shouldn't keep interrupting the woman's work. He thanked her again and headed back to where Siasha was waiting.

She didn't greet him. Instead, she was staring intently at something.

He was about to ask what she was looking at when a familiar pungent smell wafted up his nostrils. It was very faint—almost imperceptible compared to what he smelled during his battle with Siasha—but it was unmistakably the scent of magic.

But...it wasn't coming from her.

He immediately turned toward the smell and moved in front of Siasha, his stance low to the ground with his twinblade ready.

"Calm down," the witch said. "It's coming from there."

Zig kept his guard up, though his eyes followed to where she was pointing.

"What in the world...?"

A young man was leaning close to a hearth and blowing on tightly packed kindling. Flames radiated from his fingertips as he tried to start a fire. No one seemed to be minding him—was this just a commonplace sight?

Unbelievable, Zig thought.

"No way," Siasha said in amazement. "I never would've thought they used magic here."

"Is he a witch?"

Siasha shook her. "No, he's definitely human. I've been observing him for a while. Everyone has mana; the level depends on the individual, but it would seem that using magic is a thing over here..."

She threw her head back as if she were savoring the fact that they arrived in a continent where they unexpectedly found people like her.

How do I even describe this vague feeling bubbling up inside me? Siasha thought. *I don't have a name for it, but it's not unpleasant.*

Zig counted himself fortunate that she was so lost in thought that she didn't see him grimace. Magic was extremely powerful, and anyone that could use it was potentially dangerous. From what he could tell, the young man didn't look like he was capable of destruction, but still...

"Perhaps it's time to abandon wishful thinking," he muttered to himself.

"Did you say something?" Siasha asked.

"No, it's nothing. I was able to borrow an empty barn for us to sleep in tonight. We'll head out tomorrow at sunrise."

"Got it! Where to next?"

Thoughts about magic lingered in Zig's mind as he began to talk about the next leg of their journey.

Considering there are monstrosities roaming around, he thought, *I doubt the humans living on this continent would refrain from using magic if they could. They probably have some offensive spells. Not on the same level as a witch, perhaps, but who knows what someone underpowered can come up with? I need to come up with a strategy.*

Zig continued to ponder what the future held for them as he led a beaming Siasha to a barn on the outskirts of the village.

"I think I'd like to work," Siasha said.

It was the second day since they'd departed the village and began to make their way to Halian. The witch's sudden statement made Zig stop in his tracks.

He thought over her words and then resumed walking. "For what reason?"

Siasha put her hands on her hips and smiled. "I want to blend in with humans!"

He gave no reply, so she continued, "At this point, it's difficult for me to live without using magic. I mean, it's been all I've known for over two hundred years..."

"I bet," he remarked, trying to hide his surprise at the mention of her exact age.

"That's why I wanted to live in a quiet place that wouldn't attract too much attention and gather information first."

"Right. That was my plan as well."

His mind drifted back to the conversation they had at the village. Magic existed in this society, and using it was so commonplace that it wasn't met with hostility. All this was information he still needed to wrap his head around.

In the meantime, Siasha was still speaking. "However, if there's no problem with me using magic here, I'm thinking maybe it's better for me to try and blend in instead of drawing attention to myself by being distant."

Anticipation glimmered in her blue eyes, a sharp contrast to the resignation he saw when they'd first met.

"I'd like to learn about the positive aspects of humans," she said. "All I've seen are negative ones so far because I've never focused on the good."

"Oh yeah?" Zig asked.

She pouted and glanced at him reproachfully. "Isn't this the part where you're supposed to ask what led to my change of heart?"

He couldn't help but chuckle at her expression. "Why the change of heart?"

"See, was that so hard?" Siasha said smugly. "Well, I'll have you know..."

She trailed off and Zig followed her gaze to see why.

A giant boar stood in the middle of the road. It was about as large as a cow and covered in bristles and a dull-colored carapace. Its tusks were about half as long as its body and sported signs of wear and tear, likely from many previous battles.

"That's a...boar, right?" Siasha whispered.

Zig unsheathed his weapon and went into an offensive stance. "Maybe, but I've never heard of an armored boar before."

The boar aggressively struck the earth with its hoof, staring them down with bloodshot eyes. It saw them as enemies and was preparing to charge.

"Hmph!" Siasha fumed as she channeled her anger into a spell. "How dare you interrupt me just when I was getting to the good part!"

An earthen spike erupted from beneath the armored boar. To their shock, instead of penetrating through the creature's seemingly defenseless underbelly, the spike snapped.

"How hard is this thing?!" Siasha seethed.

The armored boar, while seemingly unperturbed by the attack, seemed to mirror the witch's hostility. It squealed in anger and charged for them.

It was fast, too fast for them to try to outrun.

"I'm going to draw its attention," Zig said. "You take care of the attacks."

Zig moved forward and lunged to the side to avoid the charging boar, using the momentum of his dodge to spin around and slash at its left abdomen. The blade scraped against the armor but left no mark.

The mercenary clicked his tongue in frustration and tried to put some distance between them. Although he didn't deal any damage, the boar turned its attention on him. He kept running, starting a dangerous game of tag in the hopes of pulling it away from Siasha.

There was nothing wild about how this boar gave chase. It was using all four of its legs to grip the ground, allowing it to quickly change directions. Zig feinted and dodged its attacks, slashing at parts of the boar's body that weren't covered in armor as they passed each other.

Siasha watched Zig and the boar, gathering and manipulating her mana as she waited for an opening.

The boar was beginning to slow down as it continued to bleed from the small wounds that covered its body. Zig deftly dodged its charge once more, but the creature forced itself to come to a halt and reared up to swing its tusks toward him.

This was the attack Zig was anticipating.

"Huuuff!"

He shrugged off the boar's tusks with his blade, countering it with a powerful strike to its unarmored knee just as it was about to come back down on its front legs. The twinblade sank straight into its flesh. Zig was careful not to get the blade caught in the bone and, with a swift slice, severed the boar's leg clean off.

He jumped out of the way just in time to avoid being crushed by the boar as it lost its balance and tumbled over.

Now it was Siasha's turn.

Two earthen spikes thrice the size of her usual ones impaled the boar through its sides. The mana she spent time gathering allowed her to increase their hardness, enough that they could penetrate through the creature's armor.

A third spike burst from the earth directly below its head, silencing its squeals of pain.

"That was one terrifying monster."

Zig glanced at the boar's carcass as he tended to his sword. Anyone that took a direct blow from those tusks didn't have any chance of surviving.

They were able to defeat it thanks to Siasha's strong offensive powers, but he didn't want to imagine how many lives it would take trying to kill the creature with a blade alone.

"I never expected monstrosities to be this strong," Siasha said.

If these *things* were wandering everywhere, being out in the open was probably dangerous even for a witch. It was much safer for her to get lost in the hustle and bustle of a human town.

"Hmm..." Zig approached the dead boar after putting his weapon away.

He eyed the side carapace, the creature's largest piece of armor. Some areas were cracked due to the earthen spike, but it was still large enough to be of use.

He took out a knife and tried to carve it from the body.

"What are you doing?" Siasha asked.

"This is a decent piece of armor," he replied. "I could probably sell it. Plus, I've been craving meat."

"I imagine any meat from this thing is going to be quite tough."

Even with Siasha's magic, it took some time for him to remove the carapace that seemed to stubbornly want to stay attached. They also took the boar's tusks—a collector might be interested in purchasing them.

Once they set aside the parts they hoped to sell, Zig turned to butcher the boar for its meat. However, when he cut into its flesh, something white and threadlike popped out.

"What is that?"

It looked like the kind of parasite found inside of wild animals—except it was the size of a worm. The thing wriggled what looked to be its head from side to side as it crawled out of the body and plopped on the ground.

Many more followed in droves, squirming out one after another.

Zig silently put away his knife, gathered his things, and started walking away. Siasha followed closely behind, feeling her hair standing on end.

"Just great," he murmured. "I don't even get any meat."

"I don't think I want any meat for a *long* time."

Witch and Mercenary

CHAPTER 2

ADVENTURERS

S EVEN DAYS HAD PASSED SINCE THEY DEPARTED THE village.

It took them two days longer than expected to reach Halian, as Siasha wasn't used to traveling and Zig had to adjust his pace to match hers.

Halian was larger than he had thought, with lots of people bustling about. A decent number of them were armed, yet they didn't look like mercenaries or soldiers—the types of people Zig would've expected to see carrying weapons. His curiosity was piqued.

"Seems like a big enough place," he said dismissively.

In contrast, Siasha seemed to be at a loss for words, her mouth open in amazement as she wildly glanced around. It was clear as day to anyone who saw her that she was a country bumpkin visiting for the first time.

"Zig!" she said excitedly, "Zig, what is that?"

He looked to where she was pointing. "Looks like an advertisement for a play."

"What about that?" She pointed in another direction.

"That's a type of ice candy. It's made by freezing milk."

Zig followed Siasha, patiently answering her unceasing questions as she darted around like a child in a toy store.

"Then what's that?"

"That's... Uh, what *is* that?"

Siasha was pointing at a humanoid he had never seen before. Their body was covered in fur, with ears poking out the top of their head instead of the sides. To his surprise, Zig realized they were a wolf standing upright and walking on two feet. And yet...they didn't seem to be one of the monstrosities.

The wolf-person was wearing clothes and biting into an apple like a regular human would. No one around them was reacting, which meant that creatures like these must also be pretty common, just like how using magic was acceptable back at the village.

Zig glanced around and noticed several other animals walking around on two legs. They were having conversations, so it appeared that they could communicate as well.

"People come in all different shapes and sizes, huh?" Siasha sounded impressed.

"And...we're just going to leave it at that?" Zig rebutted. *Whatever kind of creature that is, it's definitely not human.*

The amount of things that his mind needed to process seemed to just increase as they continued to walk around.

"I understand your curiosity is nowhere near satiated," he said, "but we need to get money for now. We can't do anything until we get our hands on some of the local currency."

Not to mention they were getting in the way. Since the moment they entered the town, people passing by purposely went out of their way to avoid them and their haul of monster parts.

Siasha glanced at the parts of the armored boar strapped to Zig's back. "Right. Where do you think we could sell that stuff? Maybe at an armory?"

"Maybe? I wonder if they have manufacturing methods to make armaments using materials from various animals."

The original plan was to try and sell the pieces to someone who collected oddities. On their home continent, there was a demand for fine items such as stag horns and the like for use as decor.

"But the animals here aren't normal," Siasha persisted. "These tusks are incredible."

"You have a point," he said. "I suppose there's no harm in stopping by."

They walked along the main road trying to find a suitable shop. It wasn't too long until Zig heard a familiar sound: the clanging of metal. They stopped at a large armory with plenty of customers lined up.

"Welcome!" A female clerk greeted them as they stepped inside. "What are you looking for?"

"I'm looking to sell these pieces." Zig showed her what he was carrying. "Can I do that here?"

"Yes, we can do that," she said giving Zig's haul a quick once-over. "Please bring them over here."

She led them to the back of the shop. Zig handed his items over one at a time so she could examine them.

"Whoa! C-can I get a hand over here?" The clerk staggered as she tried to pick up the carapace.

Zig felt a slight twinge of anxiety as he watched several other employees slowly carry it away.

"The examination process will take a little time," the clerk said. "Please feel free to look around inside while you wait."

Zig nodded, and he and Siasha browsed the shop to see what they had for sale. The armory was rather unusual, with many of the weapons and armor made from organic material instead of metal.

Zig's expression darkened. "This is a strange shop," he mumbled.

"What do you mean?" Siasha came over when she heard him.

"There are practically no mass-produced items. Everything is unique."

"What's strange about that?"

"Soldiers aren't big fans of armaments that aren't manufactured in bulk," he explained. "They're harder to manage and make creating battle formations a challenge because you have to consider each person's weapons. It also makes instructing troops less efficient."

"I see... But wait, don't you use an unusual one yourself?"

Given Zig's description, a twinblade would classify as a unique weapon.

"I can wield a spear too," he said. "I was a halberdier when I was part of a mercenary group back in the day. Now that I work alone, there's a little more flexibility with what I can use. I tried out several options before settling on this. Most people who fight—and not just mercenaries—are usually trained in the basics of all kinds of weapons."

Shops that sold one-of-a-kind items did exist on their home continent, but their patrons were wealthy clients looking for decorations rather than practical weaponry.

"Does that mean the target clientele of this shop isn't soldiers or mercenaries?"

"Most likely. Though, if they're not catering to either group, I don't understand how they're making enough money to keep such a big shop running."

"That's true. It's hard to imagine what kind of person would need all this stuff."

The two of them were still deep in thought when the clerk returned.

"Sorry for the wait," she said. "We're willing to offer you 500,000 dren for the plated boar tusks and carapace. How does that sound?"

Several of the customers browsing the other armor and weapons looked over in their direction. Zig couldn't tell from their reactions if the amount being offered to them was high or low—the currency "dren" was itself unfamiliar to him.

"That's fine," he agreed.

"Great! I'll bring the payment immediately."

He nodded, fully expecting that they got ripped off, but what choice did they have? Glancing at the other customers, it didn't seem like the clerk was cheating them.

The clerk laid the money out on the counter, filling a tray with an impressive number of coins. After counting them out, she put them in a bag. There were exactly fifty coins, so Zig surmised that each one was worth 10,000 dren.

"If I may," Zig said as he took the bag, "what's the going price for your most orthodox blade?"

"Let's see...an iron longsword would go for around 50,000 dren or so," the clerk replied.

"Got it. Thanks."

Zig, now with some idea of the local market prices, turned to leave. However, the clerk called him back.

"I have a question for you as well, if you don't mind," she said.

"What is it?" he asked.

"Were you the one that defeated that monstrosity?"

"No. It was her." He gestured to Siasha.

The clerk's eyes drifted to the witch, who returned her gaze with a vague smile.

"Thank you for your patronage," the clerk said. "We hope to see you again in the future."

"What was that all about?" Siasha asked quizzically as they left the shop.

"Who knows?" he said, trying not to grin. "Anyway, today was our lucky day. We sold those items for a better price than I was expecting."

"The amount seemed much lower than what we got for my jewels. Is it different over here?"

"You can't compare them. If we're talking about where we came from, the amount of money to buy an iron sword here could feed you for about a month. Well...without lodging costs."

"So you're saying this amount covers our living fees for about half a year?" Siasha marveled. "That's not bad at all!"

That would give them plenty of time to look for work. Now that they had local currency, they could finally get down to business.

"First thing's first," Zig said.

"Yup," Siasha agreed as if she read his mind.

"Let's get some food."

"Yay! I'm up for anything but hardtack!"

Zig and Siasha found a random eatery nearby and shoveled down their first proper meal with gusto. They ate without making any small talk until they were satiated enough to pay attention to some of the conversations happening around them.

"How's it been going lately?" they overheard someone asking.

"Those monstrosities have been actin' up as of late. I've gotta make sure and warn our new recruits about 'em."

"It's that time again, huh? Sounds like there's money to be made."

"Speaking of, didja hear? A real nasty one showed up near the highroad. The guild's put out a bounty on it."

"Yeah, our leader's looking for people to take on the job right now."

"Same here. The guys at the top are all gung-ho about it, but they can't come up with the numbers. I wouldn't be surprised if it's not too long before they propose we join up with your clan and make a coalition of sorts."

"Actually, we ain't got the numbers either. It's bloody hard to get enough adventurers over fourth class on the same page."

There was that word again.

"Adventurers, huh...?" Zig murmured. "The lady back in the village mentioned them as well."

"I've never heard of that profession before," Siasha said. "I guess it's a job for exterminating monstrosities?"

"Then why call them that? If they're exterminating pests, wouldn't 'hunter' be more appropriate?"

"I don't know if defeating the boar is in the same vein as exterminating a pest," Siasha mused.

"Are you interested in adventurers, Miss?" One of the employees had come to clear their table and seemed to have overhead their conversation.

Zig started to answer but cut himself off when he saw that the server had his attention on Siasha.

The witch smiled sweetly, catching on that the mercenary wanted her to answer. "I am. I just came here from a neighboring area, so there are a lot of things I still don't know. Would you mind telling me what adventurers do?"

The server grinned and launched into an explanation. They listened raptly despite the man going on tangents with unnecessary details, but they finally were able to get the gist of the job.

Adventurers exterminated monstrosities under organizations called guilds. They earned commissions based on the type of beast slain and could also earn money by selling materials obtained from the creature's body parts. Although guilds technically managed the adventurers, the system was very flexible. Individuals were free to form their own adventuring parties or join an adventuring clan.

"Sounds a lot like a mercenary group dedicated to exterminating monstrosities," Zig remarked.

"Mentioning something like that in front of adventurers is a big no-no, sir," the man warned.

Zig was puzzled. What was it that he said that made it taboo? "Why is that?" he asked.

"Adventurers detest being lumped together with mercenaries," the server said. "They don't like the idea of being compared to people who take others' lives for a living. They're proud of being free spirits who answer to no one. At least, that's what they claim."

"Umm..." Siasha shot Zig a concerned glance, but he looked unperturbed.

"It's a bit deceptive if you ask me. There's not that much of a difference between killing people or killing monstrosities to make your living; it's just a matter of preference. As for that talk about being free and doing as they please, what it all comes down to is there's a demand and it's a way of making money."

"Right..."

This man, despite his playful demeanor, seemed to have a strong sense of his own ideals—even if others may view them as a bit extreme.

"But because of that demand," he continued, "you should be careful. Many of the mercenaries around here are *those* rag-tag criminal types."

Zig felt like his mind froze for a few moments before he understood what the man was saying.

"Are you saying there's less need for mercenaries because there's been a decrease in the number of wars or conflicts around here?" he said slowly.

"A decrease? That's putting it mildly! Aside from minor scuffles, those kinds of things just don't happen here anymore."

"That's impossible!" Zig couldn't believe what he was hearing, but the man's tone and expression told them he wasn't pulling their leg.

Zig remembered the wolf-person he saw on the main road. Humans as he knew them had been fighting each other for hundreds of years over things like differences in their own skin color or culture—they would never have been able to tolerate another form of intelligent life.

"It's because of the monstrosities." He shook his head in denial.

"They've been active since way back," the man scoffed. "Whenever a large-scale conflict occurred in the old days, hordes of monstrosities would apparently show up and storm the camps. They would face attacks equally, and the creatures caused massive damage to both sides. So, as a result of this happening again and again..."

There were no more wars. It wasn't that they didn't occur, it was that they couldn't. Conflicts ceased to exist in these lands...at the cost of monstrosities freely roaming around.

Zig didn't know whether that was a good or bad thing.

"That's how we got the adventurer occupation," the server finished. "If you two think you've got what it takes, why not give it a try? You can quit if it's not for you, and you can rise to the top as long as you've got the skills."

"We'll think about it," Zig said.

"So, Miss, if you've got some free time, how about—" The employee's attempt at hitting on Siasha was interrupted by angry bellowing coming from the back of the shop.

Zig sighed heavily as he watched the man reluctantly step away. "To think such a thing would be possible..."

He thought he was getting used to surprises, but this went far beyond what he could comprehend. Conflict was inevitable as long as humans existed. Even if they were graced with a period of peace, war always returned. There was never a time when mercenaries couldn't find work. It was hard to believe that a single external factor could force all people to work together.

"Are you okay?" Siasha asked with concern on her face.

"I need to concentrate on the job at hand," he said. "I'll think about what to do next when that time comes." He looked at her. "Right now, you should focus more on worrying about yourself. Do you have any idea what kind of work you want to do?"

"Somewhat."

"Oh yeah? What would that be?" Zig already had a good idea, but he figured he should ask, just in case.

Siasha glanced over at the table where they overheard the men talking earlier. "I'd like to try being an adventurer."

It was a valid choice, a way for someone unknown to make decent money as long as they were up to the task. The time it would take to develop the skills needed would typically be the biggest barrier to success, but Siasha was a witch. Even if people here could wield magic, they were nowhere near her level.

It also made more sense for her to be an adventurer than to try a normal job after being alone for years. Siasha as a clerk or a server seemed like a waste of her talents.

"Why not?" Zig said. "I think you'd be good at it."

"You do?" she asked.

"Uh-huh."

They left the restaurant after asking another employee for directions to the nearest guild and set off. They stopped to buy a few provisions along the way, so it was around sunset by the time they arrived.

The guild was housed in a majestic building filled with people coming and going about their business. Siasha was a ball of nerves as she stood before the doors. Even the simple task of going in was perhaps daunting. Zig had been handling everything until that point, and just having an imposing presence, like when she sold the jewels, was likely not going to work this time.

Siasha looked at Zig anxiously. "Wh-what should I do?"

She seemed completely lost. There was no trace of her usually calm and collected demeanor.

"Calm down," he advised. "They're not going to take you seriously if you keep acting too suspiciously."

"I don't want that!" she squeaked. "Should I go in with a bang and show them my superiority?!"

That had the opposite effect of what I was intending, Zig thought as Siasha frantically scrambled to cast a spell. *How can I get her to cool her head? What was it that worked for me as a kid again?*

Zig stepped in front of Siasha as he sifted through his memories. Slowly sliding his hands under her arms, he lifted her as if she was a child.

"Zig...? Whoa!" Siasha cried out. "Hey! Put me down!"

People walking by glanced over to see what the commotion was about but continued on their way, unconcerned.

Siasha struggled in protest, but she wasn't as strong as he was, and she could only flail about in his grasp.

Realizing that Zig wasn't going to let go of her, she stopped struggling and slowly calmed down. "What was that for?" she asked as she dangled in the air like a kitten.

"Have you calmed down?" Zig asked.

"Yes, mostly," she said. "This is embarrassing."

Not wanting to prolong her mortification, he put her down and placed his hand on her head. "It's not unusual to be nervous when you're facing something completely new," he said. "But you need to do this if you wish to live among humans."

"Right."

"I won't tell you not to be afraid of making mistakes, but go about this in a way that one day you can look back and laugh."

"I'll try."

"Good." He roughly patted Siasha's head.

She flinched and batted his hand away. Fixing her messy hair, she took a deep breath. The tension seemed to leave her body as she exhaled.

"Just watch me," she said.

"Will do," he replied matter-of-factly without glancing back at her.

Spurred on by his comforting tone, Siasha threw open the guild's doors with renewed vigor.

All eyes turned to them as they entered. Instead of blatant stares, the adventurers threw sidelong glances as they continued about their business. The looks they gave Zig were appraising, as if they were gauging his strength. The looks they gave Siasha, on the other hand...showed they were captivated by her beauty more than anything else. Siasha headed straight for the reception area, too focused on her task to notice the attention.

Fortunately, the reception counter wasn't crowded, perhaps due to the time of day. Noise emanated from the attached dining hall, with adventurers regaling their triumphs of the day, reflecting on mistakes, and making new plans.

"How may I help you today?"

The person attending the counter was a woman. Siasha felt a small wave of relief.

"Would it be possible to register as an adventurer?" she asked.

"A new registration, is it?" the receptionist asked. "For the both of you?" Her eyes went to Zig.

"N-no," Siasha stammered. "He's my attendant. I'll be the only one registering."

"Understood. Please fill this out." The receptionist handed her some papers. "If you can't write, I can do it for you."

"I-I'm fine."

"Also, we'll need one drop of your blood. Please extract it using this and drip it on here."

Siasha looked a little confused but took the needle the woman held out to her. To her surprise, she sensed magic in the needle and papers. The enchantments didn't seem dangerous, so she calmly started to complete the form.

Once she was finished, the receptionist looked them over.

"You're missing this part and this part here." She pointed at some blank spaces on the papers.

"Oh! S-sorry about that..." The witch hastily made her corrections.

Despite making a couple of mistakes, Siasha finally submitted the forms and the paper containing the drop of her blood.

The receptionist's eyes widened slightly when she checked the paper with Siasha's blood, but the witch didn't seem to notice.

However, Zig did.

Realizing that he was staring, the receptionist loudly cleared her throat. Zig tore his gaze away and looked around the hall to distract himself.

Confirming that everything was in order, the receptionist filed the papers away. "Lastly, I'll conduct a brief interview with you," she said. "I'll also provide more details regarding our activities."

"Okay." Siasha's posture straightened as she mentally reassured herself that the process was nearly over.

"You don't seem to have a weapon from what I can see," the receptionist commented. "Are you a magic user?"

"Yes," the witch replied.

"Do you use offensive or defensive magic?"

"Huh? Um..."

The unexpected question made her freeze on the spot. Siasha didn't know much about the magic being used in these lands and didn't want to come up with a hasty answer.

"We're from the middle of nowhere," Zig cut in, seeing her dilemma. "She's been using magic without formal instruction, so she's not too familiar with the basic principles." While he wasn't an expert himself, he figured he could come up with a somewhat plausible excuse based on their past conversations.

"Is that so?" the receptionist mused. "We can lend you reference books or even arrange for an instructor if you like. Feel free to think it over."

The concept of reference books caught Siasha's attention. "All right."

She mostly used magic through instinct, so she was very curious to learn what the principles were and how they worked.

"Do you have plans to join a party with others?"

Siasha's mind was already drifting toward the knowledge that lay within the books when the receptionist's question snapped her back to reality.

Teaming up with others, huh? she thought. *I've never really thought about it since I've always fought on my own.*

Before all this, she would have immediately said no, but now...

"I'm not sure."

"All right," the receptionist said. "It isn't a requirement, but we highly recommend that you partner with someone who can fight on the front lines. It's very dangerous for magic users to get into close-range encounters."

The receptionist's statement was one of the reasons why Siasha went from refusal to work with a team to being uncertain. She recalled her battle with Zig. He was a mere human—he couldn't submerge an entire town or burn it to the ground in a sea of fire. And yet, she lost the upper hand as soon as he got too close.

He said it was a matter of their compatibility, but the entire incident was incredibly frustrating. Despite her best efforts at casting close-range magic, it was undeniable that magic users were at a disadvantage in a melee. Since monstrosities were so durable, she needed to minimize the chances of them being able to close the gap as much as possible.

"We can introduce you to other members who are looking for a party if you put in an application to the guild," the receptionist said. "However, you're required to complete a certain number of requests before you apply. Applications may also be denied based on the applicant's conduct or their rate of request completion, so please keep that in mind."

Siasha nodded, paying attention to the detailed explanation on the guild's regulations and other important information. If she wanted to blend in, she had better commit them to memory.

From what Zig could tell from listening in, it seemed like Siasha was getting a reasonable introduction to the guild. Sure that there would be no other issues, he glanced at those that were still staring at them.

Most had their eyes on Siasha. The men were surely staring because of her good looks, while the women appeared to be jealous. It didn't seem like anyone realized that she was a witch.

There were two ways the others were looking at Zig. The first was curiosity due to his unusual weapon. The second was calculating as they tried to assess his strength. While it was common knowledge that you couldn't accurately gauge someone's capabilities just from observing them, a good look could give you an idea of if they were competent or not. Those who were looking at him with a calculating eye were the ones who could most likely see and understand Zig's abilities.

He briefly returned their gazes with a sharp glare. His scowl was so terrifying that the adventurers froze and involuntarily reached for their weapons. However, they soon realized that Zig was only posturing and quickly regained their composure. Normally, he wouldn't care that they were trying to size him up, as he was used to it as a mercenary, but he was on protection duty.

So far, he noticed countless things that were different from back home, and now he noticed yet another: There were a lot of women in the guild. The capabilities of men and women were obviously different—even talented women who dedicated their lives to the sword were physically no match for a decently capable mercenary. There were no female mercenaries on the home continent—or if there were, they hid their figures so well that he couldn't tell. That was just how life was back there. But judging from where he stood, around twenty percent of the occupants were female. They all had slender arms—so thin that they didn't look like they could wield a sword.

It was such a strange scene for Zig that his head was still reeling when Siasha completed her registration process. She bowed to the receptionist as the woman gave her a small card.

She turned to Zig and proudly showed him the card. "I'm an adventurer now."

"Yeah," Zig said as he snapped out of his reverie. "That's great."

"Thanks. Now I can take the first step. Although it's a bit late tonight, so I'll have to wait until tomorrow to actually start working."

"Should we go back?" he asked.

"Apparently, there's a reference room on the second floor. I'd like to stop by there and borrow some books if that's okay?"

"Sure."

The door that led to the reference room was at the end of the hallway. Inside, they were met with the scent of old paper and the sight of bookshelves lining the walls.

"This is amazing, isn't it?" Siasha said.

Siasha seems delighted, Zig thought. *She must really love books.*

They spotted someone who seemed to be the librarian at the other side of the room and made their way over. Zig perused the shelves while Siasha spoke with the librarian.

The shelves were filled with complicated books. Even if he could technically read them, Zig felt that it would probably be way over his head.

"Oh, what's this...?"

One of the titles caught his attention: *The Illustrated Guide to Monstrosities*. Zig took the book off the shelf and started to flip through it. It contained a lot useful information like the names, ecology, and likenesses of various monstrosities.

"Zig."

He looked up at the sound of Siasha's voice, not realizing that he had read a good chunk of the book already. He closed it and returned it to the shelf.

"Are you good to go?" he asked.

"Yes, but it's going to cost money."

"Just to borrow them?"

The librarian then explained that the money was used as collateral. The amount would cover the price of the book and would be given back depending on its condition when returned.

With a polite bow, the librarian assured them that if there was nothing wrong with the books beyond the usual wear and tear, they would get the full deposit back. Thus, it was very important to treat them with care.

"Okay, that makes sense," Zig said as he pulled out his wallet. "So, how much are they?"

Siasha looked uncomfortable. "They're...one hundred and fifty thousand each."

"O-oh?"

He glanced at Siasha and noticed she was holding two books. A few beads of sweat trickled down his face as he calculated the total.

"Um, I've got plenty of time, so I can just come back here and read them..." she said sheepishly.

He took out the necessary money and placed it on the tray. "They've got the knowledge you need, right?"

After counting out exactly thirty coins, he pushed it toward the librarian. She took the amount, recorded the number on Siasha's guild card, and confirmed the return date.

Siasha bowed appreciatively to Zig as she took the books. "Thank you so much."

"Don't worry about it," he said. "I hope you get a lot out of reading them."

"I will!" Siasha beamed happily.

As the librarian watched Zig, she thought to herself, *He would've looked so cool if only he wasn't so sweaty.*

After waking up early and eating breakfast, Siasha and Zig left their lodgings and headed to the guild. Despite the early hour, there was already a decent amount of people milling about and examining the requests posted on the boards.

"See you in a bit," Zig said.

Siasha disappeared into the crowd to start looking for a job she could take for the day, while Zig turned away from all the commotion and headed back to the reception area. There was a different receptionist on duty today. She noticed Zig and asked if she could help him with anything.

During her registration, Siasha had asked if non-guild members could accompany her on jobs and was told it was possible as long as they put in an application, so Zig had decided to do just that.

Apparently, the procedures were very simple and taken advantage of by quite a few members, mostly by people who carried the guild member's equipment, but monstrosity researchers would sometimes apply as well.

"I'd like to apply to accompany a member."

"This is your first time, right?" the receptionist asked. "First, you'll need to fill out this form."

Zig filled out the form—which looked much less complicated than Siasha's adventurer paperwork—and handed it back to her.

"There are no restrictions on companions," the receptionist explained, "but be aware that you'll need to act carefully since you have no guarantees or protections from the guild. Also, the guild will not get involved in any disputes you have with another adventurer."

"What should I do if one attacks me?"

"Please file a report with the military police."

"That sounds like a great plan of recourse," he said, his voice dripping with sarcasm. "I'm so grateful, I think I might cry."

The receptionist didn't bat an eye. "Thank you for understanding." She gave him her customer service smile and handed him a card. It stated that he was allowed to accompany an adventurer—most likely Siasha—on her jobs, but the guild was not responsible for anything that happened to him. In the eyes of the law, he was only a normal person and would be judged accordingly. But of course, dead men told no tales.

His application complete, Zig went back to the job request boards. It looked like Siasha had selected her job for the day, but she wasn't alone. There were two rugged-looking men sitting next to her.

"Good grief," Zig muttered to himself.

Considering how attractive she was, it wasn't surprising that men flocked to her. If he was unlucky, this might end up being a more troublesome bodyguarding job than he'd bargained for. But, as it was, there was nothing he could do about it for now.

Zig sighed as he approached. However, the snippets of conversation he could hear were quite different from what he was expecting.

"I see, so that's how magic is simplified?" Siasha asked.

"Exactly. You're a quick study, Siasha."

"It's all because you're such a good teacher!"

"Aww, shucks," one of the rugged-looking men said bashfully. "You're gonna make an old man blush if ya keep that up."

Zig stopped in his tracks at what he was hearing. Siasha noticed him and waved him over.

"Zig! This is Bates and Glow—they're veteran adventurers! They've been teaching me so many things about the profession."

The two men looked over at him. Bates was the one she was speaking with, while Glow was silently listening to their conversation.

"Ya got yer head on straight there, brother?" Bates asked as he motioned around. "Leavin' such a cute girl here all by herself." The other adventurers that were watching from a distance—most of whom were young men—averted their eyes at his glare. "There's a bunch of young bucks in heat swarmin' 'round these parts."

It seemed these two had stepped in to protect Siasha from the ill intentions of the other men. Zig realized just how much he'd underestimated the effect she had on others.

"I'm sorry," he said apologetically. "Seems like you had to take care of her."

"Ah, it was nothin'," the man Siasha had introduced as Glow replied. "It's all part of an adventurer's job...to look out for newbies."

"He's right," Bates agreed. "We just hope ya return the favor and help someone out if ya make a name for yourself someday."

"So that's how the cycle works," Siasha said thoughtfully. "I understand."

Both she and Zig couldn't help but be impressed by the good example being set by these expert adventurers.

Bates shot Zig a meaningful glance. "We'd be happy to introduce you to a prospective adventurin' partner, but it doesn't seem like you'll be needin' one, eh?"

Zig suddenly realized that he had seen his face before. Bates was one of the few people he stared down yesterday.

"You're not an adventurer yourself, eh?"

"No," Zig replied. "I'm her bodyguard and porter."

"That's good. Ya better not try anythin', ya hear?"

They really were stand-up guys.

After Siasha and Zig thanked them once more, the two men returned to the rest of their party. Zig watched them walk away and turned to ask Siasha about the request she chose to take.

"I accepted a request to cull some pouch wolves," she said. "Apparently, they're oviparous, and they incubate a bunch of eggs in their stomach pouches."

"That's very interesting and all," he said, "but I'd rather know some of their traits and how dangerous they are."

"Oh, right."

Siasha seemed to be the scholarly type and liked to research the things that caught her interest, so Zig figured she already had some information.

"They're a highly fertile monstrosity, so there are regular requests to cull them," she explained. "When their numbers get too great, they leave the forest to find food, so that's where we should be looking for them. As for their risk factor, it seems there's not much of a difference between them and regular wolves."

So basically, they're dangerous in packs, Zig thought.

A well-coordinated pack of wolves could cause problems for even a seasoned mercenary. That's probably why requests for a party of adventurers to cull them were so common.

"It doesn't seem like a job for a greenhorn," he remarked.

"That's why I picked it," she said. "It looked like the most difficult one that was available for me."

That was probably another reason the young men in the guild were so intrigued by her. Although most of their interest likely stemmed from ulterior motives, perhaps they also wanted to stop a beginner from doing something so reckless. However, they didn't know her like Zig did. Siasha may be a novice adventurer in their eyes, but her combat prowess was second to none.

"That's a huge first step," he commented. "Are you aiming for the top already?"

"Kind of. A lot of benefits come from raising your adventuring rank. There are some magic reference materials that can't be disclosed until you become a certain class, so that's my first goal."

"If you don't mind me asking, are reference materials made by humans even going to benefit a witch?"

The capabilities between the two races were so different that it didn't seem likely that human knowledge would be of much help to her.

Siasha nodded. "Absolutely! All I've done is briefly glance over the books, but to be honest, humans here appear to use their mana much more effectively than me."

Zig was stunned by her answer. "Seriously?"

"Humans can use small amounts of mana effectively, and they've worked tirelessly to come up with methods that improve those results. Many of them have contributed to this research over hundreds of years. How could someone like me, who's only been doing self-study for around two hundred years, even hope to compete? When you have a great amount of mana, you end up being complacent with a little inefficiency."

If Siasha was this amazed, the people here must be considerably more skilled than he initially gave them credit for, Zig realized. Humans, a weaker species, had made such great efforts to effectively utilize the little power they had that even a witch was taking her cues from them.

"Additionally, they've designed tools that allow anyone to use magic!" Siasha exclaimed. "There are so many things I still don't know, so I want to learn!"

With the way she spoke, this was perhaps the first time Siasha was interested in something so much that she was ravenous for knowledge.

"I'm just happy to hear you've got a goal in mind," Zig finally said. "Should we head out soon? How far is the location?"

"About seven days by foot," she said. "But...we can be there in an instant if we use a different method."

"Come again?" Zig said, puzzled. *How could someone instantly arrive at a destination that was seven days away?*

"You'll see. Just follow me." Siasha walked toward the room to their left. There was a line of adventurers waiting to go in. Each group was shown inside after each member presented their card at the reception desk. The line moved along smoothly, and it was soon their turn. Siasha presented her own card and exchanged pleasantries with the receptionist before proceeding inside.

"Card, please."

Zig showed his companion card for the receptionist to inspect. Handing him his card back, she glanced toward the room as if to signal where he needed to go. In the middle of the room was a stone slab engraved with shimmering letters. Siasha was examining the letters with great interest.

"Stand in the center," a man in a robe instructed.

Following his instructions, they made their way to the middle of the slab. Once the man confirmed they were in the correct position, he waved his hand and uttered an incantation.

The slab started to glow.

The light continued to expand until it was the only thing they could see.

Zig gasped in surprise as both he and Siasha were engulfed in light so bright that he couldn't keep his eyes open.

Their vision returned as the light faded.

But they were no longer in one of the rooms at the guild. Instead, an unfamiliar forest spread before them.

"What just happened...?" Zig said as he looked around.

Glancing behind himself, he noticed what seemed to be the ruins of a stone building. It was covered in moss and looked so dilapidated that it was clear no one had lived there for a long time.

"That was one of the ancient magical tools: a transportation stone," Siasha explained. "Apparently, when one is created using specific materials and imbued with a magic circle, it can be used to travel to the location of another transportation stone. It's an ancient form of magic that people haven't been able to replicate in the present day."

"No way," Zig said. "If the public caught on to these things, the whole country—no, the entire world—would be turned upside down."

"It's not that flexible of a system," she said. "They're locked to certain places, and if you try to move them, they cease to work anymore."

Zig's first impression was that these transportation stones could be used to travel between the continents, but it looked like they weren't *that* convenient. The only use they seemed to have was to provide adventurers an easy method of travel to various locations so they could hunt monstrosities.

The forest they arrived in was vast rather than dense. Visibility wasn't bad, but the same thing could be said for their quarry—it would probably be difficult for them to get the jump on a pack of wolves.

"We need to walk about thirty minutes to the west of the transportation stone to reach our destination," Siasha said. "Shall we go?"

"All right."

Sunlight shone through the foliage overhead as they made their way through the trees. Siasha wasn't physically strong, but living in forests in the past had made her adept at maneuvering through them.

After a while, they arrived at a clearing. It was filled with grass that reached up to their knees, but strangely enough, no trees. It was as if they were avoiding the area.

Beyond the clearing, the forest grew denser. It was dimly lit and overgrown with thick vegetation, and a lukewarm breeze blew out from its depths. Listening to the wind, Zig picked up on the sound of something pushing past the undergrowth.

"Siasha."

"Right."

She seemed to have picked up on the sound as well because she was already taking a battle stance. The wolves emerged, spreading out as though to surround them. There appeared to be at least five wolves.

"What do you want to do?" Zig asked.

"I'm going to attack. Can you please take care of any stragglers that come our way?"

"Got it."

The creatures hadn't yet pounced, perhaps watching to see how the pair would respond. Siasha began to cast a spell. The pungent smell reached Zig's nose as he kept an eye on their surroundings.

Before the wolves completely surrounded them, spikes burst from the ground in a circular pattern with the two of them at the center. They sent grass flying through the air, hitting areas she expected the wolves might be hiding.

Some of the spikes struck true—skewered wolves slumped limply from their tips. Their hides didn't seem to be very thick, as the points penetrated cleanly through their bodies.

However, Siasha's spell didn't wipe the pack out. Zig believed at least five more were lying in wait.

The spikes had only claimed three.

A couple of pouch wolves crept up on them from the rear. They darted through the grass and pounced. Zig whirled around and thrust the lower blade of his weapon toward an incoming pouch wolf.

His weapon sank into its neck, killing the wolf instantly. Drawing the blade from the corpse, he used the momentum to slash upward at the second one as it dove to follow its companion. He thrust the blade into the wolf's abdomen and slammed its body to the ground.

He looked back at Siasha to see her attempting to skewer one last wolf that was trying to get away. With their small numbers, the wolves didn't seem to be much of a threat.

"I guess that's it, huh?" Siasha said. "Let's start removing some of the parts."

Apparently, what they had done with the armored boar before was the custom for adventurers. Removing parts of the monstrosities they killed served both as proof of completing the job and as a way to make money by selling them.

"What are you going to take?" Zig asked.

"The pouches," she replied. "They're very durable but also light. I heard they can be processed into things like rucksacks or waterskins as well. What are you doing?"

Zig was trying to cover his nose and mouth—was it because corpses tended to stink?

"Uh, it's nothing," he said quickly. "How about we split up the removal duties?"

"I know I may not look like it, but I'm very good at skinning things!"

Siasha started to enthusiastically peel the hide from one of the wolves. True to her claim, she was quite dexterous at it. To remove the pouch, she stuck her hand inside and lifted the area around it. The odor was so offensive that her eyes were starting to water.

"Eww!" she complained. "What is this? It smells so foul!"

"I bet," was Zig's dry reply.

"How can you stand this, Zig? Wait...you're plugging your nose? That's so unfair! How did you even know to do that?"

"I didn't *know*, per se."

He just figured it was unlikely that a wild animal would keep the inside of its pouch very clean. The smell was probably trapped in there for a long time and approaching toxic territory.

Siasha let out a long string of complaints as she removed the pouches, making sure not to touch the innermost parts directly.

As soon as she finished getting the parts she needed, Siasha went to wash her hands, sounding close to tears as she complained. "Bleeech. This smells so bad...and it's not coming off!"

Zig chuckled from the sidelines. But his smile immediately faded as he glanced toward the forest. Siasha noticed the sudden change in his behavior and ceased her complaints, her eyes darting around their surroundings.

The mercenary strained his ears. In addition to the sounds of the rustling grass, the breeze carried the faintest echoes of a battle in the distance.

"Someone's fighting," he said.

"I can't hear it, but it's likely another party. Some of the other adventurers took the same request as me. But, hmm..."

She looked pensive. Despite having read through the magic reference books, her knowledge was still incredibly basic. Theoreticals aside, she wanted to see what magic looked like in practice. The reference books even mentioned that seeing and experiencing magic for oneself was an excellent method of deepening your understanding of it.

"Zig, can we go watch?" she asked.

"Sure," he replied. "I wanted to see how combat is done over here anyway."

Their minds made up, Zig dashed toward the sounds, Siasha following behind him.

Time was of the essence.

As the din of battle grew louder, the pair quieted their steps.

"Be careful not to reveal yourself," Zig said. "You can't blame anyone for trying to cut you down if they catch you spying on their battle techniques."

"Got it."

Zig was still driven by a mercenary's mindset—everyone he knew had a trick or two up their sleeves that they didn't want to reveal to anyone else. After all, that knowledge could be the deciding factor in a battle being won or lost.

However, this way of thinking seemed to be exclusive to mercenaries. While it wasn't unusual for mercenaries to fight together on the battlefield one day and cross blades the next, adventurers didn't seem to be as cutthroat. Perhaps that was why they didn't see mercenaries in a good light.

Zig and Siasha didn't know how the party they were watching would behave, so they slowly crept behind some nearby trees to take a peek.

A party of four adventurers were fighting six pouch wolves. There were already five pouch wolf carcasses lying on the ground.

The party seemed to be well balanced, with two members at the front and two in the back. One had a sword in one hand and a shield in the other. He held off the wolves attacking them so that the other fighter beside him could finish them off with his longsword. Behind them, an archer and a magic user struck any wolves that were trying to attack from their flanks.

Everyone's movements were smooth and fluid, showing how well they coordinated with each other. The monstrosities, unable to take advantage of attacking as a pack, met their ends one by one.

"So, that's how you deal with them," Zig muttered.

It was a fine display of battle tactics. Each member had each other's back as they worked to reduce the number of attackers. Zig's own combat style seemed clumsy in comparison. His was like balancing on a tightrope—one little misstep could spell the end. They, on the other hand, weren't using methods that relied on the fighting prowess of the individual but were working together to bolster their strengths and cover their weaknesses.

Zig observed their techniques intently, hoping that he could steal them for himself.

It didn't take long for the battle to come to an end. After confirming the last pouch wolf was dead, the party split into two groups: one standing guard and the other removing the parts.

Zig replayed the fight in his head, trying to memorize every last detail.

"That was incredible, wasn't it?" Siasha said.

"Yeah, I gleaned a lot more than I was expecting," Zig replied. "How about you? It didn't seem like they were using any flashy tricks."

"It was more than enough, actually. When humans cast spells, they..."

The scent of magic wafted up Zig's nose. Siasha continued to explain, unaware of what was going on. This smell was unfamiliar to him...almost like grass. Since it wasn't the pungent odor he associated with offensive magic, it didn't send his internal alarm bells ringing, but he still turned in the direction the scent was coming from. It seemed to come from where the adventurers were removing the spoils from their kill.

What kind of magic could they be using?

It was then that he noticed some of the scenery seemed to be wavering slightly. He stared at the shimmering sight in silence.

"Zig?" Siasha said uncertainly.

Are my eyes playing tricks on me?

The archer and the man with the shield were the two members of the party that were keeping watch. That made sense, tactics-wise. Which meant the swordsman and the magic user were retrieving the parts.

Wait...the magic user?

The person in question was using a knife to cut out the pouch. He seemed to be aware of the terrible stench they gave off because he was wearing gloves and covering his mouth. It didn't look like he was using any magic.

The hair on Zig's arms began to stand on end.

The light from where the sun shone slightly through the trees was unnaturally refracting about thirty feet behind the magic user. Zig could make out a hazy silhouette floating, its sights set on its prey.

Zig realized that the distance he'd been making sure to maintain so he wouldn't be caught meant that he wouldn't be able to reach them in time.

"Behind you!" Zig shouted.

At his warning, the archer immediately notched an arrow in that direction and sent it flying toward whatever was quickly approaching.

The arrow struck true, but it didn't seem to cause much damage to *whatever it was*. However, the attack did cause *it* to slow down, giving the swordsman the smallest opening to grab the magic user and leap aside.

Whatever it was quickly scooped up the corpse that the magic user was carving for parts into its mouth and tore it into pieces.

Blood gushed out, staining its mouth red just as the rest of the creature's form began to solidify.

Hovering in the air was what looked like a twenty-five-foot-long shark. However, its head and backside were elongated like a snake, and its body was a blackish-brown color. Its vacant eyes darted around restlessly. The most grotesque sight of all was its gills: They undulated whenever it breathed, showing the adventurers the bright red filaments inside.

"A ghost shark?!" one of the adventurers cried out. "What's it doing in a place like this?"

"It must've been lured by the smell of blood!" one of their companions shouted. "We're not prepared to fight one of those things. Retreat!"

The ghost shark turned invisible once more, leaving no trace despite being covered in blood from the archer's arrow. Anyone paying close attention could see its shimmer against the scenery, but if they looked away, it would be difficult to track again.

"Listy, don't take your eyes off it," the swordsman ordered. "It won't attack as long as it knows it's being watched. Lyle, Malt, let it take the corpses if it wants. Listy, Lyle—you two take the rear. We're going straight back. Everyone, out!"

The archer and the man with the shield sprang to obey their leader's instructions, falling back and keeping a close watch on the ghost shark. Slowly, the party made their retreat.

The ghost shark, seeing that its prey managed to escape, began to feast on the wolf carcasses instead.

The swordsman kept a watchful eye on the shark as his party withdrew. Once everyone had safely retreated, he quickly scanned the vicinity, trying to find who had warned them; however, the owner of the voice was nowhere to be found.

✦ ◆ ✦

Zig and Siasha made it back to the guild as soon as they could and gave their report—conveniently leaving out the part about the ghost shark.

"Good job!" the receptionist praised. "Those are impressive results for your first day. We look forward to seeing your future endeavors, but please make sure to keep them within your capabilities."

"Okay."

Siasha had done very well for her first day on the job. She sported a wide grin as she returned to Zig.

"How was it?" he asked.

"Pretty good, if I do say so myself. I got 25,000 dren."

"Nice job!" Zig commented. That amount wasn't bad for a day's work.

"If I complete four more requests of this level," she said, "I'll go up to the next class too."

"You can rise up in the ranks that quickly?"

Siasha then began to explain how promotions worked.

After acquiring ten points, you could move up to the next class. Completing requests deemed appropriate for your current level earned you one point. Finishing a job meant for the next rank up got you two points; however, if you failed, you lost double the points.

That meant floundering on a higher-level assignment cost you four points in total. This made it difficult to take on requests rated above your class unless you were very confident.

"You can also be docked points if the request isn't properly fulfilled or for bad conduct," Siasha further explained. "And apparently, if you successfully do one the guild specifically asks of you, you can earn extra points."

Zig nodded. "Well, I'd say that slow and steady wins the race over being devious and trying to earn brownie points."

"I agree. If I go the route where I get one extra point, I still only need to do four more."

More adventurers filed into the guild hall as they continued to chat; among them was the party they encountered earlier.

"Was it really okay that I didn't report that monstrosity?" Siasha asked.

"I'm sure those guys will say something," Zig assured her. "Besides, I doubt they'll buy the excuse that we were passing by and just so happened to see everything."

The party had been very careful about keeping an eye on their surroundings, so any statement would sound extremely suspicious.

"I'll probably be docked points for bad conduct if they find out we were spying, huh..."

"Yup."

"Really?" they heard the receptionist gasp. "You encountered a ghost shark?"

"Yes," the swordsman replied. "It's still early in the breeding season for the pouch wolves. They were probably driven out by it."

"Thank you for your report. It seems only fitting that someone of your caliber would be able to make a ghost shark retreat, Alan. This might be the first time I've ever heard of one catching a party unawares and *not* leaving a trail of victims in its wake."

The ghost shark's special ability made it incredibly difficult to detect, so requests to hunt them were only issued after someone reported a casualty. It was exceedingly rare to discover them before-hand. Fortunately, there weren't many casualties due to their small population, which was why the guild hadn't issued any extermination orders or developed proactive countermeasures.

"About that..." the man named Alan said. "We actually didn't realize it was approaching either. If someone passing by hadn't called out and warned us, I'm sure one of us would've been killed."

"Oh, really?" the receptionist asked. "Who was it?"

Alan shook his head. "I don't know. It all happened so quickly, and they were far away. From how they were dressed, it looked like adventurers." He thought for a moment. "On that note, I have a favor to ask of you."

"You want to know which parties were in the forest today?"

"Can you do that?"

The receptionist looked contemplative. Protocol stated that they usually weren't allowed to give out that kind of information, but... exceptions could be made if the reason was legitimate. But how much should she reveal?

"I can tell you the number of parties that went to the forest," she said, "as well as their names and the times they departed and returned. That's all."

"That's more than enough," Alan said gratefully. "Thank you."

The receptionist held up a hand. "On one condition."

"And that is?"

"If you find them, I want you to inform the guild as well. We would like to know the techniques that can penetrate the ghost shark's undetectability."

"I can't promise that they'll have what you're looking for. I'll talk to them about it, but you can't press them if they refuse."

"That's fine." She handed him a sheet of paper. "Here you go."

Alan took the list and walked back to where his party was waiting.

"O-oh no!" Siasha began to panic. "He's coming this way!"

"Just act confident," Zig said calmly.

He tried to pacify the dismayed witch as Alan headed their way. However, the swordsman walked past them, not recognizing the pair.

Siasha deflated, looking immediately relieved.

"I know this is way after the fact," she said as they left to get some dinner, "but maybe it would've been easiest to just leave them to die."

She wasn't wrong.

"True, I guess," Zig said.

If they'd just sat back and watched, the monstrosity probably would've wiped out the entire party and they wouldn't have to think of excuses that could paint them as shady.

"Still, we learned a lot from watching them," he continued. "It was only fair for us to give them a warning, right?"

"You do have a point," she conceded.

"If you come across others in a similar pinch, it might not be a bad idea to lend them a hand, even if it's just a little."

Siasha looked perplexed. "Even if they don't seem like they'd be useful to me?"

"That's right. When living in human society, the important things are: don't make enemies and gather some allies."

"Allies, you say?" she asked, scrunching up her face. "That sounds difficult..."

After living so long with nothing but enemies, Siasha couldn't fully comprehend being told to work together with others.

"I'm not saying you need to find people who won't betray you no matter what," Zig said. "More like...people who might have your back if they see you in a spot of trouble. You know, have many connections even if they're shallow. It'll definitely benefit you in the end."

"I don't really get it, but...if it's your advice, Zig, I'll give it a try."

They ended the conversation at that and searched for a new eatery to try.

"How about that one?" Siasha suggested, pointing at a seafood restaurant.

The town of Halian was along the coast, so surely a place serving seafood wouldn't be terrible.

"All right, let's go."

They entered the restaurant and took a table at a corner. Once they placed their orders and the server headed to the kitchen, Zig turned to Siasha.

"You were telling me before," he said, "but how is human magic different?"

"To put it simply," she replied, "they've automated it. Remember when I told you about the process of invoking magic?"

He dug through his hazy memories. "Wasn't it something along the lines of scooping it up, manipulating it, and then giving it a form?"

"That's right! They've automated the process up to the part where the mana is manipulated."

"You can...do that?"

"Think about the transportation stone. The letters that were carved on it were magic seals that already contained the technique necessary for the spell. All it needs to activate is a flow of mana."

"So you're saying you need to figuratively engrave spells into your body?"

"To be more precise, what's engraved has to be purposely left incomplete."

Ah, so that's how it works, Zig thought.

If a technique was imprinted in its entirety, the user would only be able to cast that one spell.

"But won't that skew the type of spells you can do in a particular direction?" he asked.

"It's always been hard for me to remember spells that weren't my forte," Siasha said. "What they're doing is a very effective technique to have as one of the cards in your hand, even if you're a magic specialist. It means you don't have to waste time worrying when the moment comes to use it."

That made sense to Zig as he looked back on his mercenary experience. At times when you needed to make decisions on the spot, having too many choices could prove detrimental.

When an enemy attacks, should you try to dodge or block? If you retaliate, would it be better to use magic or a sword? Since you've already prepared what you were going to do, there would be no floundering at that crucial moment. Another benefit of this magic system was that it would be easy to designate roles when forming a party.

"Of course, there are disadvantages as well," Siasha continued. "It prevents you from making detailed adjustments, but I think the overall boost to effectiveness is more than worth it. Human innovation sure is impressive."

"If I imbue myself with some magic words, can I use magic too?"

"Nope. You, or should I say, people from your continent, don't have any mana. That's probably why you can smell when magic is being used."

Well, that was disappointing news. It would be very useful to add a projectile or something to his arsenal without adding another item to carry around.

Preemptively smelling magic had its uses too, but if he was given a choice between smelling it or using it, he would pick the latter in a heartbeat.

Their conversation was winding down when the food finally arrived. Zig had ordered *aglio e olio* spaghetti with seafood, while Siasha selected a paella.

"Whoa, this is amazing," Zig marveled, his mouth watering at the aroma of his meal.

They struck gold by picking this place—the portions were large and the prices reasonable. He made a mental note for them to eat here again.

Siasha also seemed happy with her selection. The paella was packed with chunks of shrimp and shellfish and looked just as delicious as his spaghetti.

"This one is really good too!" she said cheerfully.

"How about we trade some?" Zig suggested.

"Yes, let's! I've been eyeing your pasta as well."

They ended up sharing their food and even ordering a few extra dishes. With a job well done and a restaurant that served excellent fare, dinner was very satisfying indeed.

"There's something that's been on my mind," Zig said apprehensively as they drank their post-meal tea. "There seems to be a good number of female adventurers. Putting magic use aside, I wonder if they can handle a sword."

Taking biology into consideration, it would make sense if most were purely magic specialists, but he had seen women wearing the garb of melee fighters as well.

"The people here are constantly fortifying their bodies with magic," Siasha said. "Women usually have more mana than men, so they're about the same in terms of physical prowess."

"What?" Zig leaned forward in his chair in disbelief. "That's bad news. I don't know how much they can fortify themselves, but it means I'll probably lose to someone who has equal physical ability to me, right?"

"Hmm." She thought for a moment. "About that... What did you think about fighting the pouch wolves?"

"Nothing really. They'd be a bit annoying to face as a pack, but individuals didn't pose any threat. They might be a handful for a rookie mercenary, though."

"Then we have a roughly similar understanding. It'd be difficult for a novice to keep up, but not so much for someone with years of experience."

Something about that information didn't sit right with Zig. Even if women were slightly awkward in combat, their physical capabilities being enhanced would more than make up for their shortcomings.

"This is just speculation," Siasha continued, "but I think the raw physical ability of the people here is lower. This physical fortification happens on a daily basis, probably without them really being aware of it. I don't know whether they reduced their overall physical strength due to supplementing it with mana or if they were originally weak and developed mana to enhance themselves, though. It's the same thing with those monstrosities—they're able to maintain those massive bodies through mana fortification. As a result, there's a narrow gap between the abilities of men and women, allowing both to play an active role in combat."

Zig found himself relaxing a little at Siasha's explanation. In addition to his inability to use magic, he feared the physical ability he relied on wouldn't hold a candle to the people living here. With some of his worries alleviated, another question popped into his mind.

"How come I didn't notice them fortifying themselves?"

"Because it's not necessary to manipulate mana that influences your own body," she replied. "It's only used to supplement movements. It seems like they're not just compensating for physical ability but their bodies as a whole. Without mana, they'd probably be unable to properly heal from disease and die."

So it wasn't an additional benefit, Zig realized, but a natural ability. Even if it sounded amazing, having to constantly augment yourself with mana came with its own downsides and challenges as well.

"Since we're on the topic of magic," Siasha said, "that monstrosity used it too."

"Right," he said. "It was just luck that I picked up on it."

He recalled the sharklike monstrosity they encountered in the forest and its ability to swim through the air while concealing its massive form. A nasty foe indeed.

He looked thoughtful. "If monstrosities can use magic like that, we'll need to gather intel on them in advance."

Maybe I should look into finding an informant over here, he thought. *Is that what I really need, though? Perhaps consulting with someone who specializes in monstrosities would be better.*

Another idea came to him. *Oh, or I could check out* The Illustrated Guide to Monstrosities. *That looked like a good book. I want to keep our expenditures down, but we should go back and borrow it.*

His musing was suddenly interrupted by someone in a nearby table discussing monstrosities.

"Did you hear there was a ghost shark sighting?"

"Yup. Seems like Alan and his party were able to drive it off."

"That's some impressive stuff. Those guys have been on fire lately. They should be hitting fourth class pretty soon, right?"

"I'm so jealous. But since they didn't dispose of it, I'm guessing the guild will put up an official notice soon."

"The last one ended up being a wild goose chase, so I hope they get it right this time."

"Still, it's unusual for the guild to have incorrect information."

"So, they're fifth class adventurers..." Siasha murmured. "They did seem like a capable party, so that makes sense."

"Is fifth class good?" Zig asked. Judging from the number alone, it sounded about average.

"Bates said that more than half of the adventurers registered with the guild are seventh class and lower."

That confirmed his suspicions—anyone ranked above seventh class was pretty competent. It sounded like the party they encountered were nearing the end of fifth class and close to leveling up.

So they're at the lower end of what the guild considers advanced? The group was more powerful than he initially thought. They probably had considerable influence that allowed them to get the information they needed.

"That might be bad for us," Zig said.

The probability of that party not finding them was low.

"Let's just pray they're not the petty type..." he sighed.

The incident occurred on the morning of their third day of continuously hunting pouch wolves. Zig watched as Siasha, still sporting bedhead, seemed to finally wake up as they ate breakfast.

"I'm tired of this!" Siasha fumed as she tore the piece of bread she was eating perfectly in half.

"Hmm..." Zig rubbed his chin thoughtfully, trying to figure out the reason for her sudden explosion. This was only the second day in a row he served her bread for breakfast. They had meat last night and fish the night before that.

She can't be tired of the food already, he thought. *What else could it be?*

"Ah, is it the tea?" he asked.

"No, that's not what I'm talking about," she snapped while slathering a liberal amount of jam on the bread.

Taking a big bite, she chewed vigorously and washed it down with a gulp of tea. She had no complaints regarding her tea and sugary meal, so he assumed they weren't the cause of her outburst.

"I meant that I'm tired of hunting the same type of monstrosity all the time," she sighed.

"Oh, that's what this is about."

They had been taking the same request for the past three days since it was such efficient work, but it seemed the excitement of fighting pouch wolves was wearing thin.

Zig, however, looked puzzled, as if he couldn't understand the reason for her boredom.

"You're not bored, Zig?" she asked.

"My work has always involved fighting people. Doing it three days in a row wouldn't give me much pause."

"Oh, right..."

He was a mercenary, someone who killed people for a living. In hindsight, it was a bit silly to ask if he ever got tired of fighting the same foe.

"Do you want to take a day off?" he asked.

"That's... No," she replied reluctantly. "I'll still go."

Despite tiring of the work, Siasha's desire to quickly rise through the ranks meant that taking a day off was off the table. However, she didn't seem to be feeling her best at the moment.

If this kept up, she wouldn't be able to perform well, and there was a chance that being emotional could lead to small mistakes. Unfortunately, Zig doubted she would be willing to take some time off if he told her to. After thinking for a few moments, he remembered a piece of advice he once heard from a senior mercenary.

"Why don't we wrap up early today and go out for a bit afterward?" he suggested.

"Go out?" she asked. "Like where?"

"We could go clothes shopping. I'm sure it's troublesome just having that one outfit, right?"

Siasha always wore her black witch robes while they were working and donned the linen clothing she bought on their home continent during their downtime. Other than those two garments, she had nothing else.

"There's not a woman alive who doesn't get excited about having clothes bought for her."

A senior mercenary—one who considered himself a bit of a ladies' man—had given Zig those words of wisdom when they were drinking together. He wondered if that same advice was applicable to a witch.

Zig didn't have much experience with women. Of course, he used to stop by brothels to relieve his physical needs when it was necessary, but those were just business exchanges and all he did was pay money for services rendered; it wasn't like he was having pleasant conversations with them. With no other point of reference, he had no choice but to rely on his colleague's advice.

Siasha looked slightly confused. "Shopping for clothes, you say...? Hmm."

I should've known there'd be a big difference in how human women and witches perceive these things, he thought. *Since she's been on her own for so long, she's probably not too worried about appearances.*

...Did I just make a big blunder?

He casually raised a hand to get Siasha's attention as she inspected her outfit.

"Of course, we don't have to if you're not interested," he said. "We could alwa—"

"What about you, Zig?" Siasha interrupted. Her eyes were cast down and her fingertips played at the edges of her garment. "Would you prefer it if I dressed up?"

There was an unusual hint of formality to her tone, which confused him. She was acting a little different than usual. Zig got the feeling that answering in the affirmative would be the most prudent course of action.

"Yes. That would be good."

"Is that...so?" Siasha began playing with her hair, twirling it around her fingertips.

Zig wasn't sure if he said the right thing, but she seemed to be in better spirits.

"All right," she said. "Let's get work over with quickly and go shopping afterward."

Zig felt a wave of relief that his client's mood had significantly improved. "Sure."

Apparently, that piece of advice he received about buying clothes was right on the money. He was concerned the same principles wouldn't apply to a witch, but judging by how quickly she brightened up, witches had the same interests as human women.

He owed that playboy acquaintance a big thank you—not that he'd ever see the guy again.

Siasha cheerfully finished the rest of her breakfast and started to prepare for their departure. She was even happily humming to herself. If the prospect of getting new clothes delighted her this much, she must've been really dissatisfied with her linen ensemble.

Content with how he completely handled the situation, Zig finished his tea and began to get ready for work himself.

Their work for the day ended without any major incidents. Unlike the first day, they didn't encounter anything out of the ordinary, and they returned to the guild's reception area after slaying several pouch wolves. There was no one else lined up around at that time of day, so Siasha was able to immediately give her report.

"All right, great job today," the receptionist remarked. "Seems like you finished up quite early."

"I'm planning to go shopping with Zig once we're done here," Siasha said.

The receptionist grinned. "That sounds nice. Taking care of your physical health is important, but finding ways to de-stress is also essential for adventurers. You two have—" Her smile suddenly disappeared. "Oh dear, looks like your companion is getting an earful again."

Siasha followed the receptionist's gaze to the other side of the hall and saw a few young men loitering around Zig. It was too far away to hear what they were saying, but it was obvious they weren't having a pleasant chat. It seemed like this group of young adventurers had decided to mess with Zig while he was waiting for Siasha.

The witch stroked her chin incredulously as she took in the scene.

"I've been wondering this for a while now, but doesn't Zig have an intimidating appearance?" she thought aloud. "Why would they give someone who looks as tough as him so much grief?"

This wasn't the first time young adventurers had tried to pick a fight with him. Anyone could see they were jealous because he was the ever-present third wheel that kept them from getting too close to the beautiful Siasha.

If Zig's menacing aura and stature didn't deter them, something had to be off with their sense of self-preservation.

The receptionist scratched her cheek with a strained smile. "Well, there *is* a reason for that..."

"They're lookin' down on him 'cause of all of his muscles," a deep voice finished her sentence.

Siasha turned around to see an amiable-looking man with a bald head and a similar burly physique to Zig approaching the counter. He shot her a wink.

"Bates!"

"Howdy, Siasha," he said, raising a hand to acknowledge her greeting. "How's your adventurin' been goin'?"

"Very well, thanks." After turning in some paperwork, he glanced over in Zig's direction with an amused expression.

Still confused about Bates's earlier statement, Siasha decided to prod him for more information. "Why would they look down on him because he's muscular?"

"Enhancin' your body with magic is important for adventurers," he replied, "'specially for those on the front lines. It's not an exaggeration to say that the worse ya are with enhancement arts, the more ya have to increase your physical strength. Guys who have to train so much that they get all bulky is a sign of underdeveloped enhancement magic... At least, that's what the young pups who are just gettin' used to it love to say."

"Oh...well, I suppose I can see where they're coming from," Siasha said, though was not entirely sure she agreed with that philosophy. "However, it doesn't seem like toning one's body would be a waste of effort either."

"I dunno what gives 'em that impression." Bates stroked his chin thoughtfully. "But I can't deny that honin' enhancement skills makes ya seem visibly stronger than workin' out. It's true that guys with less mana have to bulk up in order to supplement their physical form. Like me, for example."

Bates also had a well-trained physique, but he had many accomplishments to his name, so no one ever gave him a hard time. Zig, on the other hand, was still practically a nobody.

The receptionist sighed as she gave Bates's documents a once-over and stamped them. "There are people who judge a book by its cover wherever you go. Once they get it in their heads that something is 'right' they lose all sight of everything else."

Bates took the paperwork back from her and stuffed it in his pocket.

"Well, that's the reason why a certain number of 'em give muscular guys a hard time. After a while, they usually improve to the point where their enhancement magic hits a plateau and then arrive at the obvious conclusion that they'd be stronger if they trained both magically and physically. I supposed you'd say it's the folly of youth."

"I see," Siasha said. "So that's why." It finally made sense why only younger men messed with Zig.

"His docile nature plays a part in it as well. If those whipper-snappers tried that kind of crap with any veteran adventurer, they wouldn't live to see the next day."

Siasha had never seen Zig use physical force of any kind outside of battle. The adventurers on this continent tended to see red if someone disparaged them, so perhaps they saw Zig as soft because he never fought back.

Zig was ignoring the jeers the men hurled his way, but when he saw Siasha was done with her report, he got up from his seat and deftly dodged the adventurers who tried to grab at him. They protested, saying they weren't done talking yet. Some of them tried to follow Zig but froze when Bates gave them the stink eye.

At the sight of the veteran adventurer's menacing glare, the blood drained from their faces, and they crept away with their tails between their legs. Zig gave Bates a grateful look, which the old man responded to by casually raising a hand.

"Sorry for the long wait, Zig," Siasha said apologetically.

"Are you good to go?" he asked.

"Yes. Let's head out."

They left the guild and walked down the street lined with armor-ies and other shops that catered to adventurers. Their destination was the center of the shopping district, which was an area densely packed with shops selling general merchandise and other sundries.

Instead of choosing one of the used clothing shops on the outer edges, they entered a tailor shop with a regal storefront. Waiting inside was a middle-aged tailor and his daughter.

"Welcome!" the woman said. "Oh, you've brought someone with you today?"

"Yes." Zig gestured to Siasha. "I'd like to get some clothes for her."

It didn't escape Siasha's notice that the mercenary and the tailor's daughter were already acquainted. Had Zig shopped here before?

"What's this, Zig?" Siasha said. "Do you come to shops like this often?"

"Of course not," he said. "Well, not usually, but I had no choice."

The tailor's daughter laughed. "This wonderful customer has such a large body that he couldn't find a single garment in the used clothes shops that would fit!"

The young woman hadn't meant any ill will by spilling the beans, but both Zig and her father silently facepalmed at her statement. Siasha couldn't help but giggle—it sounded like the type of problem Zig would have.

"Wow, what a looker!" the tailor's daughter commented. With Siasha's unearthly beauty and wide smile, she looked positively radiant. "There must be more to you than meets the eye, sir." She smacked Zig on the arm several times, captivated by Siasha's beauty even though they were both women.

"She's just my client," he responded, glancing around the shop.

The young woman hadn't lied—he couldn't find any used clothing that worked with his frame, so he had been forced to have a custom order made. As he only regularly requested the same pieces for himself, he had never taken a good look at the garment designs for women.

"What type of outfit would you like?" the tailor's daughter asked Siasha.

She immediately turned to Zig. "What kind of clothing do you like, Zig?"

It's your outfit, he wanted to say, but he held his tongue after recalling their conversation from that morning.

She was likely trying to pick clothing with an eye for style for the first time in her life. It would be cruel to ask her to choose on the spot without offering even a few words of encouragement.

Deciding that it was his duty (this one time) to help her pick something, Zig decided to rethink what he would say.

"Do you know your size?"

"I have a general idea," she said. "But if you asked me to give you numbers..." She mumbled something about not being sure.

Zig put a hand on her shoulder and gave the tailor's daughter a wink. "She's in your hands! Take all the time you need."

"Understood!" the tailor's daughter declared. "This way please, Miss."

"Huh?! U-um..."

"There's no need to worry about a thing!"

With Siasha being ushered to the back of the shop for measurements, Zig turned his gaze to the tailor who had silently watched the whole scene play out. The well-coiffed, middle-aged man gave Zig a silent nod before starting to instruct him in the art of selecting women's clothing. The tailor was well versed in the psyche of vulgar and useless men who knew nothing about the type of garments that would delight women and taught Zig accordingly.

"You have such amazing proportions..."

The envy in the tailor's daughter's tone was palpable as she looked at Siasha admiringly. If Zig or the tailor felt the same way, they had kept that opinion to themselves.

That Siasha fit into the display version of the garments with little to no altering was proof of the tailor's daughter's words: On this continent, she had the ideal figure.

"I feel...a little embarrassed," Siasha said sheepishly.

She was wearing a dress of black and muted blues. The skirt had high slits, exposing a good amount of leg, though her modesty was preserved by the short pants and undergarments she was wearing underneath. The cut of the dress and the underclothes made it easy to move around—an asset when it came to running and fighting.

The ensemble included a cape with fur embellishments and elbow-length gloves, as well as a knife belt and pouch to go around her waist. To complement the look, the tailor's daughter had her put on sturdy-looking, calf-length boots. Her glossy black hair was accentuated by a decoration Zig had selected while waiting for her to get dressed. It was the same blue as her eyes and added a brilliant pop of color.

"What do you think, Zig?" Siasha asked anxiously.

I don't think I've ever seen a better example of someone lacking self-awareness, he thought.

Siasha already had a lovely face. With her otherworldly aura and eyes of captivating azure, she had a bewitching charm that good looks alone couldn't surpass. The new garments served only to further enhance her beauty.

"Yeah. It's fine," was the only reply he managed to muster. *Sheesh, it's not like you're a virgin,* he internally berated himself.

The silly grin the tailor's daughter had plastered all over her face was also starting to get on his nerves.

"Really?" Siasha gave a satisfied smile. "I'm glad to hear that."

She didn't know what was going on in his mind to elicit the rather stilted reaction but understood those words were a sincere compliment.

◆ ◆ ◆

Over the next few days, Zig and Siasha continued to hunt pouch wolves. Despite being repetitive, the payout was decent and the request was still the most lucrative way to get the points she needed to achieve the next rank.

And it seemed that retail therapy had done the trick, because Siasha happily carried out her work with no more complaints. Just to be safe, they always sought their quarry far from where they first encountered the ghost shark. Despite Zig's worries of an attack, they were able to finish the job without incident.

It was on the fifth day that Siasha asked Zig if she could handle the slaying, with him only standing guard in the vicinity. She wanted to make adjustments to the lethal force needed to kill monstrosities, as well as test to see if she could keep her distance.

The day ended without any trouble, and Siasha headed straight for the reception area upon their return to the guild.

"Congratulations," the receptionist said as the witch made her report. "Your rating has passed ten points, so you've been promoted to the ninth class!"

"Thank you very much," Siasha said. *It's about time,* was what she was thinking, but she held back her exasperation and made a show of looking very grateful for her promotion.

"It's incredibly impressive how you've achieved the next rank so quickly. But..." the receptionist gave a look of concern, "you're working too much, so please make sure to get some rest. You're more likely to make careless mistakes when you're tired."

"I'm working too much?" Siasha asked. "How often do adventurers usually take jobs?"

"The average party takes a day off every other day. Even high-level parties work a max of two days in a row before resting for one.

To be blunt, it's highly irregular to find someone like you who works solo every day."

What I'm doing is irregular, huh? Siasha thought. *I didn't want to do anything that would make myself stand out... It's a bit of a pain, but I guess I'll have to take a day off occasionally.*

"You're...right," she said. "I may have been pushing myself too hard. I should take this opportunity to rest for a bit."

"Please do. Also, since you've surpassed the required number of requests, you're now eligible to be introduced to parties. Are you interested?"

"Um... I'll hold off for now." If she was going to team up with humans, Siasha needed a better grasp on what spells they commonly used.

Fortunately, the people here didn't seem to have the ability to sense the amount of mana someone possessed. As long as she didn't use any large-scale spells, she could still fly under the radar.

The receptionist nodded. "Understood. Also, you've become quite the hot topic here, Siasha. If anyone tries to solicit you, please report them to the guild and we'll take care of it."

"I'm a...hot topic?" she echoed. Siasha wasn't quite sure what that meant, but it didn't sound right after thinking about how much she didn't want to stand out.

"Female adventurers aren't particularly rare in and of themselves," the receptionist said, "but in addition to being a promising novice, you're someone with good looks who works solo. To be honest, there's probably something wrong with the men who *don't* try to approach you."

In the past, Zig had also mentioned something about her being attractive, but she'd never had the chance to compare her looks to others. The concept of beauty wasn't something she fully understood after being alone for so long.

Zig never reacted like that toward me, so I assumed it was just flattery...

The mercenary was rough around the edges and didn't outwardly express his feelings, preferring to show them through his actions instead. He was dependable, but she had a difficult time reading him.

The receptionist looked thoughtful. "I assume they've stayed quiet because you've been ineligible to join a party until now, but I don't doubt that you'll be receiving plenty of invitations soon." She frowned. "Many of the youngsters don't pay attention to what's going on around them, so they may approach you even when your male companion is around."

Siasha hoped a menacing glare from Zig would ward anyone off, but from what the receptionist was saying, it probably wouldn't be enough. She was starting to get the feeling that there were times when a man's lust superseded his desire to live.

"Understood," she finally said. "I'll report anyone who bothers me before Zig takes care of them."

"I get the feeling a lot of situations are going to be the latter. Is he powerful?"

In her time with the guild, the receptionist saw and interacted with many types of people. Even if she wasn't a proficient warrior herself, she had a knack for spotting them.

"Very," Siasha said succinctly.

The receptionist sighed, the witch's answer confirming her suspicions. "It would be much appreciated if you let the guild know before it goes that far..."

With a little giggle at the sight of the receptionist's grimace, Siasha bade her goodbye and headed for the dining hall.

"Over here."

Zig called out to Siasha, his hand raised. Even without the gesture, he was hard to miss—his massive frame stood out from the rest of the crowd. She walked over to him and showed him her card with a smug smile.

"I got my promotion," she said proudly.

He lightly clapped. "Congrats."

Her face then crumpled into a dissatisfied pout. "She also told me that I need to take a break...that I've been working too much."

"Well, she's got a point." Zig didn't sound surprised. He'd expected that might be the case.

"But I don't even feel tired!"

"You're supposed to rest before you get to that point." He couldn't suppress a small smile at her annoyance. "You need to be in optimal physical condition when you go to bed and wake up. If you keep pushing yourself, you're just asking to be a sitting duck when the unexpected occurs."

"Fine," she huffed.

Zig could somewhat empathize. Being asked to step on the brakes right when you've found something you enjoy was an experience he also went through.

When his swordplay began to improve, he had been so excited about the prospect of getting stronger that he started swinging his weapon around like a madman...until one of the veteran mercenaries beat him to a pulp to make him stop.

"No more pouting," he said gently. "Why don't we go out tomorrow? I found a large shop that deals in magic items—"

"Did you say magic items?!" she piped up. "I'm in, I'm in!"

Zig chuckled at how quickly she jumped on board at his suggestion.

"Let's go right after breakfast!" she said before quickly changing gears. "Oh, can you hold on for a moment? I'm going to borrow more books."

"Sure."

That was another reason why Siasha had been so eager to get promoted: She had already read through most of the books available to her as a tenth-class adventurer. Ranking up meant getting access to more reading material. Aside from completing requests for the guild, the only other thing that had kept her occupied the past few days was reading.

As he watched Siasha walk off, Zig decided to order a drink.

"May I sit here?"

He looked up to see a woman dressed in loose-fitting vestments. Her silvery hair and feminine figure caught his attention, but the most distinct aspect of her appearance was the piece of cloth draped over her eyes.

What is she, a blind priestess? Zig wondered.

He quickly glanced around the dining hall. There were a decent number of people, but it wasn't completely full. There had to be a reason why she chose to sit next to him.

His senses told him that this woman was anything but ordinary.

"Go ahead," he said.

Zig pointed to the seat across from him with his chin, cocking an eyebrow as he poured water from a jug into a cup and offered it to her.

"Thanks."

The woman gracefully sat down, resting her chin in the palm of her hand. When he handed her the drink, she accepted it and took a sip. Even if she couldn't *see*, he was well aware that she was observing him. Shrugging off her scrutiny, he sipped his tea, keeping his face completely blank. They continued to drink until the woman, who seemed to have reached the limits of her patience, broke the silence.

"You're not going to ask why I'm here?"

"I thought you wanted to share a table with me?" Zig replied politely.

The woman stiffened at his genteel demeanor. When he said nothing else, she proceeded to speak.

"I'm looking for someone on Alan's behalf. He wants to thank them for their help."

"Thank" them, huh...

"Oh yeah?" he said. "I don't know anything about that. I think you're barking up the wrong tree."

"I met with all the other parties who were working on that request on the same day and time. They also said they didn't have any idea. Don't you think that's strange?"

I knew this was going to end up biting us in the ass.

Making enemies out of one's peers was nothing but trouble—though he couldn't help but feel suspicious that the trail had led back to them in such a short amount of time.

"I've looked into the other parties," the woman continued. "While they weren't weak by any means, it didn't seem like any of them had the capabilities to see through a ghost shark's tricks. There was only one group that I didn't have any information on."

So that's what it was, Zig realized. They ruled out the rest of the suspects for being too ordinary. Siasha was also in the spotlight as an up-and-coming novice. The connections made sense.

"However, the guild member in that party was female. Alan said it was a male voice that shouted the warning. I thought it would be another swing and miss, but wouldn't you know it, apparently that girl always brings along a male companion to carry around her things."

The eye-masked woman seemed to be staring at him, waiting for a reaction. Zig returned her stare, his expression stony.

"I was surprised to finally meet you, though," she said. "It's hard to believe you merely carry around luggage. I've never met an attendant who was quite so...big."

"I'm a seasoned professional," he said. "A veteran porter in my own right."

"What about the weapon you carry?"

"How else am I going to defend the luggage?"

"I see."

His expression didn't waver.

The eye-masked woman seemed to realize that her approach was going nowhere, and her tone grew stern. "Let me be frank with you. I—"

Her face suddenly turned pale.

It was as if something within her was violently churning, and her body broke out in a cold sweat. Her breathing grew more and more ragged, and she felt a growing need to start massaging her stomach. Clenching her teeth, the woman desperately tried to stop the floodgates from opening.

"Are you okay?" the man across from her asked.

"Y-yes. I'm fine." Just responding made her feel like she was teetering on the edge of the brink.

"Are you sure about that? You shouldn't force yourself to keep it in. Seems like you're dying to use a restroom, huh?"

The epiphany hit her like a load of bricks.

That bastard!

The man had been sipping tea the whole time and never once touched the water.

He leered at her with an infuriating smirk. "Oh, right. You were going to ask me something? I'm feeling charitable at the moment, so I'll tell you whatever you want to know...slowly and in great detail."

Her face twisted into a hateful glare. "You shithead...!"

"What do you mean? I believe the one who needs to shit is *you*."

"Tch!"

Zig watched in amusement as the eye-masked woman scurried off. She was obviously in a hurry, yet she kept her movements incredibly slow to avoid triggering...an accident.

Siasha returned just in time and shot the woman a curious look. "What's with her?" she asked.

The mercenary shrugged. "Beats me."

The next day after breakfast, Zig and Siasha headed to the magic items shop.

Unlike how humans only imbued themselves partially to simplify the magic activation process, magic items were fully engraved with a particular spell. However, the enchantment alone wasn't enough. Depending on the intended use, the items also needed to be molded into specific forms using certain materials. When it was used to cast magic, the design supported the spell's activation. The design specifications weren't that particular when it came to simple spells, like ones that produced small flames or purified water; it was the stronger incantations that were stricter with their forms and components.

While extremely useful, magic items were supposed to be used to make up for a person's weaker attributes rather than boost their superior techniques. They also couldn't wield a magic item stronger than their own spells because they lacked the mana to activate it.

"Whichever way you slice it," Zig muttered in disappointment, "someone like me who can't use mana at all is shit out of luck..."

In contrast to Zig's inner gloom, Siasha was as excited as a kid in a candy shop, examining all the wares for sale and asking the employees question after question.

I should just leave her be for a bit, Zig thought.

He decided to look around the shop himself while he waited for her. It was fascinating to see the various magic items they had in stock.

"Whoa, these aren't cheap," he said to himself.

The small stuff was affordable enough, but the price skyrocketed when it came to magic items used in battle, such as those for attacking or defense. It was like seeing an auction being held before his eyes—the price rose incrementally with each object he looked at.

But one item made him stop in his tracks.

"Is this a dagger?"

Most of the magic items so far were things like gem-embedded bangles or other types of accessories. Judging from the deep indigo color of the blade and the weapon's peculiar design, it didn't appear to have any sort of practical use.

"Are you interested in this one?" one of the employees asked.

Zig looked at the blade closely. "Is this also a magic item?"

"Technically speaking, it's more of a magic implement than a magic item," they explained. "Rather than being imbued with a specific spell, it's a weapon that's been constructed from a material with special properties."

"How's that different?"

"The main difference is the weapon itself possesses a unique effect. Unlike magic items, it doesn't have to be activated with mana before use. This blade is fashioned from indigo adamantine, an ore with magic dissipation properties. Basically, it can cut through magic."

A blade that can cut through magic?

He never would've guessed the weapon was that powerful. But something didn't quite seem to add up. "Since it's only a dagger, wouldn't the magic strike you before you could cut through it, though?"

"It would."

Well, that sucks. The gears in his head started turning. "Is this the longest size they're made in?"

"Of course not, but if you're after something longer, you'd be better off checking a weapons shop. As for the price..."

Zig glanced at the item's price tag: 1.5 million dren. A big price for that small of a blade. He couldn't even imagine what something full-sized would cost.

"...It would be quite pricey as a weapon," the employee continued. "But we do also carry indigo adamantine arrowheads. They're quite effective against monstrosities that use protective magic."

Aha. That could work.

Something the size of an arrowhead would be reasonably priced and reusable. They might be a good to use as a last resort.

"How much do the arrowheads run?" he asked.

"We sell a set of three for 500,000 dren."

Zig's blood ran cold.

Reasonably priced...huh.

"Thank you and please come again!" an employee called after them as they left the shop.

While Zig had left empty-handed, Siasha had purchased one small trinket, something that looked like a little tube.

"What did you get?" he asked.

"It's a magic item that produces light," she said. "The brightness and time you can use it depends on how much mana is used for activation. I think it'll come in handy."

She often read books at night, so it would probably be useful as a reading light.

"All the items that can be used in battle were too expensive," she said sorrowfully. "I won't be able to afford them for a while. But just window shopping was fun!"

"There were magic wands, right?" Zig asked. "What were those for?"

"They're close-range weapons for magic users—blunt weapons that implement a sort of gimmick. Apparently, they cause an explosion if you activate them while striking something."

That could be dangerous, he thought. *But it wouldn't be a bad idea for a novice to have a blunt weapon. She wouldn't have to worry about the details of swordplay, since just smacking her target would be enough. Although...it wouldn't be necessary with those earthen spikes.*

"By the way, I heard someone defeated that ghost shark," she said.

"Oh?"

He didn't know how strong the creature was, but trying to track it down and kill it didn't seem all that easy.

"Those monstrosities have an incredibly honed sense of smell, so they're almost guaranteed to show up if you leave some bloody carcasses around. Apparently, it's common practice to surround it and then bombard it with attacks as soon as it starts to feed."

"It doesn't notice the people sneaking up on it?"

"Not if you douse your entire body in grass juice, I guess. I heard it doesn't have very good vision."

The measures sounded a little extreme, but it was a fine battle tactic if it was that effective. He assumed the ghost shark to be quite cunning despite its large size, but apparently it was weak in close quarters as well. However, that didn't mean adventurers should underestimate its power. Measures could be taken if a party member was aware of its presence, but it was difficult to notice it before it claimed a victim.

"Do you have an idea of what you want to do after tomorrow?" he asked.

"Pretty much," Siasha replied. "I'm thinking of going after sky squids or blade bees or maybe both."

Zig hadn't heard of either one. *I can wager a guess about the bees, but what's a sky squid?*

He looked puzzled. "By squid...you mean the sea creature?"

"Yup. I've only read about them in this book, but they seem just like the marine type."

Siasha took out the book in question and handed it over to him. Glancing at the spine, Zig realized it was the same *The Illustrated Guide to Monstrosities* he had read in the reference room. She opened the book and showed him a bookmarked page.

SKY SQUID

Lives in the treetops, using its tentacles to freely move between the branches.

Primarily feeds on small animals, but large specimens may attack humans. They spring down from above to capture prey by holding it in place with their tentacles. After stabbing their proboscis into their prey, they inject digestive fluid to break down its internal organs and consume the resulting liquids.

It is easy to recognize the victims of a sky squid because their corpses are completely hollow. If you come across these husks, keep a careful eye on the canopy above you.

They are surprisingly clever and can't be caught by simple traps.

The flesh of these monstrosities is considered delicious and fetches a high selling price. The proboscis is also delicate yet durable, so there is a demand for them as medical supplies and for other various uses.

"So there are also squid on land here," Zig mused. "That method of feeding seems pretty grotesque, though..."

"I wonder what they taste like?" Siasha said.

That's her first thought when it comes to this obviously dangerous creature? Zig thought, slightly alarmed at her brazen statement.

"As for blade bees..." she continued, "they have a blade-like protrusion that extends from their posteriors. They don't seem to be venomous, though."

The mercenary gave a nod at that information. *So pretty much a case of what you see is what you get.*

"But they could be the more dangerous of the two if they're like normal bees," he said. "It might be tough to handle if they attack as a swarm."

"They do build large hives, but it should be okay if we don't attack one directly. Worker bees go out to hunt in small numbers, so we could pick off some when they're away from the hive."

A small group would probably be manageable for them. Siasha's magic allowed for better crowd control than him attacking with his twinblade.

"Why'd you settle on those two types?" Zig asked.

"Two reasons. The first is that the commission is good, and the second is that the two species prey on one another."

"So they're both predator and prey to each other? Is that even possible?"

Zig wasn't an expert at ecology, but he couldn't help but wonder if that would throw the ecosystem out of whack.

Siasha had done her research. "It's not unusual for the role of predator to change based on numbers, terrain, surprise attacks, or size. The blade bees have numbers; the sky squids have size. The victor is determined by their circumstances when they fight."

Which meant the battle would be won or lost based on the luck of the timing.

Even in the natural world, the strongest one doesn't always automatically win, Zig thought.

"Anyway, I figured if I found one, it wouldn't be too difficult to find the other," she reasoned. "I was thinking of accepting the blade bee request and selling any sky squids we happen to come across for parts. Blade bees don't seem to have a lot that's worth selling, but they can be dangerous if their population grows too much, so there are always requests to cull them."

It sounded like Siasha had put a lot of thought into her plan. Zig could see that she was vigilant when it came to collecting pertinent adventurer information and coming up with the most efficient and financially lucrative ways to increase her rank.

"Got it. I'm guessing that means I'm on sky squid duty?"

"Yes, please. Whether I get sucked dry as a bone or not is all in your hands."

"Sounds like an important mission. I'll do everything in my power."

They continued to talk about their plans as they headed back home.

It was another perfect day for adventuring. Zig waited at the dining hall while Siasha went to the request boards. He was sitting in a chair, trying to stifle a yawn, when he heard someone approach.

"May I sit here?"

That's the same opening line as that woman from yesterday.

If it was someone who knew her, he was going to give the same response. "Go ahead."

But when Zig poured the newcomer a cup of water just like he'd done the day before, there was hesitation in his voice.

"Th-that won't be necessary. I'm not thirsty."

That confirmed that this person knew or had talked to the woman with cloth-covered eyes.

The man sitting across from Zig looked to be around his own age, with a mop of red hair and a longsword in his hand. From his build and posture alone, Zig could tell he was a man of considerable prowess.

"The name's Alan. Alan Clows."

"I'm Zig."

"Nice to meet you, Zig. Okay, I'm just going to be direct here: Were you the one who warned us back then?"

Zig appreciated his directness—the man seemed like he was merely confirming what he already knew. Which meant there was no point in dodging the question.

"What are you going to do with that information?" he asked.

"Nothing," Alan said. "I just want to say thanks."

"Even if the person who shouted was spying on you to steal your battle techniques and just so happened to pick up on something else?" Zig pressed. "Do you still feel indebted to them?"

Alan didn't miss a beat. "Of course. Obviously, the thought of being spied on doesn't sit well with me, but it's a small price to pay for my friends' lives. I'm just grateful for the help."

"I see."

Zig couldn't entirely rule out the possibility that this man was putting on an act, but he was never good at discerning someone's intent just by looking at their eyes.

The other man's words sounded sincere—at least to Zig's ears. If the cat was already out of the bag, there was no point in trying to skirt around it. He just needed to be prepared to kill all of them if they decided to retaliate.

Zig lifted both his hands up, as if in surrender. "Yeah. It was me."

Alan chuckled. "Heh, I wasn't expecting you to actually own up to it."

"I don't like beating around the bush."

"Regardless, thank you." Alan bowed his head in a show of appreciation. "Because of you, my friends are all still alive and well."

Zig casually waved off the gesture. "Don't worry about it. Like I said, it was just a coincidence."

"You didn't use some special technique to detect the beast?"

"Not at all. I just happened to see some inconsistencies in the light. If it wasn't for that, I wouldn't have noticed at all."

He conveniently left out being able to smell magic. After all, him detecting the ghost shark's presence purely by coincidence wasn't a complete lie.

"You're not an adventurer, are you?" Alan asked.

"No. I'm a porter and bodyguard."

"There are a lot of rumors flying around about your client," the swordsman commented. "She's quite a promising newcomer."

"So I've heard."

"I'd like to do something to show my appreciation, but since you're not an adventurer...would cash suffice?"

"I don't need to be paid for what I did."

Alan shook his head, unwilling to back down. "Come now. Don't be like that."

Despite Zig's attempts to decline, Alan didn't look like he was going to back down. Zig supposed this stubbornness was also what had pushed the man to such a high rank despite his young age. Sensing that Alan wouldn't leave him alone unless he made some sort of concession, he threw out the first thing that came to mind.

"You owe me one, then," he said. "Just return the favor at some point."

Alan thought for a moment before nodding. "Hmm...I suppose that's a good compromise seeing as I can't think of an alternative at the moment. But I will definitely make it up to you."

"I'm not going to hold my breath, but we'll see."

"Well, let's leave it at that for today. Oh, by the way...Elcia is furious."

It took Zig a second to remember, but there was only one person that had a reason to be pissed off at him.

"Oh, the woman with the eye mask?"

"The...*what*?" Alan gaped at him. "Elcia's a highly acclaimed third-class adventurer! I wouldn't be so reckless around her if I were you."

A third-class adventurer, huh, Zig thought. *That's a completely different tier compared to where Siasha's at now. I guess she's a force to be reckoned with?*

"Her digestive system wasn't that impressive," the mercenary said bluntly.

"Never ever say that to her face," Alan laughed wryly.

He got up and walked away, Zig silently watching his retreating back.

"Was I being too cautious?"

From what he could tell, this Alan guy didn't mean him any harm. The values where he was from and the ones on this continent seemed to be different...

"If that's the case," he said to himself, "I may have gone a little overboard yesterday."

He'd resorted to that underhanded tactic because he thought she was using some sort of magic with her gaze. Why else would she hide her eyes?

But maybe he'd been a little too paranoid.

"As long as it doesn't blow up and get out of hand..." Zig muttered under his breath as he waved Siasha, who had just returned from the request boards, over to him.

Despite being able to get the request they wanted, Siasha didn't exactly look enthusiastic.

"What's wrong?" Zig asked.

"I suppose it can't be helped," she said, "but there are a lot more people now."

The request in question was aimed at eighth-class adventurers. Since the majority of adventurers were seventh class and under, jobs for those ranks naturally had the most competition.

Which meant...

"There's a high probability we'll encounter others on the same job," Zig pondered, "so we may end up squabbling over our quarry."

That wasn't surprising—everyone was looking to make money. The request they were fulfilling was lucrative and most likely popular. The more takers, the higher chance of getting into disputes, likely over the most efficient hunting spots or who got to stake claim on kills.

"And we're basically small fry since we're newcomers," Siasha said.

Zig could already imagine how troublesome it would be if they happened to venture into some veteran adventurer's territory. It would be wise to assume that any good hunting spot had already been claimed by someone else.

"In any case, let's go and check it out," she continued, "If it doesn't work out, we can consider the next step."

"I guess that's all we can do."

Now that Siasha had taken the job, breaking the contract would mean paying a penalty fee and taking a hit to her reputation—both were situations she wanted to avoid.

The pair quickly set off for the transportation stone and waited in line until it was their turn to be sent to the forest. Once they arrived there, they headed east, the opposite direction from their pouch wolf hunting grounds.

Their expressions darkened once they arrived at their location. Other adventuring parties had already set up camps, surrounding a giant hive from a respectable distance.

"This is worse than I anticipated..." Siasha murmured, her face tinged with disgust.

She was looking at a large hive that likely belonged to the blade bees. About two-thirds of the hive was buried underground, with bees about the size of a small child flying in and out of an exposed opening. Unlike normal bees, they were black with the occasional white stripe running across their bodies. Instead of stingers, they had slender, curved swordlike blades.

The adventurers were lying in wait, with most spread out along small clearings. These sections gave them more space to fight, but due to their numbers, each party also had to take care not to overlap with the others.

Countless blade bees were entering and exiting the hive, but because they could fly, there were very few passing through the glades where the adventurers camped, thus limiting the potential for combat.

"Blade bees make their hives underground," Siasha explained. "When they get too large, they start to stick out like that."

"Wouldn't taking out the whole hive significantly reduce their numbers?" Zig asked. "It might be annoying to deal with the part that's underground, but there are ways to work around it, right? Like flooding it with oil or something?"

Zig thought he had asked a very reasonable question, but Siasha answered him with a funny face. "When the blade bees lose their queen, the largest of them becomes the next one. Even if a hive is destroyed, it's only a matter of time before they construct another one. Also..."

She paused a moment, looking reluctant to continue her explanation.

"Also, I don't think the adventurers would be on board with it," she finally said. "This place is basically a meal ticket for them."

Zig nodded in understanding. "So that's how it is."

The adventurers would be in an uproar if they completely eliminated the blade bees. By keeping the hive alive, they could consistently hunt them and earn a living. In the grand scheme of things, these monstrosities didn't pose that much of a threat since everyone knew how to properly deal with them—and earn a living while they were at it. Their survival was a safe yet stable method of making money.

"I won't say it's wrong," Siasha commented, "but anyone with that line of thinking probably shouldn't refer to themselves as an 'adventurer.'"

Her words made sense—clinging to a quick and easy source of income was far from being adventurous. Even farmers needed to get creative when facing uncertain weather conditions and pests every day.

"Although, it's not like there's absolutely no danger involved. I've heard that people have occasionally gotten too close and been attacked by a swarm of blade bees on all sides after getting caught in the crossfire."

Zig could tell there was a lot she wasn't saying aloud. As some-one who was truly enjoying the profession for what it was, it was probably difficult for her to accept these types of behaviors from her colleagues.

"Must be nice, running your mouth like that!" someone snarled. "You sure talk a big game for a little girl who's still wet behind the ears."

They both turned in the direction of the voice.

"Excuse me?" Siasha asked.

Another adventuring party was glaring at them with open hostility.

What the hell? Zig thought.

There were a lot of people around, but they'd made sure to keep their distance from all the other groups. They weren't making a big fuss either; no one should've been able to hear their conversation.

Siasha was so shocked that she was at a loss for words.

Scanning the party's faces, Zig saw that one of them—the man that had called them out—had a unique feature. Jutting from the sides of his head were pointed ears.

They were long and narrow, like the tip of a rounded spear. The ears also looked perfectly proportional for his size, so they couldn't be just a freak mutation. Maybe he was part of a race that was unique to this continent? If those ears weren't just for show, this man probably had superior hearing abilities.

Zig internally scolded himself for their careless mistake. He already saw how fundamentally different people were here compared to their home continent. After seeing the walking wolf when they first entered Halian, he should've known there would be other races. However, he had been too used to interacting with just humans that it slipped his mind.

"I apologize for my rude comments," Siasha replied. Her tone turned defiant as she accepted the fact that she'd been overheard. "But I don't understand why someone would defeat the purpose of this profession just to make a profit."

"You don't know a thing about us!"

To Zig, it sounded like the man knew perfectly well what he was. More than anger, there were traces of self-loathing in his spluttered words. Having the truth pointed out by Siasha, who looked like a young girl, probably touched a nerve.

The mercenary could feel the men's animosity growing by the minute, but Siasha seemed oblivious. She probably didn't notice feelings such as hostility when it didn't involve any murderous intent.

"Of course, I don't. I'm—"

"That's enough, Siasha," Zig interjected before she could provoke them even further.

Siasha looked at him, startled. "Fine," she muttered. It was clear she still wanted to speak her mind, but she backed off meekly after seeing the stern expression on his face.

Zig gave her a pat on the shoulder and turned back to face the men. "Sorry about that," he said apologetically. "She was just irritated since it's so crowded around here."

"Hmph, you're just a coward who follows this woman around like a dog," the man said contemptuously.

Zig felt a murderous rage welling up inside him. For a moment, all he saw was red. He quickly pushed the feeling down, forcing himself to stay calm. Thankfully, the men didn't seem to notice and turned around to walk away.

Siasha's shot a fierce glare in their direction as she quietly watched them leave. Only when their forms were but tiny specks in the distance did she finally speak.

"Why did you stop me?" she said reproachfully.

"There are far more humans like that than you'd imagine," he admonished. "It's best not to make enemies of them."

Siasha didn't say a word and averted her eyes with resentment; she didn't seem satisfied with his answer.

"One more thing," Zig softly chuckled, amused at her pouty behavior. "Not everyone is strong. You have to come to terms with who you are and weigh your ideals versus reality."

"Do you do that too?" she asked.

"Yeah." To him, it was commendable to always want to improve and aim higher. However it wasn't right to impose those values on others. "Even if you come across someone you don't agree with," he said, "just chalk it up to having a difference of opinions. Always butting heads will only lead to endless arguments."

His explanation must have made sense to her because she was starting to calm down.

"Okay."

"However, you don't need to understand them or associate with people like that. Just keep doing what you've been doing until now."

Not everyone was strong, but it also wasn't right for them to hinder those who were or wanted to be by forcing them down to their level.

"All right," she said, mollified. "For the time being, let's do something different today."

Now that she'd gathered her wits about her and changed her mindset, Siasha was quick to decide their next course of action.

"You mean cancel this request?" he asked. "Wouldn't the costs outweigh the benefits if you do that?"

Siasha wouldn't go down in ranking by losing reputation, but a cancellation would create a deficit she would have to make up before she could earn more points to move up to the next class.

"I'm not canceling anything," she explained. "Once all the other adventurers have started to go home, we can quickly take care of a few blade bees ourselves. Until then, I want to explore the area and see if we can find a monstrosity with a high population that seems easy to kill."

It looked like the new plan was to focus on finding a plentiful quarry that Siasha could easily turn in for requests.

"All right," Zig said. "What about the money?"

"For the time being, I'll put less emphasis on work that brings in high commissions and focus on earning points so that I can get past the ninth- and eighth-class ranks. Once we get there, both the pay and number of good requests should significantly increase. I'll just have to hold out until then."

"So that's your plan. Sounds good."

She was back to being efficient, except she was now concentrating on the future instead of the present.

Armed with their new strategy, the pair bypassed the hive and headed further into the forest.

After detouring from the hive, Siasha and Zig explored deep within the forest. There were many insect-like monstrosities in the area, and they could hear buzzing sounds coming from here and there.

"I know the blanket term is monstrosities, but does it count for bugs?" Zig asked.

Wouldn't a name like "insectrosities" be more suitable for them?

"There's a proper term for creatures in the insect family under the monstrosity genus, but no one really ever uses it," Siasha said. "Apparently, it's not uncommon for people to further simplify creatures' names and just refer to them as 'bees' or 'squids' and the like."

"I guess it comes down to the easiest name so everyone knows what they're talking about," he mused.

The two continued to make small talk as they inspected their surroundings, but so far all they could find were small clusters and hives. There didn't seem to be another plentiful species propagating in the area nor was there any big game.

"There sure isn't a wide variety here," he commented.

"That's because this is blade bee territory," Siasha remarked. "They probably only create small colonies because they'll be discovered if they grow too large."

True, or the larger groups were already devoured.

Maybe the blade bees posed a threat to everything in the forest.

Zig casually put out his hand so that it was within Siasha's sight.

"It could also be that many of the monstrosities here lie in wait until the right opportunity presents itself," he said.

"That's a good point."

He made a fist, pointed his thumb down, then held up two fingers.

Two enemies were nearby.

Siasha nodded in understanding and silently moved behind Zig.

The mercenary took a few more steps forward.

There was a rustling in the trees above him, followed by the sound of something swooping down.

It was a pair of sky squids in mottled patterns of green and brown, both around the size of a petite woman. They dove toward him, tentacles outstretched in hopes of entangling their prey.

Siasha's stone projectile shot out from behind him, knocking both squids down. However, neither seemed very hurt as they slowly staggered back up and tried to escape after their failed attempt to attack.

It was Zig's turn.

He slashed their tentacles clean off as they tried to grab the branches of a nearby tree. Both squids lay dead before they could even leave the ground.

"Hm, doesn't seem like earth magic works well on them," Siasha said with a scowl, unamused that the squids were still alive and kicking even after taking a hit from one of her spells.

Perhaps the flexible and slimy nature of these creatures allowed them to withstand the impact of stone projectiles and earthen spikes. On the other hand, fire or electricity would probably be more effective, but using those means would render any valuable parts unsellable.

"They might be an incompatible enemy for you," Zig said as he began to flay their newly captured prize. "Think positive: At least we can sell the meat."

To his surprise, the squids' flesh, previously a mottled green and brown, had turned pure white after their deaths.

"Why did the color change?" he asked.

"It's the same mechanism as normal squids," Siasha replied. "I read their coloration changes when they become aggressive. Oh, you can't eat the tentacles, so don't bother with them. The fins, liver, proboscis, and digestive fluid sac can all be sold."

Zig cut off the parts she indicated.

"Make sure not to damage the sac. It will spoil as soon as the contents are exposed to the outside air."

"What's this thing even used for?"

If exposing its contents made the digestive fluid sac useless, did it have any sort of value?

"It's a highly prized item for taxidermy; it apparently produces some amazing results."

"I honestly admire the people who think to use stuff like this."

"Right? You just have to respect the insatiable curiosity of artisans."

Zig finished cutting up the squids and glanced around. They were fairly deep into the forest, and there were no other adventurers nearby.

"We're lucky these sky squids attacked us," he said. "It would've been hard for us to detect them first with this camouflage." He hadn't smelled anything either, so they weren't using magic to alter their coloration.

"They probably thought they had a chance because there's only two of us and I'm small," she said.

"You have a point. Joining a party is probably a good way to avoid getting jumped by monstrosities that specialize in being covert."

Stealthy monstrosities tended to have inferior combat capabilities in close quarters so they wouldn't want to attack large groups of humans who could fight back. When hunting these creatures, safety in numbers seemed like the safest tactic.

Siasha considered his words. "When you put it that way, that shark must've been fairly powerful considering it relied on stealth."

The ghost shark had been lying in wait as well, but it was highly aggressive even when faced with multiple opponents—probably because it was so fast that it could escape even if it was captured, and its stealth ability enabled it to disappear before one's very eyes.

Even if they both relied on stealth, the sky squids completely paled in comparison to the ghost shark.

"Zig, Zig, Zig!"

The excitement in Siasha's voice pulled Zig from his thoughts.

"Hm?"

"Look at that!"

He glanced in the direction of her outstretched finger.

Two types of monstrosities were locked in combat: the blade bees and one he had never seen before.

It resembled an ash-gray caterpillar, but what stood out the most were its legs. Several pairs extended from its sides, though they were long and spindly, like those of an insect. It was using them to agilely dart around.

A stinger protruded from its tail.

It deftly dodged the blade bees and flailed its tail, knocking its attackers to the ground.

"I believe that's a rockworm," Siasha said. "It may look like a caterpillar, but that's the adult form."

"Looks pretty strong."

The creature was facing around a dozen blade bees and slowly reducing their numbers without sustaining serious injury to itself. Considering how many it was fighting, escaping didn't seem like an option.

Granted, its movements were quick, but it appeared to have solid defenses as well.

"It's one of the stronger monstrosities around these parts," she explained. "They're usually hunted by parties of seventh-class adventurers."

"Yeah, that makes sense," he said.

"Zig, let's kill it."

The gears in his head started turning at her proposal.

Killing it is possible. It's fast, but not nearly fast enough that we can't handle it.

However, fighting off a swarm of blade bees would be much more difficult for him to do solo. The other issue was the guild.

"Is it okay for you to take down a monstrosity that's above your rank?"

Adventurers were limited to requests that were only one level above their current class. Would Siasha get in trouble by fighting something two classes above hers? That was Zig's main concern.

"I wouldn't be able to fight one ordinarily, but there are exceptions to the rules. I'm permitted to defend myself if it attacks me. If I can defeat it, I'll get paid the commission as well."

Those rules probably didn't apply if the monstrosity was slow or noncombative. However, this rockworm was both quick and aggressive. It was a good enough excuse.

Zig nodded. "Understood. What about its parts?"

"Rockworms don't have much that's usable. All we need is the stinger on the tail, so feel free to hack at it to your heart's content."

As those words left her lips, the battle between the monstrosities came to an end with the rockworm crushing the final blade bee to death in its jaws.

Zig dashed forward.

He tried to keep his footsteps light, but perhaps the rockworm had a keen sense of hearing as it seemed to sense his movement anyway and turned toward him.

In that case there's no need to hold back, Zig thought as he increased his speed.

Siasha released a spell just before he reached the creature, but the rockworm managed to dodge her earthen spikes, using its long legs to wiggle around them.

No, it didn't have good hearing. Now that he was up close, Zig could see fine hairs growing all over its body. They must've been what the rockworm was using to detect movement coming from the air and the ground.

Even after evading the spikes, the rockworm didn't lose its balance. Instead, it stuck out its jaw, ready to crush anything in its path.

Zig ducked to the right to avoid it, trying to cut off some of its legs along the way. The rockworm quickly whirled around and began to chase after him without losing any momentum. Thanks to its many legs, the monstrosity had incredible balance and was adept at sudden changes of direction.

"Tch!"

Zig had no choice but to step back as he swung his sword. He'd lost his momentum, so he wasn't able to injure it, but a side swipe to the jaw was enough to deflect the rockworm's trajectory.

He crouched down to avoid a swipe of the creature's tail and prepared himself for when it turned around and charged at him once more. Before it could engulf him in its jaws, Siasha cast another spell.

The rockworm sensed the motion and once again tried to dodge. However, instead of earthen spikes, a long wall burst horizontally from the ground. It launched the front half of the creature's body in the air, putting it off balance.

Its precious legs kicking helplessly in the air, the rockworm tried to squirm and right itself.

Zig leapt on top of the wall, cleaving through its exposed belly in one sweeping strike. The rockworm's head went flying through the air as the rest of its body slumped lifelessly to the ground. Its jaw continued to twitch for a few moments before it stopped moving.

"That's it?" Zig muttered as he started to wipe off the gunk that covered his twinblade.

Despite how quickly he'd dispatched it, the sheer speed and agility of its legs made the creature a formidable foe.

"Either enemies can sense my spells coming or they're just plain ineffective lately," Siasha groaned, her face twisted in annoyance.

"Don't say that," Zig said. "You really helped me back there."

Her spell's timing had been perfect—it would've been far more difficult if he'd had to fight the rockworm by himself.

"Thanks," she said. "But this experience seriously makes me want to purchase some magic items. It's not very convenient relying on just one attribute."

"You better save up, then."

Zig left the rockworm harvesting to Siasha while he gathered up the blade bee carcasses.

"Still, it did our work for us," the witch said. "This many blade bees should be enough to fulfill the request."

"You're okay with that?"

"Yes. The rockworm killed the blade bees, and we killed the rockworm—to the victor go the spoils."

I guess it's not too different from corpse looting on the battlefield, Zig mused.

"This should be enough for today," Siasha said as she put her knife away. "Let's go home."

"All right."

Loaded down with materials obtained from the various monstrosities, the two of them turned and headed back down the same road they'd come from. When they reached the blade bee hive, they found that there were still many adventurers present. It seemed to be taking some time for them to finish up as each party was taking turns in culling the specific amount listed in their request.

They glared at Siasha and Zig suspiciously when they emerged from within the forest. Upon seeing their overflowing bounty of monstrosity materials, their expressions darkened with envy, jealousy, contempt, and annoyance—their eyes made no secret of their feelings toward the pair as they passed.

Zig spotted the adventurers from earlier that afternoon among the crowd. Siasha, on the other hand, didn't pay them a moment's notice. She kept walking without so much as a backward glance.

Upon returning to the guild, they reported their completed request at the reception area as usual.

"Another job well done today!" the receptionist praised. "Looks like you brought a lot back with you."

"Would you mind appraising it?" asked Siasha. "Oh, and this is proof of something else we ended up killing."

"Sure. Let me take tha—"

The receptionist paused when she saw what Siasha was handing over.

"Isn't this the mandible of a rockworm?" she said slowly.

"Oh, so *that's* what that monstrosity is called." Siasha's tone was laced with false appreciation, as if she was thankful for having learned something new.

Zig wondered if her response sounded like a blatant lie to him only because he knew the truth.

Regardless of whether or not Siasha's faux ignorance was also obvious to the receptionist, she erupted in anger.

"You should've known better! Rockworms are monstrosities that require the skill of around seventh-class adventurers!"

"That may be true, but...it randomly attacked us," Siasha said. "We had no choice but to fight back. We tried to run away, but it was so quick that fleeing wasn't an option..." Her voice trailed off as she feigned a sullen expression.

Seeing Siasha's glum face, the receptionist's expression softened and her voice became gentler.

"I apologize for shouting," she said. "If those were the circumstances, then it can't be helped, but please try not to do such reckless things."

"Yes. I'll be more careful."

The receptionist appeared to be truly worried about her—the realization made Siasha feel a painful twinge in her heart.

"Anyway, this is quite impressive," the receptionist commented.

"It's not an easy feat for two people to take down a rockworm on their own. I'll inform my superiors about what happened. It's the guild's policy to provide reasonable accommodations, so I don't think anything negative will come of this."

"I appreciate it," Siasha thanked the receptionist and walked back to Zig. "She got mad at me."

"It is what it is," he said.

"But strangely, I didn't feel too bad about being scolded."

"Probably because it wasn't superficial; she was legitimately concerned for your safety."

"You think so?"

"Most likely."

Her report finished, Siasha headed off to borrow some books from the reference room while Zig waited in the dining hall.

"May I sit here?"

Again?

It felt like this was a daily occurrence by now.

He didn't even need to look at who it was—he would recognize that voice anywhere considering it was someone he saw practically every day now.

After a long pause he said, "Go ahead."

"Thanks," the receptionist replied as she took a seat across from him.

"Aren't you on the clock?"

"I'm taking my break at the moment."

There was silence afterward. Zig didn't have anything to say to her; the receptionist, however, was looking him up and down.

"Do you mind if I ask you some questions?" she finally said.

"Sure. As long as I don't have to answer anything I don't find favorable."

"That's fine. Were you ever an adventurer in the past?"

"No."

"Then, were you ever in some sort of profession that involved combat?"

"Yes. I've been a mercenary for a long time."

The receptionist's eyebrows twitched slightly—she didn't look excited to hear that.

"You're a mercenary?"

"Do you have a problem with that?"

"N-no, it's not that..."

"I can understand if you do. I heard the mercenaries around here are an unsavory sort."

"It's not like that where you come from?" The receptionist leaned forward a little, now more interested in his background.

"People who frequently break their contracts soon find themselves without work," he replied. "The punishments are quite severe since it also hurts the reputation of the mercenary band they're affiliated with."

"I see. I'm sorry for my assumptions."

"There's no need to apologize. Truth is, I used to make money killing people."

"Right. So what's your relationship with Siasha?"

"She's a client who's hired me to be her bodyguard."

The receptionist tried to be nonchalant, but even she couldn't fully conceal her disgust. Mercenary work obviously didn't sit well with her. It was a natural reaction for someone who'd always walked the straight and narrow.

"I'll take your word for it," she said. "She's an incredibly promising adventurer—so studious and likely a future role model."

I figured she had a good reputation, Zig thought with a mental sigh, *but I never thought it'd be that stellar. She even talked about not wanting to be conspicuous. Looks like she's way beyond standing out at this point.*

"Please make sure to keep her well protected," the receptionist continued. "She's an indispensable human resource for the guild."

"You don't have to tell me that—it's my job. I'll keep her safe as long as I'm getting paid."

The disgust on her face deepened.

That's probably not what this lady wanted to hear, he thought.

"Thank you for making that clear." Her tone turned cold and businesslike. "We look forward to your continued support."

She rose from her seat and went back to work. Her reaction told him that perhaps due to the town's culture, she held other things in life with more regard than money.

In all honesty, Zig felt the same way.

Money solved a lot of problems, but indulging in it too much could cause someone to lose sight of what mattered the most. He could name several instances in the past where it happened to him.

He didn't know if the receptionist had gone through a similar experience herself, but even if she hadn't, her education and knowledge were apparently enough to lead her to the same conclusion. If that was the case, he wouldn't want to mess with another like her.

"Still, the reality is you're not going anywhere without money," he said to himself.

Seeing Siasha coming down the stairs, Zig got up from his seat. She was carrying an extra book, likely thanks to their larger than usual payday.

"What should we do now?" she asked. "Go home?"

"Would you mind if we stopped by the armory?" he said. "I want to get some repairs done."

Hacking away at monstrosities caused a lot of wear and tear on his weapon. Zig had been taking care of the upkeep himself, but it was reaching the point where he wanted to get it professionally sharpened.

"Of course. Why not get a new one while you're at it? You've been saving up money lately."

"A new sword, huh..."

The thought of a weapon made from locally acquired materials piqued his interest...

The fangs and claws of monstrosities were incredibly robust, not to mention far more durable than normal iron swords.

His twinblade relied on using weight and centrifugal force rather than sharpness. And because it had to be durable, it was also large and heavy. However, if materials from monstrosities were used...they could possibly be rather sturdy and incredibly light at the same time. Their raw power might be decreased due to the lower weight, but there were plenty of ways to work around that. Sacrificing a little power for higher mobility came with the benefit of having more options.

"Depending on how much it costs, it might not be a bad idea," Zig said.

"We can ask them about a variety of things, including an estimate for a weapon price."

"Let's do that."

After getting a snack at one of the food stalls, they headed to the armory they'd visited when they first entered Halian. It was filled with adventurers stopping by after completing their work for the day.

"Welcome!" the clerk said cheerfully. "Thank you for your patronage from before. What can I help you with?"

It appeared the clerk remembered them. They probably made quite the impression as the customers who'd lugged in that back-breaking tusk.

"I'd like to get my weapon sharpened," he replied. "And I'd like to look for a similar weapon while I'm here. Do you have anything in stock?"

"A double-edged sword?" she paused for a moment. "Very few people use them, so I don't believe we have something like that in the shop. There might be some in storage, though. Let me speak with the person in charge there."

Zig realized that while he called his weapon a twinblade, it was known as a double-edged sword here. Perhaps it was like back in the home continent—weapon names differed depending on the region.

After handing over his weapon to be sharpened, there was nothing to do but wait. They were browsing the shop's selection of mysterious-looking weapons when the clerk returned.

"We only have two weapons that meet your specifications," she said, pushing a cart before them. It contained two twinblades: one with single-edged straight swords and one with double-edged longswords.

The single-edged one had a greenish hue, the blades curved at an angle in a shape reminiscent of an insect's claw.

"This masterpiece is made from the entire claw of a razor-bladed decapitator mantis."

Forget biologically *inspired*, this sword was the real thing.

"It's so sharp that it's actually cut off the arms of people who've tried to wield it while being unfamiliar with this weapon type."

"Oh."

Zig grimaced at the clerk's sales pitch. Was that what a prospective buyer wanted to hear? She didn't seem to notice his reaction and continued to describe the weapon in detail.

But Zig already knew this one wasn't the weapon for him.

It wasn't that he couldn't handle the blade; he was just looking for something more reliable. The sharper the blade, the more fragile it was. They weren't suited for consecutive combat or battles of attrition. After all, twinblades focused heavily on weight and centrifugal force, so they took a beating in battle. This one was just a razor-sharp longsword—not in line with the weapon's concept at all.

"...And that pretty much sums it up. Now, about this other one..."

The clerk had either wrapped up her explanation fairly quickly or noticed that Zig was no longer paying attention because she then started talking about the second twinblade.

"This one was carved from the horns of a double-horned blue beetle."

"Can I try holding it?" he asked.

The clerk nodded, and he picked it up. It was slightly lighter than his own weapon, and the bluish blades appeared to be thick and sturdy.

"I'd like to give it a try if that's possible," he said.

"This way, please."

He followed the clerk as she led him to a small open area near the armory's forge. There were a few large piles of kindling there that could be used as practice dummies.

"It shouldn't be a problem if you take a few swings out here."

"Thanks."

Once he made sure the clerk was well out of the way, Zig began swinging the blade. Since it wasn't his usual weapon, he started out slow to try and get a feel for it. With each flourish, he tested out its center of gravity, grip, and the distance between the blades as he swung.

The craftsmen working nearby stopped their hammering to watch Zig. He didn't notice the eyes on him, however, as he was fully absorbed in brandishing the sword.

The sound of the blades whipping through the air gradually grew louder and louder, eventually reaching the ears of the customers inside the armory. The more in tune he became with the blade, the quicker his swings became. The weapon was now spinning so fast it was practically impossible to make out what type of weapon he was using.

"Try hitting the armor now," the clerk said as she stood to his side, pointing at a scrap piece of armor.

"Is that okay?"

"Go ahead."

The words were barely out of her mouth when Zig used his built-up momentum to strike the armor with all of his might. He swiped at its side so that he wouldn't damage the base it was resting on, squarely hitting the rib guard.

The armor immediately crumpled like a piece of paper, the top half spinning wildly as it flew through the sky.

"Nice work," the clerk commented.

Zig looked over the weapon. The blade was still hot to the touch from the powerful blow, but he couldn't make out even the smallest blemish.

"Impressive," he murmured.

The weapon was well balanced, and he had no qualms with the reach or weight. He knew monstrosities provided materials of excellent quality, but he had no idea they were *this* good.

He wanted it, that's for sure. But a weapon like this...

"How much is this?"

Despite feeling that it was going to cost more than he could pay, it was perhaps a sense of longing that propelled him to ask anyway.

"One million dren."

"I figured as much..." His head drooped.

"However..." He quickly looked back up. "This is a piece that's been resting in storage without a buyer for some time. You might be able to strike up a deal with the craftsman who made it."

"Really?"

"Yes. Very few people wield double-edged swords, so we've actually been wondering what to do with it. Okay, saying *very few* is an exaggeration. To be honest, as far as I know, there's no one else in town who uses them."

"Not even one?"

"There was one in the past—the person who sold us that other sword."

She pointed at the green twinblade.

"I see."

Heh. I wonder why.

"Would you like to try bartering?" she asked.

Zig thought for a moment. Even if he could haggle the price, the most he could afford to pay was around 500,000 dren. Even if they were itching to get rid of this weapon, a fifty percent discount seemed too much to ask.

Considering the materials and cost of labor, 800,000 dren was about as much as he could expect.

"It's a shame, but I think I'll pass," he said. "I don't have enough money."

"Oh? So, if you *did* have the money, would you be willing to buy it then?"

"What's that supposed to mean?"

Maybe she was offering to put it on layaway? Even so, she said herself that no one else could use it, so would another buyer even show up?

"If you're okay with it, we could do a deferred payment plan," the clerk offered. "Of course, it would require an initial deposit to start."

"A loan, huh..."

That proposal was a siren song. He knew the horrors firsthand from watching countless men fall victim to temptation. There were even some who lost their lives to slavery after being forced to retreat from a job and their clients disappearing. These men had banked on a huge payday just over the horizon, only to find out they'd been swindled.

It had been painful to see their stunned faces as their belongings were confiscated before they were stripped of their clothes and shoved into a carriage.

"N-no, I don't want to do that," he said as the memory sent chills running down his spine.

The clerk looked disappointed. "Are you sure? That's a pity to hear."

She didn't press the matter any further and hauled both weapons back to the storage room. Zig then put in a request for his sword to be sharpened and left the armory.

"Oh? He didn't end up buying it?" one of the craftsmen asked the clerk as she was putting away the double-edged swords.

"No. It's a shame, right? All he ended up doing was asking us to sharpen his current weapon."

"Indeed... This is just made of metal. What a waste, considering his talent with a blade."

"You think so too, Ghant?"

The craftsman—Ghant—stroked his beard. "I've never seen anyone handle a double-edged sword like that before. The novices just do some flashy moves that are all for show, unlike that young man. I can tell he's quite experienced."

The clerk was slightly surprised—it was rare for the somewhat crotchety craftsman to offer such high praise.

"I tried to offer him a loan plan, but all the blood drained from his face, and he ran away."

Ghant guffawed. "Haha! What else were you expecting?"

The clerk giggled for a moment before her face turned serious.

"Ghant, how much do you think you can lower the price?" she asked.

"Hm... There aren't as many double-horned blue beetles around these days, so probably not that much."

"I understand that it's an excellent blade, but as a business we can't keep holding on to merchandise that is never going to sell."

"Yes, well, I know that, but..." Ghant stuttered, trying to come up with a retort.

"Even if you have to give a little leeway on making a profit, wouldn't your pride as a craftsman be satiated by having the blade wielded by someone who is worthy of it?"

"Satisfaction doesn't put food on the table."

"*Ghant.*"

"...800,000."

"You're joking, right?"

The look on her face told him that she wasn't going to back down on negotiating. Ghant sighed, his resolve crumbling.

"750,000."

She silently shook her head.

"700,000!"

"How many years has it been since you made that thing?" she admonished.

"650,000!" he snapped. "I can't go any lower than that!"

Sensing that this was about the best compromise she could get, she nodded. "All right, we have a deal." She chose to ignore his dejected expression. "Okay, well now it all comes down to him..."

No matter how much she whittled down the price, it would be all for nothing if the man earlier wasn't interested in buying.

"I got the impression he liked the feel of it, but it's hard to say for sure without knowing how much he has. I would wager a guess in the range of 300,000 to 400,000 or so."

She gave herself a pat on the back. She finally found a customer who might be willing to buy this weapon that had been collecting dust for a very long time.

"It pays to be in the good graces of such a skilled customer," she said to herself.

She wasn't doing this out of the goodness in her heart—the clerk was also looking out for her best interests.

"Are you sure you're okay with not buying anything?" Siasha asked when she noticed Zig returning empty-handed.

He was feeling a small twinge of regret already. "I found something I liked, but it was out of my budget."

He couldn't afford to go broke just so he could buy a sword. Weapons were tools of the trade—items purchased to *make* money.

"I can buy it once I've got some savings set aside," he said.

"Sounds like we're both focused on raising money for the foreseeable future then," Siasha said. "In order to do that, I need to get my adventuring class up."

"In the end, I guess it all comes down to that," Zig agreed.

At this rate, taking days off was going to start feeling like a burden—probably not as much as it did to Siasha, but still.

"No, I can't think like that," he mumbled. "If you stop enjoying your days off, you're not even a human being anymore."

"Hm?" Siasha looked at him curiously.

Zig shook his head, trying to expel that dangerous line of thought.

"By the way, it seems like you can bring your own materials in as well," she supplied.

"Bring materials in?" he asked.

"You know, have an armament made for you using pieces of a monstrosity you've killed. All you need to do is pay a fee for the equipment and the cost of labor, so it's much more economical than buying an item at full price."

"So it's similar to having something you've hunted prepared for you at a restaurant?"

Acquiring a weapon at a reasonable price was quite an attractive prospect. As long as he could get his hands on the fangs or claws he wanted from a monstrosity, it would be possible to forge his ideal weapon.

"There's just one problem, though," Siasha cut in.

"What's that?"

"You need to have connections to a weaponsmith," she said. "The number of people who want special orders is far more than those who can make them, so it's not as simple as them making weapons one after the other. In order to get preferential treatment, you need to either have a personal connection or pay some extra money."

"I figured there was a catch."

And because they came to this continent from far across the sea, their connections were woefully nonexistent. Saving up to have a weapon specially made with materials he acquired to save on costs defeated the purpose.

"Slow and steady wins the race, I guess…" he finally said.

"There are always checks and balances in place."

Struck once again by the harsh realities of the world, the pair headed back to their lodgings.

CHAPTER 3

PRINCESS OF WHITE LIGHTNING

ZIG WAS AN EARLY RISER.

Upon waking up, he washed his face and began stretching. He would take his time doing these exercises, working on improving his flexibility. Anyone who fought for a living knew that keeping limber was essential—not only did it lead to fewer injuries, but it also kept you agile.

However, the mercenary knew many within his field that found stretching not only tough but boring, so they avoided the exercises. Unlike stamina or strength training, it was hard to see physical results, which didn't help motivation.

Zig wasn't a fan of it either. However, his stretching routine made a big difference in keeping himself fit. People who slacked off on stretching knew full well that they were only hurting themselves. Maybe the persistence to keep up with such a tedious routine could itself be considered a talent, he thought with amusement.

Once his body was loosened up, Zig went for a run.

He jogged around the periphery of the city, carrying his sword—which weighed about the same as a person—on his back. The first people that death came for on the battlefield were those who stopped walking. It could be due to injury, lack of stamina, or willpower, but whatever the cause, anyone who lost the ability to walk was sure to lose their life as well.

The simple act of walking gave a person the capability to trudge through mountainous terrain to attack the enemy from behind, shoulder heavy burdens to deliver supplies, and even flee from battle with a fallen ally on your back.

To Zig, wars and conflicts all came down to the ability to move.

And so he ran to keep his strength and stamina up, because one never knew when this old habit would one day be the difference between life and death.

After returning to their lodgings, Zig went to the nearby well to fetch water and wash up. He got back to his room just as the sun was starting to rise and went next door to wake up Siasha.

She was sleeping with her arms and legs wrapped around the blanket—a clear sign that she'd stayed up late reading again. With nothing but a nightgown on, her pale shoulders and legs were bare. Her long, glossy black hair fanned across the bed.

Zig looked away as he lightly tapped her on the cheeks a couple of times. "It's morning now, wake up."

"Ungh..." She mumbled something, but Zig couldn't make out the words.

He poured some water into the washing bin and wet a small towel before placing it on the witch's face.

"Eeek!" Siasha sprung up from the bed before locking her vacant eyes on him for a few moments.

"Good morning," Zig said.

"...Morning," she said blankly.

"Let me know when you're ready to go."

"Okay."

He left Siasha in her half-asleep state and went back to his room. Although the witch wasn't a morning person, she wasn't the type who would go back to sleep. Once Siasha shook the last dregs of slumber from her body, she was ready to start work.

It wasn't long after Zig finished his own preparations when he heard her say, "Sorry to keep you waiting."

She stood at his doorway, completely alert, dressed, and neatly groomed. There wasn't a trace of sleepiness about her.

"Shall we?" he asked.

"Yup, let's go."

They both headed out of the inn. People were starting to fill the streets as they made their way to their usual food stall where a long line of men looking to fill their bellies before starting their day of work were waiting.

The stall faced the main street. As the pair approached, a delicious smell greeted them.

"They still have meat pies left!" Siasha squealed.

"Oh, that's good news."

After buying their breakfast, they walked down the road toward the guild.

It was shaping up to be another typical morning.

"An...extermination squad?"

The guild, as usual, was a lively place. Siasha was registering her request for the day when the receptionist extended an unexpected offer.

"That's right," the woman said. "The higher-ups decided it shouldn't be a problem for you to join."

Was this part of those "accommodations" the receptionist mentioned the other day? Siasha wondered. Things were progressing faster than she expected.

"What exactly does the extermination squad do?" the witch asked.

"It's a group of adventurers that cull specific species of monstrosities from time to time. Their goal is to deal with populations that are getting out of hand."

Monstrosities multiplied in a variety of ways. The guild roughly categorized them into colony types, whose numbers were continually replenished through building hives and the like, and breeding types, whose populations would dramatically increase after periods of mating and rearing their young.

Colony-type monstrosities were dealt with by issuing regular extermination requests, so their numbers never exploded.

The problem was the breeding-type. These creatures weren't an issue if they had low fertility, but some monstrosities produced an astronomical amount of young. This was often the case for those that carried no threat individually, so they sought the continuation of their species through producing great amounts of offspring.

"The guild itself issues a special request in order to thin out their numbers," the receptionist continued. "Due to the nature of the job, magic users who can take out monstrosities by covering a wide area are considered the most suitable members, so we reach out to them."

"If it's just magic users, isn't it dangerous if any of the creatures get too close?" Siasha asked.

"A swordfighter often joins, so that's usually not an issue. Also, it's not a hard job, so the payment reflects that."

A swordfighter likely wouldn't get much action if a pack of magic users were systematically bombarding the enemy with spells. It sounded like easy money since they just had to clean up the survivors. However, if Siasha understood correctly, the pay wasn't very high.

"The benefit is that you'll get a large increase toward your next rank," the receptionist said. "The guild can't afford to pay much, so this is their way of compensating those who accept one of their direct requests."

"I'll do it!" Siasha said without hesitation. Increasing her rank took priority above pay.

"Usually, this request is reserved for those who are seventh class and above, but based on your achievements the other day, they made a special exception for you."

"I'm honored to hear that, but is it really okay to accept such special treatment?"

If special exceptions were made based on merit alone, she thought, it wouldn't be long until the strong and powerful decided to seize power and form a dictatorship. Rules and codes were in place for this very reason, and they worked because they couldn't be easily broken.

"You don't need to worry," the receptionist assured. "These types of things only happen when someone is just starting out."

What's that supposed to mean? Siasha couldn't discern the intentions behind those words.

"I won't probe into your personal life, but the two of you have plenty of combat experience, right?"

"Well, I guess so."

"We sometimes have people like that come our way. Maybe they were previously knights or lived in a rural area with no guild to record their achievements, but they still have experience killing monstrosities. Having those who are beginners in name only stuck in the lower ranks doesn't do them or the guild much good."

Now Siasha understood. "That's true."

"The credibility of the guild is also at stake if members aren't ranked at an appropriate level for their abilities. That's why they make provisions to streamline such people up to seventh class as quickly as possible."

That all sounded fair to Siasha. It seemed like the guild put some thought into handling people from various backgrounds.

The receptionist handed her some paperwork. "Fill in the required fields and bring it back to me tomorrow. You'll be departing three days from now in the morning. You'll be on-site for two days, so make sure to come fully prepared. The guild will provide some food, but it's not a lot, so you should prepare some provisions of your own as well."

The explanation continued for a little while longer. Once she got all the details, Siasha bid the receptionist goodbye and she and Zig headed out to work. They used the transportation stone to get to the forest and headed out.

They passed by the hive and the crowd of adventurers who were there to hunt the blade bees and continued onward until they neared where they had encountered the rockworm.

"I was hoping we might find another one, but it doesn't seem like it'll be that easy," Siasha said.

"Those things don't show up around here very often?" Zig asked.

"No. If monstrosities of that class frequented this forest, it's unlikely anyone seventh class and below would be granted permission to enter."

It was purely thanks to their luck that they ran into one yesterday, although it probably would've been bad luck for any low-ranking adventurer who happened upon it instead.

"We're going after sky squids today," Siasha said. "We probably look like delicious snacks to them after last time."

While the chances of encountering those creatures were slim if they went around with a large group, the two of them alone would likely attract quite a few.

"You're right about that," Zig said. "In fact, we've already got some incoming."

He had sensed three squids moving parallel to them as they walked for the past few minutes. The witch and mercenary might've looked like tasty treats to the squids, but little did they know the feeling was mutual.

"All we need to show proof of killing them are the proboscis and digestive fluid sacs," Siasha instructed. "Let's take some of their meat back with us today. I already spoke with the restaurant we ate at before about having them prepare it for us."

"When did you do that?"

Apparently, once Siasha had her heart set on something, she was quick to take the initiative to make it happen. Zig, marveling at her proactiveness and thinking of the meal later, prepared to greet the monstrosities with his sword.

The day after completing their sky squid hunt, Zig found himself walking through the town. He didn't have a particular purpose in mind, wanting to simply wander around and visit places he had never been to before.

"Oh?"

He stopped before what looked like a small, privately-owned shop. It was tucked away in a back alley that was so dimly lit that one was unlikely to notice it unless they already knew it was there. From what he could tell, the sketchy-looking establishment was likely an apothecary.

"Very interesting," Zig murmured as he headed toward the suspicious shop.

"You think I should rest tomorrow?" Siasha said the previous evening, her tone puzzled.

It was the evening of the day they'd taken care of the sky squids.

They sat inside the restaurant, waiting for the kitchen to prepare the sky squid meat they'd brought back.

"Yes," Zig said. "Since this extermination trip is going to include making camp, there's a lot you need to prepare. Plus, getting a sound sleep in stressful conditions is harder than you think. It would be a good idea to rest up and make sure you're ready."

"Hmph..." Siasha pouted, then thought for a moment. "I guess I can do that. It just so happens there's something else I need to do."

She didn't look thrilled at the prospect of taking a day off, but his logic seemed to have urged her to see it as necessary. As she accepted her circumstances, a man emerged from the kitchen, bearing their dinner.

"Oh, finally!" Siasha exclaimed.

Steam rose from the platter of exquisitely prepared squid steak as the server set it before them. The white flesh was grilled to perfection, with the red sauce providing a beautiful contrast.

"That sure was some fresh meat you brought in," the man remarked. "Your preservation methods were top-notch."

"I just did as you told me to, Mr. Owner," Siasha said.

So he's not just any employee, Zig thought, *but the owner of the restaurant himself.* He was bald with a swarthy complexion, and had a well-toned frame that put most adventurers to shame.

"What kind of sauce is this?" Siasha asked.

"It's a tomato chili sauce," the owner explained. "It's quite a delicacy, made by lightly frying garlic and then stewing it with tomatoes and onions."

Siasha and the restaurant owner's animated discussion regarding the food was enough to make Zig's mouth water.

"I'd love to chat more," the man said, "but how about you give it a taste?"

"Right," Zig agreed. "It would be a shame not to try it while it's still hot."

"Okay, let's eat!" Siasha declared.

Zig cut a piece of squid and brought it to his mouth. The slightly acidic sauce perfectly accentuated the rich flavors of the meat. It had just the right amount of spiciness, and the aroma of garlic served to further whet his appetite.

"Mm, delicious," he commented.

"Mr. Owner, this is so good!"

"Yeah, yeah..." The restaurant owner tried to wave off the compliment, but he looked more than pleased with their lavish praise.

The two proceeded to gobble up their dinner in silence.

"What are you going to do tomorrow, Zig?" Siasha asked as they relaxed with post-meal tea.

"I was thinking about taking a walk around town since it seems like we'll be staying here for a while," he said. "I'd like to start gathering information."

"Hmm, that sounds interesting!" Her enthusiasm gave way to annoyance as she nibbled on the rim of her cup. "Oh...but I've got that thing I need to do..."

"If I find a place that's good, I'll bring you there with me on our next day off."

That made her perk up. "You will? Okay, I'm looking forward to it!"

"This is even more extreme than I was expecting."

It was the day after their lavish meal at the restaurant.

After discovering the alley with the suspicious-looking shop, Zig immediately went in to take a look around.

The place *was* an apothecary, just like he had guessed. However, the drugs on sale were far more dangerous than those used to cure ailments. The display cases were stocked with sleeping pills, poisons, and even stimulants—a far cry from the usual medicinal items.

"I doubt... No, I'm *sure* they don't have permission to sell stuff like this," he murmured to himself as he browsed.

They had a product that looked like tobacco, but when he held it up to his nose, it smelled faintly sweet. Likely some sort of narcotic.

"This might be a different continent, but some things never change."

Places like this always emerged in populated areas because where there were people, there was money. Where there was money, the underbelly of society surfaced and claimed a piece of the pie for themselves.

It was just the natural order of things, Zig thought.

To the average citizen, these kinds of places were a blight on society, but they could also prove very useful if you played your cards right.

Zig feigned disinterest as he approached the employee, who was keeping a careful eye on him.

"Who are the big shots around here?" he asked, slipping a gold coin onto the counter.

The clerk sized him up without touching the money.

"Sir, this is just a simple apothecary," he said. "If you're not interested in making a purchase, I'll have to ask you to leave."

"Where are you getting your goods from?"

"That's a corporate secret. Please leave now."

"I see. Sorry for the trouble. Feel free to keep that as my apology."

Zig left the coin on the counter and quickly left the shop.

The moment the door swung closed behind Zig, the employee pocketed the gold coin and left through the back entrance. He walked quickly down the back alley and darted through several streets, nervously glancing behind him as he went.

Finally, he reached a small house. It was shabby and dirty, though not dilapidated or abandoned. Using a special sequence, the man knocked on the door. It opened, revealing three men with glowering expressions.

The one who appeared to be their leader rose to his feet. "What do you want? I thought I told you not to show your face around here very often! And who the hell is that behind you?"

"Angus, there was a strange man asking probing questions at the—what?!"

Someone tapped on the man's shoulder. The employee turned, seeing Zig behind him.

"Thanks for showing me the way," the mercenary said.

"Gaaaah!!" The employee whirled around and started backing away.

The men inside the house barged out of the door as tensions began to rise.

"You imbecile!" one of them snarled. "You led him straight here!"

They reached for the daggers sheathed at their waists and prepared themselves for battle. However, Zig calmly raised both his hands, signaling that he came in peace.

"Now, now," he said. "I'm not here for a fight. I want to make a business transaction."

The men didn't drop their aggressive stances. "What's that supposed to mean? What've you got to offer?"

Two of the them started to slowly scoot their way around to his rear so that they'd be able to jump him at a moment's notice.

"I'm a mercenary," Zig replied. "I'm not too different from you lot."

"Another mercenary?" the leader said. "Well, you don't look like a member of the military police, that's for sure. So, Mr. Mercenary, what is it you're looking for?"

Zig's ears perked up at the man's use of *another*, but he had more pressing matters to ask about.

He slowly reached into his pocket, making sure the movement was visible. "I want information."

The tension in the air was thick as he pulled a small pouch out. He gave it a little shake, letting them hear the clinking inside.

"I'm going to throw it," Zig said to the leader before tossing the bag to him.

The man, still brandishing his dagger, caught the bag and examined the contents. Despite the pouch's small size, it was stuffed with gold coins. The sight made it hard for him to suppress a smile.

He sheathed the dagger and addressed his companions.

"That's enough, boys," he said. "We have an honored guest. Make sure to treat him with the utmost respect. You," he barked at the shop employee, "go back now."

Those words could've sounded more ominous, but the man's tone was sincere and amiable. His two underlings sheathed their daggers as the employee fled back to the shop.

Entering the shabby house, Zig took a seat as the leader approached. The man must've either just really loved cash or he was the type to quickly have a change of heart. His demeanor turned polite, as if Zig was already a valued business partner. "I'm Angus. So, what kind of information are you seeking?"

"The name's Zig," the mercenary said. "I want to know the primary factions, territories, and trends in this town."

Angus shot him a suspicious look. "Heh? Are you new around these parts?"

"Yeah, I came here recently."

"To be honest, you could've gotten all this information above ground, but oh well…" Angus lit his tobacco and inhaled before letting out a smokey breath. A plume of purple smoke wafted through the air before he continued. "There are three things you need to know about this town: The Bazarta Family run the north, the Cantarella Family—that's the one I'm part of—run the south, and lastly, the Jinsu-Yah are in the east."

Zig had never heard of such a name. "Sounds like one of those things is not like the others."

"I'll give you a brief rundown," Angus said. "The Bazartas and us, we're what you'd consider to be your conventional mafia families. We sell drugs, run brothels, run gambling establishments, smuggle in magic items... You get the picture. We have different territories, but we basically do the same things. We sometimes get into small scuffles with the Bazartas, but we haven't had a major conflict with them for a long time."

Apparently, mafia activities were pretty much the same wherever you went. But there was still something that was bothering Zig...

"When it comes to the Jinsu-Yah... Honestly, I don't know much."

"Hey, now." Zig shot him a doubtful look.

Angus looked slightly uncomfortable. "We don't have a clear idea what they're about. They randomly migrated here twenty-odd years ago, but all we know is that they came from the east. They just showed up out of nowhere and seized territory from the Bazartas, who ran the eastern district at the time."

"And they didn't face any resistance?"

"Of course they did! The Bazartas aren't so stupid that they'd stand by quietly and give up their territory to outsiders. But in the end, they had to clear out."

The mafia were vindictive—they didn't hesitate to take revenge on anyone who caused them grief, so even mercenaries needed to be cautious when dealing with them.

A mafia that was deeply rooted in a town was a force to be reckoned with. If a group was able to pry territory away from them and still hold it today...

"So they're pretty strong?" Zig asked.

Angus nodded. "I don't want to admit it, but yes. Even our executives don't want to rumble with them. There aren't that many, so if we seriously tried to take them down, I don't think we'd lose. But...we're not willing to make that big of a sacrifice."

Whoever these Jinsu-Yah were, they were powerful enough to keep the mafia at bay.

It sounded like Zig needed to tread carefully.

"They don't really act as an organization that much," the leader said. "Each one just sort of does as they please; that's why incidents happen from time to time." He looked annoyed as he scratched his head. "There are a few that are just ridiculously dangerous. If you encounter any of them, you'd better just run away."

"They're that bad?"

"Yeah. I think they've got to be the head members of the Jinsu-Yah, but they're unbelievably strong. One of them could probably take on our boss and the members directly under him all at once."

"Wow."

These people probably had a considerable amount of skill and were very dangerous opponents.

"That's about all the information I've got," Angus said. "It's probably not worth the amount that you paid, though."

"It's fine. Much appreciated."

"Including you, we've had a few run-ins with mercenaries lately."

"You mentioned something along those lines earlier," Zig said. "I thought most of the mercenaries around here weren't much different than thugs."

Angus groaned as he crossed his arms. "You know, you kind of remind me of that other guy—you both give off the same vibe. Not like the other mercenaries you find around these parts."

"I see."

The two men rose from their seats. Zig wasn't sure whether it was to see him off or keep an eye on him, but Angus and his men walked him outside.

He nodded in appreciation. "Thanks for your help. I'll be back again."

"We're always happy to assist a customer with deep pockets," the leader said. "We also deal in narcotics—you interested?"

"Not this time. I've already got my own supp—"

The hairs on the back of Zig's neck started to prickle. He grabbed his sword and glared toward the back of the alleyway.

"Hey, hey. What are you doing?!"

Zig didn't answer Angus, his focus on the alley instead.

"Peeping isn't a very nice habit," he said to the seemingly empty alley.

Angus's expression darkened in realization.

"Oh? You sensed me even from this distance?"

A woman stepped out from the shadows. She looked to be in her midtwenties with long white hair that fell to the middle of her back. She was pretty, he supposed, but rather than finding her attractive, her aggressive expression filled him with dread.

Zig noticed she had the same kind of pointed ears that he had seen before, and she wore what looked to be some sort of traditional clothing in a style he hadn't seen anyone else in town wear.

But what caught his attention the most was her weapon, a slender longsword belted to her waist. The handle was facing away from him, so he couldn't make out the blade type, but it appeared to be longer than a typical longsword.

Angus gasped. "It's her! She's one of them! One of the Jinsu-Yah!"

"She's one of them..."

Yes, it made perfect sense. She certainly looked like she came from a migrant tribe. And if her stance was any indication, she most likely had formidable battle capabilities. To the untrained eye, she appeared to just be hunched over with a hand on her weapon, but Zig could see the tension in her body, as if she was ready to spring at any moment.

"You were spying on us, bitch?" Angus howled. "What a dirty trick!"

The white-haired woman ignored him. "I'm honestly offended that people like you lot would accuse me of playing dirty. I was just *listening* in," the woman said as she twitched her ears.

She looked past Angus and straight at Zig.

"To be fair, I wanted to have eyes on you as well," she continued, her eyes narrowing at him, "but I was afraid that man would sense me if I got too close. I suppose in the end he did. Who and what are you, exactly?"

The menacing aura and the bloodlust emanating from her was so palpable that the blood drained from Angus and his men's faces.

"I'm just a run-of-the-mill mercenary," Zig said.

"A mercenary? Really? You're not an adventurer or a member of the mafia? Just a mercenary?"

"That's right."

The woman's smile broadened at his answer. He didn't know why, but her malice was now focused entirely on him.

"So this means I caught you in the act of purchasing drugs from the mafia?"

"I didn't buy any drugs."

"But you already have some, right? I overheard you mention that."

Zig cursed himself for not noticing her eavesdropping until it was too late. At least she hadn't been able to hear what they were talking about inside the house.

"That's reason enough," the woman said. "If you're not a member of any particular organization, no one will even be upset if you die."

Was she trying to make sure no one would retaliate?

"Um, if you don't mind," Angus piped up.

Zig glanced at him. "Sure. I won't ask you to join me. Go ahead and get out of here."

"Sorry about that," he said apologetically. "I don't think she'll try anything reckless in the public eye. If you can escape to the surface streets, you might make it out alive."

With those parting words, Angus and his men fled the scene. Watching them go, the woman gracefully bent forward, her hand on the handle of the blade.

"I thought chasing after those small fry would just be a chore," she said with glee, "but looks like I unexpectedly landed myself a big fish. This is going to be enjoyable."

Zig sighed. "I'd rather not fight a futile battle when I'm off the clock."

"This is *my* work, though, so give it up. Besides, it's not futile—it's fun."

It didn't seem like she was likely to be deterred, so Zig unsheathed his weapon.

In contrast to her overwhelming bloodthirstiness, the white-haired woman's movements were discreet and deliberate. They both moved slowly, sizing each other up.

This woman has plenty of experience in one-on-one combat.

He couldn't estimate the blade's length, since only its handle was pointed toward him and she was being careful eye to keep a certain distance between them. She'd probably already gleaned that he was also proficient in one-on-one combat.

She remained silent, the smile never leaving her face.

Zig made the first move.

"Huff!"

He rushed at her and swung diagonally past her shoulder toward her chest. The white-haired woman seemed unfazed by his speed, calmly twisting out of the way to dodge the blow.

She took a step back, putting her out of range of his opposite blade, which Zig had to rotate his body to swing.

Seeing that the mercenary was continuing to go on the offensive, she launched a counterattack.

"Tch!"

There was a glint of light as she pulled her blade from its scabbard. It surged toward him with tremendous speed, forcing him to snap the twinblade up to deflect it.

A metallic sound echoed through the air. Zig took a step back to put more distance between them.

"I'm impressed you matched me," the white-haired woman said as she slowly lowered her blade.

Zig finally got a look at it. The slightly curved blade looked magnificent—thin with a single edge so sharp, it shone like a mirror.

"Where I come from, we call these weapons katana."

"Attacking straight from the draw, huh?" he murmured.

"My people practice the art of sword drawing, but this is the first time someone's been able to match my strike."

Zig glanced down at his own weapon. One of the blades had been sliced through the middle. It wasn't the most well-made weapon by any means, but it should've been considerably more durable than a common sword.

And she had sliced through it.

"I'd love to see that move again, but I'm guessing that's out of the question, right?" he asked.

"Obviously."

She wasn't going to just leisurely sheathe her sword again.

"I can't have you getting a big head over staving off one of my special moves," the woman said with a glare, the tip of her sword directly pointed between his eyes.

It was hard to gauge the blade since he could see it as a single dot. Her swordplay appeared to focus heavily on the distance between her and her opponent, made apparent by her initial draw-and-slash attack.

The white-haired woman moved once again, closing the distance between them with a gliding gait that made it difficult to measure the length of her strides. She raised her sword to swipe at him.

Zig moved to the side to dodge. She turned and aimed for his neck. Zig chose not to evade, opting to take a slash at her legs instead.

"Ngh!"

This time, it was she who withdrew to make space.

Zig had deflected her swing with the half-cut-off blade of his weapon while using the reverse side to stab into the skirt of her robe. In one move, he utilized both the offensive and defensive capabilities of his twinblade's reach.

That katana, as she called it, was incredibly sharp, but he realized it required both momentum and speed to fully utilize its menacing potential; it didn't have enough weight to cut through his own weapon in consecutive strikes. That was why she tended to use draw-and-slice attacks.

By provoking her greed and allowing her to aim for his neck, he was able to aim for her legs. His plan wouldn't have worked if he tried to go for a vital spot.

Still...

"Too superficial, huh..." he muttered.

She was able to quickly shift her body and dodge, probably thanks to her sprawling gait. It was hard to see her feet because of the clothing she was wearing, but it didn't seem like he caused much, if any, damage.

The woman looked practically euphoric. "Heh...heh heh. Very good, in fact, marvelous!"

She darted forward once more, using the same creeping steps, and unleashed a barrage of lightning-fast attacks by slashing up from the ground.

Zig took a step back and swayed back and forth to avoid them.

She reversed the blade of the katana and slashed diagonally toward his shoulder, which he deflected with the twinblade. The woman moved with the momentum to pivot her center of gravity, whirling around to slash at him from the side.

This is my chance!

He thrust one side of the twinblade into the ground to block the attack while using it as a base so he could propel himself up to kick her.

The white-haired woman blocked the attack with her left arm.

"Gaaah!"

But one arm wasn't enough to completely deflect the force of Zig's entire body.

Her bracer flew away with a nasty cracking sound, though she managed to lessen the blow by quickly jumping back. She rolled across the ground, putting distance between them before immediately rising to her feet.

"That's not a bad look," Zig said.

The back alley was anything but clean, which meant that the woman's dramatic tumbling escape had completely ruined her clothes.

"This is much more fun than I'd even dared to imagine," she breathed out.

"Well, aren't you a lively one?"

She had managed to slow some of his momentum, but his attack should've been effective in causing at least a serious injury...

A sweet aroma floated through the air.

It struck him that the woman hadn't been using any magic until now, but that smell was familiar...

It was the scent of healing magic.

Flesh wounds weren't going to be enough, Zig discerned. He would either need to knock her unconscious or land a fatal blow.

The woman swung her left arm around as if confirming it was fully functional again.

"I wonder how long it's been since I last used this," she said.

Something was off.

She was done healing herself, and yet the sweet aroma intensified. The scent, which was so sweet that it almost became pungent, prickled his danger senses.

Her tone was like poisoned honey. "But you seem like the perfect opponent for it, so I don't need to hold back."

This was bad.

"Allow me to send you to the afterlife!"

Really bad.

Light surged from the white-haired woman's body. It was only after the brilliance subsided that he realized she was enveloped in a lightning bolt glowing with a jade-green light. Her pure white hair floated in the air around her, and her green eyes, dangerous and beautiful, shone in the lightning's luminance.

"Let's go."

The woman put her hand on her blade, which had somehow managed to return to its scabbard, and rushed at him.

She was closing in. There wasn't even time to let out a yelp of surprise—she was already within striking distance.

There was another glint of light, and Zig knew he wouldn't be able to block. He tried to predict the woman's movement and the direction of her shoulders to dodge a blow that he couldn't even see coming.

"Nghhh!"

She was so quick that Zig couldn't get completely out of the way, and he felt her blade sink into his side.

The woman took another step forward, reversing the katana, and slashed down. Her left hand swung the scabbard up, performing a simultaneous attack from both sides.

"Yaaaaaah!"

"What?!"

Rather than trying to avoid or mitigate the attack, Zig dropped his weapon and charged. His movement overlapped with hers, putting them practically face-to-face. He grabbed the arm wielding her katana with his left hand while blocking the attack from the scabbard with his right gauntlet. A horrible screeching filled the air when the sheath made impact.

She's using a metal scabbard?!

But at least he managed to stop her lightning-speed attacks. For a moment, they both stood still.

"I'm impressed that you were able to block that!" she declared. "But what are you going to do now that you've cast your blade aside?"

"Hm? I just thought using a weapon would make it too easy."

"I'll silence that impudent mouth of yours!"

Zig pushed back against her, trying to control her movements. Finding it difficult, he realized that she wasn't using the lighting around her just for offense but as a variant of self-fortifying magic. It was enhancing her physical capabilities, especially her forceful charges and attacks. Whatever this was, it was far more potent than regular enhancement magic. Zig found himself losing ground, her strength outmatching his.

The woman released her hand from the scabbard. "Haaah!"

The mercenary, now without the object he was bracing himself on, went tumbling forward. With her left arm free, the woman tried to pry off his hand that was holding back her katana.

She had an opening now, but they were still too close for her to inflict a fatal blow. Now that both of his arms were empty, the white-haired woman hurled herself toward his shoulder.

The impact forced Zig to stumble back a few steps.

Gaining the space she needed, she changed to an offensive stance, her left foot forward and her blade pointing upright.

"Haaah!"

"Yaaah!"

She aimed a sharp thrust at his heart, but Zig quickly crossed his gauntlets and deflected it upward.

"Haaah!"

The woman grunted as she used the momentum to bring the blade down again.

Zig frantically pulled his arms back. His gauntlets fell to the ground, cleanly sliced in two. If he'd hesitated for even a fraction of a second, it would've been his arm instead.

Blood dripped down both of his hands.

"Why won't you use magic?" the woman asked. "Are you holding back?"

"Maybe?" he answered. He wasn't going to let her know he couldn't use magic.

"I see." She resumed her stance. "If that's the case, I'll send you to your grave without you ever getting to use your trump card!"

The woman pointed the blade directly at him.

Zig kept his eyes fixed on it as she surged forward once again.

Her thrust was so fast, he didn't hear her grunt at the effort. However, no matter how fast she was, she couldn't reach past the range of her katana. As long as she was only using it as a thrusting weapon, it all came down to attack range.

As she moved forward, Zig stepped to the side and dodged the attack. However, as soon as he did, she stopped and thrust at him a second time.

He stepped back again and kicked something up from the ground, sending the twinblade he'd tossed away earlier sailing through the air. He had used evasion to guide his way back to its location.

The white-haired woman couldn't hide the disappointment in her eyes.

Did he really think I wouldn't notice? she wondered.

"I thought you were better than that!" she screamed, thrusting the sword at him for the third time.

Zig reached out.

Two sharp sounds echoed in the air.

"Nghhh..." Zig grunted.

The woman's katana had penetrated Zig's left shoulder. Blood gushed out, the blade slicing through the muscle and crushing the bone.

Zig's twinblade, in turn, had smacked the woman straight in the face.

"A-aghh...!" Her eyes rolled into the back of her head as she collapsed.

Zig hadn't reached out to grab for the weapon to deflect her blow but rather used the handle to punch her.

Such weight behind a weapon should've been fatal, but she was still breathing. She was a tough one.

Zig gave a long sigh. He wanted to sit and rest, but he pushed that feeling aside, pulling the katana out of his shoulder and using his first aid supplies to stem the bleeding. Then he tied the woman up and took her weapon, rendering her helpless.

"She sure was strong..." he murmured.

Out of all the opponents he'd ever faced, she was easily in the top five. Her lightning-quick techniques made the battle one of his most arduous—especially since he wasn't fully able to dodge her attacks.

"She even broke my weapon."

He almost wanted to cry. Here he was, broke and with a shattered weapon, which meant more overhead costs. Reality stung a lot.

"And I beat this strong of an opponent without even getting paid for it..." he sighed. "Well, whatever. I should just kill her and get it over with."

This woman was dangerous. With her techniques, she might even be able to pass him and reach Siasha. It was best to dispose of her immediately.

Angus and his crew would probably benefit from her death, and there weren't any witnesses around, so he could kill her now and not have to worry about repercussions.

"I should probably strip her possessions first."

It would be nice to get even a little compensation to put toward getting medical treatment and repairing my weapon, he thought as he fished through her clothing.

He found her wallet and was going through it when he noticed something dangling around the woman's neck.

Something about the shape looked familiar to him, like he had seen it frequently.

An ominous feeling stirred in the pit of his stomach.

He stifled the desire to pretend he never saw it and glanced down at the card he'd taken from her neck.

"Come on, you've got to be kidding me!"

Adventurer, Second Class
Isana Gayhone

"Damn it!" Zig seethed. "Now what do I do?"

If he killed a high-ranking adventurer, someone was going to start asking questions about her cause of death. Even if it was unlikely, he couldn't risk them sniffing him out.

"She did mention something about this being for work."

Apparently, even adventurers were sent to investigate the mafia.

"Maybe I can make it seem like this was a hit...?"

No, that would be impossible. There was no way the mafia could take down someone like *that*.

And even if they somehow managed to do it, they would've needed to overwhelm her with sheer numbers. The battle would be nowhere near this scuffle they had.

Besides, if the investigation led back to the mafia, Angus and company wouldn't hesitate to rat him out. He was still thinking through the various possibilities when his shoulder wound started to fight for his attention.

"I'm not going to get anything figured out in this much pain." Zig pulled out a round pill from his belongings and chewed on it.

The pain-dulling drug was both bitter and putrid as the taste coated his tongue.

Mercenaries often couldn't treat their wounds while on the battlefield, so it was common practice to carry around medicines that dulled the pain, allowing them to continue fighting.

There were also other types of drugs, including those that shook off sleepiness so you could keep going or heightened your senses to increase your focus. While all were very powerful, they could cause lasting side effects if the one taking them mismanaged their dosage. Habitual users could even end up permanently disabled.

"It's good to know I can probably still replenish my supply," he said to himself, "but I'm shocked that even possession is a crime over here."

It was illegal to manufacture or smuggle the substances on his home continent, but he could normally purchase them at government-authorized shops. This woman using it as an excuse to fight him was baffling.

The drug started to kick in. Realizing that his pain was slowly numbing, Zig shifted his thoughts back to how to deal with her.

"Since she's an adventurer, even if I let her go now, we'll cross paths again eventually. Even so, I can't kill her. The only other option left is to reason with her. But...*reason*...with *her*...?"

The woman was as bloodthirsty as they came. Not to mention she was one of those Jinsu-Yah Angus warned him about.

"It's not going to be easy, but I don't think there are any other alternatives."

His mind made up, Zig wrapped the woman in some cloth and hoisted her up on his back.

Siasha was in her room, thumbing through magic textbooks, when she heard two sharp knocks.

"Yes?" she called. "Who is it?"

"It's me," came Zig's muffled voice. "Is now a good time?"

"Zig? I'm coming."

He must've returned already after spending the entire day gathering information. Either he finished earlier than anticipated or something unexpected had happened.

It's unusual for him to come and visit me of his own accord, Siasha thought as she headed for the door.

When she opened it, Zig was standing at the threshold, one of his shoulders dyed a deep shade of red.

Siasha's pleasant expression vanished at the sight of her blood-soaked companion. "Zig?! What happened to you?!"

"A lot. Sorry, but could I ask you for some help with this?"

"Come and sit on the bed. I'll start right away."

She immediately cleared her books off the bed and prepared to use her recovery magic. The bundle Zig set down caught her eye, but she stifled her questions, deciding that healing him took priority.

He was having trouble taking off his clothes, so she helped him until his upper body was bare.

"This is..." she trailed off in horror.

There were cuts on his flank and arm, but the worst was his shoulder. It looked like whatever had attacked even cut through the bone.

The fabric wrapped around the area was stained a bright red. After peeling the makeshift bandage off, Siasha wet a clean cloth and started wiping the wound site. Fortunately, it was clean.

She cast a spell, focusing it on the injured area. Zig's labored breathing eased slightly, but there wasn't time to talk; she needed to concentrate.

A few minutes passed by.

She was able to seal the wound and stop the bleeding, but the internal damage would take some time to heal. She put that off for later.

"Give me your arm," she said. "I need to stop the bleeding."

She could tell from his clothing he had lost a lot of blood, so she made it her priority to mend all his injuries and prevent him from losing any more strength. She cast magic on his side and both arms.

Once those wounds closed, she touched his shoulder. It had been run through by a sharp blade. It had cleaved the bone but fortunately didn't shred it to pieces.

"Unlike flesh injuries, bone can't regenerate quickly," she said woefully. "I'll have to keep applying magic to it for a while."

Compared to offensive spells, casting recovery magic expended a great deal more mana. To her knowledge, continuous casting was demanding even for an experienced practitioner. When trying to heal a grievous injury, it was common for several people to rotate and then treat the patient afterward.

Siasha's ability to cast recovery magic over and over spoke volumes about the potency of her mana as a witch.

"Can you tell me what happened?" she asked, working on his shoulder once again.

"That woman attacked me."

She glanced at the bundle Zig had brought with him. Only the woman's head was visible, the rest of her body completely wrapped in fabric. A horizontal bruise marred her otherwise pretty face.

"Alone?" she asked incredulously.

"Yup."

Siasha looked taken aback. This mercenary was practically a monster in the field, especially in close combat. It was hard to believe someone could inflict so many stab wounds on him.

But...something didn't quite add up.

Zig wasn't the merciful type. Merely capturing an enemy that attacked him first—that didn't seem like him at all.

"Why didn't you kill her?"

Instead of answering her question, Zig sighed heavily and handed her a card. Siasha, immediately recognizing what it was, scanned its contents, her eyes growing wide.

"Adventurer...second class?!"

This woman was on a whole other level. Some of the veteran adventurers had told her that anyone third class and above was bordering on superhuman.

It all made sense to Siasha now: He'd spared this woman's life because of *her*.

Due to Zig's association with her, they couldn't let anyone know he was responsible for taking down a high-ranking colleague.

"Sorry, I was too careless," Zig said, lowering his head apologetically. If he'd never given the woman an excuse to attack, this situation could've been avoided altogether.

Siasha, despite her calm expression, was internally panicking at how he was degrading himself for her sake.

"Don't worry about it!" she assured him. "You've been very good to me. At any rate, we need to think about what to do with her."

"Yeah. You're conscious, right? Is there something you want to say?"

Siasha glanced over at the woman again. At some point while they were talking, she had opened her eyes.

"I'm still alive, huh... Unggh... My face hurts..."

The bundle wiggled, and she scowled. Even though she was in pain, the woman looked at Zig and Siasha curiously.

"You didn't kill me?" she said. "If you're going to use me as a Jinsu-Yah hostage, I'd rather off myself. Just bring my head to the Bazartas or Cantarellas as an offering instead."

"What in the world is she talking about?" Siasha asked, puzzled.

Right, she didn't know anything about the mafia power struggles or migrant tribe. Zig made a mental note to explain everything. Though, there was so much information he didn't know where to start.

The white-haired woman—Isana Gayhone—was incredibly confused about what was going on, but she didn't let it show on her face. The beautiful woman in front of her didn't seem like she was part of the underworld.

Those who came from there often had some inner turmoil about not having a place in society and were jealous of those who did. She knew that all too well, because she was one of them. Isana felt some kind of a connection to this black-haired woman, like she was a kindred spirit, but it certainly wasn't because she had a chip on her shoulder.

No, this woman looked like she had found a place where she belonged.

And then there was the man. The one who called himself a "mercenary." Was a man this powerful really part of the mafia? That menacing aura and battle prowess... It seemed almost impossible that they could control someone like him. He reeked so much of the scent of blood that it made the mafia look tame in comparison.

"Well, where should I start?" the man said. "Uh, what was it again...? Gayfone?"

"It's Gayhone. Isana Gayhone."

"Oh, right, Gayhone. So, how much do you value your life?"

"How much...?"

That was a silly question. Was there a person alive who didn't value their life?

"How much are you willing to overlook if I spare your life?" he asked. "To be more specific, forgetting about, say, a narcotics possession."

"Excuse me?"

She didn't understand what he was implying. He would let her live if she turned a blind eye to a drug charge?

"That doesn't sound like a very good deal on your end," Isana replied. "Wouldn't it be easier to kill me?"

The man looked like he was mulling over something for a bit before he addressed her again.

He pointed at the woman tending to his shoulder. "This woman. She's...my client and an adventurer."

"What?"

The black-haired woman didn't speak, seeming content to just watch and let him do all the talking.

"I've been tasked with protecting her, and I also accompany her on guild requests," he continued. "I can't afford to get tangled up with the military police."

"Huh? Then, earlier today, why were you..."

Making deals with the mafia? she finished the sentence in her head.

He probably already knew what she was going to say.

"We came here from somewhere very far away," the man explained. "In order to survive in a foreign land, we needed information about the culture and customs, especially since she's working in a rough profession like adventuring. It's not as if we can completely ignore what's going on in the seedy underbelly of this place."

"In other words..."

I mistook him for a criminal and attacked him. Of course, possession of narcotics is a crime, but not such a serious one that it requires the death of the perpetrator. I assumed he was trying to join the mafia, and as a warrior, I prioritized wanting to fight to the death. Looks like I may have gone too far...

"Right, in other words, as long as you don't tell anyone I have drugs in my possession, then this can all be water under the bridge."

He seemed to have misunderstood the turmoil painted on Isana's face.

"Zig!" the woman treating him cut in. "She seriously wounded you. Just letting bygones be bygones isn't—"

"You're right," he said. "How about I also get compensation for my equipment, and you put in a good word for us as a senior adventurer? Also—and this is the most important condition—you must never lay a finger on my client. Can you do that?"

"I can do that much, but...are you sure that's enough?" Isana asked.

The man's expression turned grave. "You understand what I'm asking you, right? No matter what happens, you can't *ever* hurt her. It's not something to be taken lightly."

His tone was completely earnest. If she agreed, she needed to be prepared to uphold their deal.

"Fine, you have my word. I pledge on my people that I will never harm that woman."

"All right, you said it," he said. "And if you ever break your word, I'll annihilate every last one of your kind."

Isana's breath caught in her throat. The man was far too intimidating for her to laugh his words off as a silly threat.

He could negotiate with both mafia families if he brought them my head, she thought. *This man would be able to take on the stronger members of my people on his own while the mafia attack in large numbers to limit casualties.*

Ever since we took over the mafia's territory, they've been dying to kick us out. It's only the presence of expert fighters such as myself that holds them back. They can't do anything and won't touch us as long as we're around. However, if an ally who could take us down joined their ranks...

I'm getting ahead of myself. All I need to do is keep this promise.

"Understood," she finally said.

"Good. Then we have a deal." The man stood up and started to unbind her.

Her limbs tingled with pins and needles as she started to use recovery magic to heal her injured face.

The man sat on the edge of the bed watching her before he gazed at her weapon.

"Can I take a look at it?" he asked politely.

"Go ahead."

The man unsheathed the katana. He gasped in admiration as he examined her beloved sword, the blade so polished it reflected his face.

"This is amazing," he said with sincerity.

"Thanks." Her chest welled up with pride at his praise.

She remembered the paltry weapon the man had used in their fight.

"By the way, um..." she began.

"Zig. And this is Siasha."

He gestured to himself and the beautiful woman. She gave a slight nod in Isana's direction as she cleaned up the dirty clothes.

"Zig, why were you using such a shoddy weapon?" the swordswoman asked.

Zig looked crestfallen. "Shoddy...huh."

Perhaps he had a strong attachment to the blade—it *did* seem to be well maintained...

Seeing his face made her feel like crawling into the deepest depths of the bundle she was wrapped in.

"Oh, sorry," she said quickly. "I know everyone has their own circumstances."

"No, it's not that... I just don't have a lot of money."

"O-oh...?"

"And on that topic..." he said. "Part of the deal was that you were going to compensate me for it, right? I'm just going to be blunt: How much are you willing to pay?"

"Um, to be honest..." Isana's face turned red. "I don't have a lot of money either. I send most of it back to cover the living expenses of my people."

"Oh."

As an immigrant, she was often unable to work in one place for a long time due to conflict and discrimination. In her experience, those like her tended to find work that was unstable or paid poorly.

Working as a second-class adventurer paid well, but not enough to sustain a large group of people. It was also hard to complete jobs rapidly because they were incredibly dangerous.

"I could probably only give you 500,000 dren at the mo—"

"Oh, that amount would be fine!" Zig piped up.

"What?"

"I can provide the other 500,000." His face was full of glee as he started to pack up his belongings. "I should be able to get my hands on some decent equipment with one million dren!"

"H-hold on a minute," Isana stammered. "What kind of weapon do you expect to buy with one million dren?"

"Is there a problem with that?" he asked.

"Do you know how much I could get for my katana if I sold it?"

"Hmm...maybe two million?" Zig guessed.

Isana shook her head.

"Uh...three million?"

"Ten million," she said.

Zig froze. "T-ten..."

"That's how much it will take to fight monstrosities. Are you just starting out as adventurers?"

It was Siasha who answered for the stupefied mercenary. "Yes. I recently became ninth class. Although, we do have experience battling a monstrosity that was classified as two levels above."

They're already going at it with seventh-class level monstrosities? Sounds quite reckless.

"And you're fighting them with an iron blade?" Isana said, incredulous. "Please tell me you're joking."

"Is it that bad?" Siasha asked.

"I don't know if *bad* is what I'd call it... I'm just surprised it's still functioning. It broke from countering just one direct attack."

"Considering what kind of direct attack it countered, that's not a surprise," Zig retorted, finally recovering from his state of shock.

"The reason people use higher-quality blades is so that they *don't* break from attacks like that," Isana said. "Well, whatever. You're planning to go and check some weapons out, right? I'll come with you."

"Naw, it can wait until tomorrow," he said. "I'm still not fully recovered yet. And you probably need to do something about that getup."

Isana glanced down at her outfit. He was right—it was covered in trash and dirt from her tumble in the back alley, not to mention she smelled horrible.

I want to just soak in the tub, she thought.

"All right, I'll do that," she agreed. "My face is still hurting too. I'll come back here tomorrow."

With those parting words, Isana left the room.

"Can we trust her?" Siasha asked.

"We don't have any other choice," Zig replied.

Siasha sat down next to him and put her hand on his shoulder, casting her magic on it like she was giving the area an affectionate pat.

"Please don't be so reckless," she said softly.

"Yeah, I'll be careful."

The witch focused on healing him for a good part of the evening.

Clans were groups of adventurers who gathered and formed a faction under the banner of a particular purpose or ideology. Due to the difficulty of gathering enough people for a complex job, there came the idea of having fixed groups of people, separate from their parties, whose members were compatible with each other's working style. Those people then responded to various requests depending on their availability.

Most adventurers became part of a clan after accumulating a certain amount of experience. This was because aside from a few that required quotas or had strict rules, the camaraderie between clan members provided many benefits such as information sharing and insurance in case of emergencies.

But, of course, not everyone joined one. Common reasons were that they didn't like interacting with others or were rejected due to behavioral issues. Isana Gayhone also had a reason for not joining one, but it had nothing to do with her attitude or a distaste for working with others.

She was heading back to her lodgings when she remembered she hadn't checked in with the guild. It was already well past the time that she usually made her reports, so she knew it couldn't wait any longer. So, although she was still a complete mess, she had no choice but to stop by.

All eyes were on her the moment she stepped into the building. She was a high-profile figure, one of a handful of elite adventurers who also happened to have stunningly good looks, so this wasn't an unusual reaction. Isana was so used to these stares that they didn't even register as she walked to the reception desk.

"Sorry for the long wait," she said. "Here's my report on pickup sites used by the Cantarella Family and the list of shops that are connected to them."

"Miss Isana!" the receptionist said. "We were so worried when you didn't come back at the usual time. I was just about to request personnel for a welfare check."

"Sorry, I had a bit of unexpected trouble."

Just as Zig had feared, the guild was especially concerned about the safety of their top-ranking adventurers.

"*You* had trouble, Miss Isana?" The receptionist's eyes were wide. "No way. Is that why you look so...?"

"I didn't sustain any major injuries, so it's fine," she assured, ignoring the receptionist's curious gaze. "Anyway, please take care of the rest for me."

The receptionist nodded and went to file the paperwork. As she disappeared within the back office, Isana heard a voice calling out to her.

"Hey, Isana!"

She turned. "Norton, you're here late today."

The man looked to be in his midthirties and sported golden hair and a wide smile. He was well-built, the way he carried himself only serving to enhance his imposing presence.

"It was a big day today," he said. "More importantly, did you give the clan invite some thought?"

"Sorry, but my answer hasn't changed."

"That's too bad."

Some time ago, Norton had invited Isana to join his clan. She refused on the spot, and ever since, he'd been asking again each time they met.

"Can you at least tell me what it is we're lacking?" he asked.

"It's not that I dislike anything in particular about your group..." she said.

"Is it a matter of race? No one in the clan is going to care a lick about that."

"But I do."

She knew he had the best intentions. Norton was a good man; not only was he amiable, but he was considerate to those around him.

But that wasn't what she wanted.

Isana and her people just wanted to live in peace. They weren't seeking to be understood or help solve conflicts within the town. The only reason they had those dramatic clashes with the mafia was because they were forced to leave their previous home and were desperate to survive.

Norton didn't know this, but he dropped the subject anyway, understanding that unnecessary pestering would only put her in a bad mood.

"Anyway, what happened to you?"

"I encountered an obstacle while on the job," she said. "It ended up just being a misunderstanding, though."

Norton narrowed his eyes, his jovial demeanor shifting to seriousness. "Hmm... Anyone that gives you that hard of a time has got to be a big deal. Who was this guy?"

Isana thought for a moment.

I just said I'd keep quiet about the drugs, but I doubt that man would appreciate any unnecessary attention.

"Who knows," she said with a shrug. "Not a type I've ever encountered before."

She glanced at the counter, noticing the receptionist returning.

"Your report has been submitted successfully," the receptionist said. "Do you want your compensation in the usual way?"

"Yes, plea... Actually, could you give me an extra 500,000 in cash as well?"

"Understood. Please wait for a moment."

Isana always sent half of her commissions back to her people and received the rest in cash, but this time, she needed money to compensate that man for his weapon. She felt a small twinge of regret at having to dip into her personal savings.

Buying equipment was a huge expense for adventurers. Due to the commissions they received, people had the impression that they were earning huge sums of money, but the amount they had left after expenses was surprisingly small. It was even less if they were someone like Isana, who sent her earnings to support her kinsmen.

It was only natural that, deep down, she lamented being forced to spend some of the nest egg she'd worked so hard to save up. Still, Isana knew very well that it was a small price to pay for walking away with her life after being defeated in a duel.

If she was being honest with herself, she didn't have a right to complain even if she was stripped of her every last possession. Siasha was healing Zig's wounds for free, but considering the damages Isana caused, what he was asking for in return was paltry. Complaining about her circumstances would likely only incur divine wrath.

She took the money and finally returned to her lodgings. Tonight's dinner would have to be on the modest side.

The next day, Zig and Siasha headed to the armory to meet with Isana. The shop was lively as usual, filled with adventurers browsing and buying new weapons.

"Welcome!" the female clerk greeted as she approached them. "Oh my, you've got quite an extraordinary companion with you today." Her eyes grew wide when they caught sight of Isana.

Apparently, her notoriety even extended to a place like this.

"We're acquainted because of...reasons," he said. "That weapon I looked at the other day, do you still have it?"

"Of course! Were you able to come up with the funds for it?"

"Something like that. I'd also like to see some inexpensive gauntlets as well."

"Understood. Let's get your arm measurements first."

She called out to a nearby employee, who brought over an instrument to start measuring his arm.

"You must work out a lot," the clerk commented.

"It's part of the job," he said.

"Do you want a model that won't impede your arm movements?"

Zig answered the clerk's questions about his preference as best as he could while she took his measurements. When she finished, the clerk left to search for his requested items.

While they waited—no, ever since they stepped into the shop—he had the odd sense that people were staring. Or to be more precise, they were staring at Isana.

"Hey, isn't that...?" he heard someone murmur.

"Yeah. That's got to be her. The Princess of White Lightning."

Zig could hear the whispers coming from all around them.

"The Princess of White Lightning?" he asked, shooting the person in question a quizzical look.

"That's my nickname, apparently."

From the sour expression on her face, Zig could tell the moniker was not appreciated.

"The *Princess* of White Lightning, huh?"

"Shut up," she groaned. "I know I'm the furthest thing from one. I never asked to be called that."

It seemed like he touched a nerve, despite just wanting to tease her a little.

"My bad," he said apologetically. "Still, impressive that you've even got a nickname."

"Others have them as well. Things like Frostbite or Inferno Princess..."

"That's pretty rough."

Just the thought of those titles made Zig cringe internally as Isana grimaced.

"Seriously, I'm twenty-six already. I wish they'd just stop the princess talk..."

His eyebrows shot up. "Oh, you're my senior then?"

"You're younger than me?" she asked with surprise. "With a face like that? You've got to be kidding..."

"Leave my face out of it." Despite being teased back, the words stung. "Let's just talk about something else."

"Good idea," Isana agreed.

Siasha, who was much older than either of them at the ripe old age of over two hundred, said nothing and just looked dejectedly at the ground.

Just as their conversation dried up and everyone's feelings were well in the dumps, the clerk returned, pushing a cart with one weapon and a selection of gauntlets inside.

"I'm terribly sorry, but one of the weapons I showed you last time was purchased the other day," she said.

"The blue one?" Zig asked.

"No, the green one."

"Oh, that's fine." He never intended to purchase the other blade anyway. Zig took the remaining twinblade from the cart while Isana studied it intently.

"Heh... Looks like it's made pretty well," she commented. "What material does it use?"

"It's carved from the horns of a double-horned blue beetle."

"That's quite rare..." Isana remarked. "It should be sturdy enough at least, but it's not a magic implement, is it?"

"No, it's not," the clerk said. "If it were, the price would be quite steep..."

The employee and Isana began to discuss the weapon's features. Zig recalled that magic implements were constructed from materials with special properties, and unlike magic items, didn't need to be activated with mana.

"So how much is this?" Isana inquired.

"This piece is one million dren."

"Hmm... Well, I guess that's not horrible considering the quality of its craftsmanship."

"However," the employee piped up quickly, seeing the perturbed look on Isana's face, "I spoke with the artisan. This weapon has been in storage for some time since there aren't many people who can use it. As a business, we can't have it taking up space forever, so I'd like to offer it to you for the price of 750,000 instead."

The corners of Zig's mouth turned up ever so slightly—that was a far better discount than he imagined. Siasha couldn't help but smile herself when she noticed his almost imperceptible reaction.

"That's not bad at all," Isana said. "Choose whichever gauntlets and greaves can be combined with the weapon price to reach a flat one million dren."

"In that case..." The shop employee picked out a set of gauntlets from the cart. "How about these? They're made from the carapace of a shield bug, so they're highly durable."

Zig tried on the slightly curved gauntlets. They did feel quite sturdy, and they weren't unwieldy. However, they weighed more than his previous set.

"That high durability does come at a cost of being a little heavy," the clerk said. "What do you think?"

"Hmm..."

He stepped back and tried swinging his arms, turning a few times before adopting an oblique stance with his right hand in front of his face and his left by his chin.

The sharp sound of a fist cut through the air.

Jab, jab, straight, duck, duck, uppercut!

Zig did a few more punches before removing the gauntlets.

"These should be fine," he said.

The clerk nodded. "All right. With the weapon, the total should come out to one million dren. We will slightly adjust the gauntlets to fit you and have them delivered to the guild in a couple of days."

Isana handed her money over to Zig, who pitched in his share. Everyone watching couldn't believe their eyes.

While Zig and Siasha knew Isana was merely compensating the mercenary for the equipment she damaged during their fight, to any onlookers it seemed as though she was buying new gear for him. They couldn't help wondering who in the world this man that Isana Gayhone, the second-class adventurer known for being a loner, was with and why she was spending money on him.

The trio, however, remained oblivious as they finished paying for their purchase.

"Now we're even," Zig said, shouldering his new weapon as they left the shop. "I'm expecting you to hold up your end of the deal." He and Siasha turned to walk away.

"Can I ask you something?" Isana called out.

Siasha turned around, but Zig just looked back over his shoulder.

"Do you think it would be impossible for people like yourselves to accept someone from a different race like me?"

Zig shrugged before glancing at Siasha and tapping her on the shoulder as if to say, "This is all you."

"Like you, I'm basically a different species who wasn't accepted," Siasha said with a hint of a bitter smile. "That's why I ran away here. I think people tend to get scared when they're faced with the unknown."

"Have you found a solution to deal with that?" Isana asked.

Siasha shook her head with a sad smile. "That's a difficult question. But I don't think words or force work. Maybe there isn't an answer."

The swordswoman's face looked dejected at her response. *No matter where we go, those who are different will never be accepted, huh? We'll always be outsiders...*

"But..." Siasha's voice cut through her dark thoughts, "that's why you need to cherish those who *do* understand and accept you."

"Someone who'd accept me...huh," Isana muttered.

"You don't have anyone like that?"

That wasn't entirely true. She had been thanked many times by those who had asked her for help with a request. And Norton was always looking out for her despite her brusque attitude.

She was the one putting up walls between her and everyone else.

They don't accept me; they don't understand me. She was starting to feel embarrassed for boasting about the unfortunate hand fate had dealt her.

What am I, a moody teenager?

Isana felt a large hand rest on her shoulder, which was now slumped down in shame. She looked up, and her eyes met Zig's serious expression.

"Would you like to go on a journey to find yourself?" he asked gravely.

"As if!" she cried, embarrassment and anger simmering in her stomach as she raised her fist.

Zig easily dodged the air-slicing blow and walked off with a grin on his face. After giving her an apologetic nod, Siasha followed him.

Isana watched them leave in a huff before looking back down at her hands.

How long has it been since I last tried to strike someone, not to cause harm but due to an emotional outburst?

She'd raised a fist to Zig in a fit of anger, but what annoyed her was that she didn't even feel bad about it.

"Hmph!"

Whatever. It was time go home and drown herself in booze.

She'd already spent 500,000 dren today, so the cost of alcohol was beyond scaring her now.

With his new weapon slung safely on his back, Zig and Siasha searched for a place to have some lunch.

Siasha, who was walking a few steps ahead of him, looked back over her shoulder. "Is there anything you'd like to eat?"

"Hmm..." He tried to think of a place, but their options were limited due to the state of his wallet after the purchase.

"How about we grab something from the food sta—"

A chill ran up Zig's spine, and the hairs on his arms stood on end. It was just for a split second, but his senses had picked up on something. He looked around.

No one was there.

Whoever it was that triggered such a strong surge of alarm was hiding themselves very well.

"Zig? What is it?" Siasha's voice snapped him back to the present.

The presence was gone. A wave of dread washed over him when he realized that it had taken him time to notice because the entity hadn't been staring at him—their gaze had been fixed on Siasha.

"Siasha?" he said.

"Yes?" she asked worriedly.

"Have you done anything lately that would cause someone to hold a grudge against you?"

"Huh?" Her expression shifted to one of confoundment. "That's a random question."

"Well..."

Considering the intensity of that stare, it likely wasn't a positive one. Despite this someone being adept enough at stealth to mostly escape Zig's notice, those emotions he picked up were *extremely* potent. The fact that they were powerful enough to sense concerned him the most.

"It's nothing," he finally said. "Let's just eat at the food stalls today."

"I want skewers!" Siasha said cheerfully and immediately took off in the direction of the street lined with various carts.

As he watched her skip off in high spirits, Zig's hand curled tightly into a fist.

That's right, there's nothing wrong.

The reason I'm here in the first place is in case there's trouble.

Even if someone tries to stand in our way, that doesn't change what we need to do.

Witch
and
MERCENARY

CHAPTER 4

MONSTROSITY SWARM

Z IG AND SIASHA MADE THEIR WAY TO THE GUILD TO
join the extermination squad. Despite taking two days off,
it had been a rough couple of days, so they weren't as well
rested as they hoped to be. But work was calling, and it was time to
keep earning their stripes.

At least Zig had a new weapon. Even with an injured shoulder,
he surmised that the job shouldn't pose much of an issue since he
would only be on cleanup duty.

The guild was swarming with more people than usual—even
entry to the building had a new setup, with many adventurers lined
up in a different reception area than they normally would.

"All adventurers joining the extermination squad, please line up
here to confirm your registration!"

Following the instructions, the two went to stand in the appropriate line. Since they'd already finished the registration procedures
ahead of time, they would be able to get transported after just
confirming their identities. However, that line was long as well, so
they would have to wait like everyone else.

"Feels like it's going to be a piece of cake if this many people are
coming," Siasha said.

"Or it could also mean that an immense outbreak of monsters warrants these numbers..." Zig said.

He paused. Zig could feel the heat of people staring. Siasha was always getting stared at, so that was nothing new, but this time their eyes were trained on him.

Zig squinted suspiciously. Why were they looking at *him*?

One of the members of a party that just finished their registration gave him the answer.

"So, today you're hanging around with a different girl from yesterday?" a sulky-looking man called out provocatively. "Lucky you!"

His choice of words and tone immediately clued Zig into what was causing all of the stares. It seemed that rumors of him and Isana going out together were already spreading.

Putting her battle lust and teenage-like mentality aside, Isana was quite a fine woman—not to mention her status as a second-class adventurer. Most people probably didn't know how little money she actually possessed.

Many of the men already took issue with him always being glued to Siasha's side, so he didn't blame them for having a choice word or two if they thought he was parading Isana around on top of that.

"Must be nice," the man continued. "You're such a popular guy that you can just switch out the ladies one after another. You've got so much to offer she even dished out for your new weapon. My pride would never let me accept something like that, though."

It wasn't a stretch for an outside observer to deduce that he made Isana help him purchase a weapon. Seeming like he was switching between two desirable women and even getting one of them to buy his equipment... He could completely understand where the men were coming from.

"It's not what you think it is—" Siasha piped up.

"You're really okay with that?" the man interrupted. "That he's going after another woman when he's already got someone as good as you?"

"Like I was saying..."

"Why not leave this no-good cheater and team up with us? We'll make sure you're never bored."

Siasha went silent. Trying to resolve the situation as amicably as possible wasn't working. The men weren't listening, seeming content to just keep throwing around baseless accusations.

It was clear to all watching that she was becoming increasingly irritated by the man's attitude and accusations. Calling Zig a "no-good cheater" just turned her irritation to aggression.

"What's going on here?" someone asked from the sidelines.

"Stay out of this!" The men glared in the direction of the voice, but their faces paled when they saw who it was.

"O-oh, Alan..."

A man with an unruly mop of red hair stood glowering before them.

"It sounded like you were having a bit of a dispute," Alan said. "Is there a problem here?"

"N-no! We were just making small talk. Anyway, we'll be going now!"

The men hurried past, almost as though they were running away from Alan. When they were gone, Alan turned to Zig and Siasha.

"I hope I wasn't sticking my nose in where it didn't belong," he said.

"No, we appreciate the help," Zig said. "I was worried Siasha might explode."

"Indeed. To be honest, it was more for their sakes that I decided to butt in."

The man had a point. Zig and Alan both started to laugh.

"I got the impression they were disparaging you," Siasha said sulkily.

"You just have to laugh that kind of thing off," the mercenary said. "After all, Siasha, you've got so many years of life experience over them."

"I don't care what anyone has to say about me, but if it's you they're making fun of, then I..."

Although it was common for people to care more about the defamation directed at others than that directed at themselves, Siasha's case was unique. She was used to having various curses hurled her way, but it was hard for her to accept the same treatment being given to the very first person she had ever been able to call an ally.

"I appreciate how you feel, but you can't force your values on others," Zig gently chided. "To everyone on the outside, I look like a regular freeloader."

"But just because they don't know what's going on, it doesn't give them the right to—"

"It's impossible for other people to completely understand someone else's situation. Humans are only able to make decisions based on what they see and hear."

"Okay." Siasha's face fell.

Zig gave her a wry smile as he placed a hand on her shoulder. "You said it yourself, right? That you need to cherish the people who understand and accept you."

Siasha smiled shyly at hearing those words again. Meanwhile, Alan was watching the two of them talking with deep interest.

"You're an unusual one, Zig," he said. "There are a lot of people in this profession who start fights because they believe it's all over once someone looks down on them."

"Well, I'm not an adventurer," Zig replied. "In my world, anyone who goes around looking down on others won't be breathing much longer, so worrying about what they have to say is just a waste of time."

Anyone on the battlefield who was stupid enough to make remarks like that, whether they be friend or foe, imminently ended up dead. Being at the receiving end of teasing pissed him off in the beginning, but as the men who took part in those activities died one after another, all he eventually felt was pity.

The only thoughts that filled his head were along the lines of, "This one's not much longer for the world." It was almost like watching a sick person inch ever closer to their deathbed.

"Sounds like quite a cruel profession..." Alan remarked.

"Anyway, what are you doing here?" Zig asked. "I thought this extermination squad was for adventurers that were around seventh class."

While adventurers were limited to taking on requests that were one rank above their level, there were no restrictions on taking anything below. However, it meant they couldn't earn any points toward advancing their rank. In fact, if an adventurer was obviously only taking jobs that were under their level, they could lose points.

Zig couldn't imagine why someone like Alan would've accepted this request.

"They're coming for insurance," Siasha said. "In other words, they're our 'babysitters.'"

"Babysitters?"

"Well, that's not exactly the intention..." Alan said sheepishly before explaining. "On these kinds of extermination jobs, there's always one party made up of at least fourth-class adventurers who also joins in order to take care of any higher-level monstrosities that might show up."

From time to time, dangerous monstrosities also made an appearance during breeding seasons. Sometimes they showed up to feast on the abundant smaller creatures, and sometimes one member of the pack would be ridiculously powerful.

"Things are often unpredictable in extraordinary situations," Alan continued. "I'm sure there's a good reason for it, but we still don't understand a lot about the biology of monstrosities, and in previous breeding seasons, there have been instances where an extermination squad has encountered monstrosities outside of their natural habitats."

"Makes sense," Zig agreed. "It does sound like you'll be there to babysit us."

"You know, I'm not the biggest fan of that term," Alan said with a wry smile.

"I'll feel better knowing you're around."

From what he had seen, Zig knew that Alan and his party were quite capable—not just in terms of strength but also in their excellent situational judgment and adaptability. If a high-level monstrosity did happen to show up, they should be able to handle it.

"I'm happy to hear that," Alan said. "We'll do whatever we can."

He walked off, and that's when Zig noticed that the line had progressed considerably during their conversation. Once it was their turn, they confirmed their registration and headed to the transportation stone room.

This time, they were using one in a different room.

"We're going to a place called the Fuelle Mountains, right?" Zig asked.

"Uh-huh," Siasha confirmed. "This extermination squad is being sent to handle an outbreak of rockworm larvae."

Rockworms might've looked like large caterpillars, but they didn't make cocoons. Adult rockworms incubated their young within their bodies and gave birth to them once they reached a certain size, at which point the young would break through their parent's body, destroying it.

Since the monstrosity only procreated once, the number of young wasn't particularly great, but their survival rate was high since they were already so developed at the time of their birth. If left unchecked for too long, an entire area could end up teeming with rockworms. It wasn't necessary to hunt them every year, but caution was required if their numbers got too large.

"An extermination squad is usually put together once they're found outside of their natural habitat," Zig murmured. "Just like the one we fought the other day..."

The mercenary felt like he owed that rockworm his gratitude. Encountering it had been a stroke of good luck that led to them being among those invited to take part in the culling of its kin.

"The high-level monstrosities that could show up include hammer lizards, crag drill dragons, and rock-devourer demons," Siasha continued, "and they aren't high-level per se, but adult rockworms and saber-clawed insectoids could also be in the mix."

Zig's eyes widened. "Did you say 'dragon'?"

"Even if it's called a dragon, it's more of a subspecies," she assured him, "inferior to the conventional type. They don't have breath weapons or high intelligence like normal dragons but are quite powerful and have a strong life force."

"We've finally reached the realm of fairy tales. Honestly, my interest is piqued."

Even on the continent where they were from, dragons were considered creatures of legend, and one of the few creatures that he admired.

"Don't even think about it, Zig," Siasha warned. "Crag drill dragons are a monstrosity reserved for high-ranking adventurers, like fourth class and above. Even if you did manage to defeat one, we'd be given a stern reprimanding by the guild."

"That's too bad."

Despite the guild's policy of trying to promote capable adventurers as fast as possible, there were still limits in place. Deviating from the standard procedure would be seen as problematic.

Stepping toward the transportation stone, the two steeled themselves for another day of work.

The Fuelle Mountains were a wasteland filled with exposed rock faces rich in mineral resources. It was a dangerous area where unique monstrosities that fed on the ores and crystals roamed, but adventures deemed it so profitable that the benefits outweighed the risks.

Monstrosity extermination requests were regularly given from this region, handled primarily by parties made up of sixth- and seventh-class adventurers. There was a chance to encounter creatures such as crag drill dragons as well, but they were more commonly found in the hinterlands and wouldn't appear unless provoked. When they did occasionally show up during times like breeding seasons, the higher-level adventurers took care of them.

Zig and Siasha joined the adventurers that had arrived before them at the squad's encampment and started getting ready. More adventurers kept appearing until there were about fifty people assembled.

The average adventuring party was made up of four to six people, and ten parties in total had arrived. After confirming that all participants were present, the fourth-class adventuring party took the lead. Alan stood in front, yelling out what they could expect while carrying out their task.

"The targets of this extermination squad are rockworms! Even if they're just larvae, their numbers are vast. Do not go off on your own under any circumstances and make sure to leave enough distance between yourselves so that you can watch each other's backs!"

Some of the parties glanced at each other at Alan's warning.

"Looks like quite a few of the members have already talked this over," Zig remarked.

"That could be true, but some of them might just be joining from the same clan," Siasha said. "I've heard it's difficult to ally with others on the spot, but if you have an existing relationship, there's no need to worry."

"When it comes to teaming up with others, we're practically still amateurs. We need to be careful not to get in their way."

While they both were highly capable in combat, they were still inexperienced when it came to killing monstrosities. They hadn't properly learned all the basics of being adventurers and were novices at working in a team. And while Zig had plenty of experience with battling human opponents, these were monstrosities. It didn't seem like his years on the battlefield would be very helpful here.

After receiving more guidance on the finer details, the extermination squad moved out.

Alan's party separated into two groups: one to the left of the main group and one to the right. They would prepare for any surprise attacks from their flanks while the extermination squad handled anything assaulting them head-on. The group split into three squadrons and began to fan out horizontally.

"This time, the focus is on annihilating monstrosities with magic attacks," Zig said. "Doesn't seem like there'll be much for me to do."

"You can take it easy today, Zig. This is my specialty!"

"I'll take you up on that offer." Despite his words, he knew he couldn't completely slack off.

A few parties were already forming a front line in case anything got too close. Zig thought about joining them, but adding one more member without knowing how they could fit into the mix would probably be more of a hindrance than anything.

"I'll be in the rear," he said as he fell back. "If anything happens, I'll let you know."

"Got it."

He decided to do reconnaissance work so he could keep an eye on the entire group's movements and immediately detect anything out of place.

There was already a party acting as a rear guard. They shot Zig suspicious looks, but seeing that he was keeping his distance from them, they said nothing and shifted to patrolling the perimeter.

The scenery around them gradually began to change.

The ground was fissured, and the path they marched ran between large surfaces that were cracked and raised like blood vessels. The chasm was so large, it could accommodate the entire extermination squad comfortably.

However, there were many dead ends in addition to branching paths.

Most of the small creatures on the path that spotted the large group coming their way made themselves scarce. On the rare occasion one of them tried to attack, it was quickly dealt with by magic or an arrow.

There really isn't going to be anything for me to do here, is there? Zig mused to himself as he kept an eye on the perimeter.

The party on rear guard duty approached, its members looking at Zig curiously. Finally, one of them spoke.

"Hey, can I ask you something?"

"What is it?" Zig asked.

"Is it true you were with Isana?"

Looked like they also heard the rumors and wanted their curiosity satiated.

"Yes, it's true."

Zig's straightforward answer sent the men into a tizzy.

"Seriously? Th-then, is it also true that she bought you a weapon?!"

"Not exactly," he said. "She broke my weapon, so she was compensating me."

"R-really? What do you mean by compensating you?"

"She attacked me due to a misunderstanding," he explained. "Not only did she break my weapon, but she ran that sword of hers through my shoulder."

"Wow..." another of the party said in awe. "That sounds...like quite a tragedy."

"It sure was. Are all the top adventurers like that?"

"Um, it does seem like most of them are a bit strange..." The man who answered had a look that Zig couldn't read.

As far as Zig had seen, in many professions, those that rose to the top tended to be odd ducks. It seemed like adventuring was no exception. He continued to talk with the men as they walked.

Suddenly, the front squadrons came to a stop.

"Looks like we're on the enemy," one of the men said as a voice from the front warned them to proceed with caution.

If Zig strained his eyes to look, he could make out a swarm of monstrosities emerging from one of the branching paths of the chasm. They seemed to ooze out, one after another, until the ground was covered with them.

Rockworm larvae stampeded toward their prey, sending up a cloud of dust in their wake.

The parties began to form battle lines as the magic users lined up in two long horizontal rows. The advance guard moved to protect them from both sides, weapons ready to deal with anything that got too close.

"Here they come!" someone from the vanguard yelled. "Magic users, prepare to attack!"

The adventurers began to cast their spells. Various pungent odors filled the air, the smell so intense that Zig couldn't help but grimace.

"Aim... Fire!"

At the signal, the magic users let loose their spells.

The myriad of spells obliterated a large portion of the rockworm swarm, causing the survivors to lose some momentum as they now had to climb over the bodies of their fallen brethren.

The first line of magic users moved back to start preparing their next spells, while the ones behind stepped forward.

"Second wave, fire!"

A deafening roar filled their ears as more monstrosities were sent flying through the air.

There were some adult rockworms as well, but at this point, they were just sitting ducks. The rockworms' greatest advantages were their speed and the mobility their many legs provided. However, in such a cramped space and against opponents who stuck to their tight-knit formation, they couldn't utilize their abilities.

"Seems like it'll only take ten minutes or so to finish this lot off," Zig muttered under his breath as he watched the scene—which could hardly be called a battle—play out in front of him.

Seems they have things under control, so I'll shift my focus to patrolling the rear, he thought.

But just as he was about to turn around, he spotted something from the corner of his eye.

"What was that?"

About to dismiss it as a figment of his imagination, Zig froze as he recalled what happened with the ghost shark. Giving the entity his full attention, he noticed another type of monstrosity appear from a side path.

It was covered in a light brown carapace—about six and a half feet tall and walking on two feet. Not only did it look able-bodied, but its long claws implied a vicious aggressiveness. Due to their length, it would be better to call them blades instead of claws—they were so long that they touched the ground if the creature stood upright and lowered its arms. Its face resembled that of a long-horn beetle, complete with large, undulating mandibles.

And it was swiftly approaching them from the side path.

"That's got to be one of those unexpected monstrosities," Zig said to himself.

More of them began to appear from either side and suddenly charged toward the extermination squad. Zig started to move to meet the incoming threat when the words of one of the rear-guard members stopped him in his tracks.

"It's going to be okay."

"What's that supposed to mean?" Zig protested.

"What do you think it means?" the man replied, glancing toward the two flank guards. "This is why we have *them* here. Just watch."

The members of the extermination squad looked unperturbed by the monstrosities attempting to ambush them. The creatures continued to charge forward, stomping as they ran across the ground.

They were even faster than the rockworms.

A red-haired man appeared, blocking one in its path.

The monstrosity flailed its claws in an attempt to cut down the obstacle, but the man deflected them with his longsword. Seeing its first attack miss, the monstrosity took a swing with its other set of claws only to find its opponent was no longer there.

The man had sidestepped in time with his block, pivoting so that he positioned himself behind the creature. He swung, cleaving into its torso with a horizontal sweep of his longsword.

It tumbled to the ground, twitching for a few moments until it stopped moving.

Alan, having slain the monstrosity in a flashy show of swordplay, moved straight on to the next incoming creature.

A cheer rose from the extermination squad, secure in the knowledge that they only needed to concentrate on defeating the monstrosities approaching them directly.

"Well, what did I tell you?" the man next to Zig said.

"So, that's how it is."

It was a fine display, just as one would expect from a fourth-class adventurer. As long as Alan and company were around, they wouldn't need to worry about any unexpected guests.

"Still, that was a rather pitiful one—a saber-clawed insectoid, that is."

"What kind of monstrosity is it?" Zig asked.

The man began to fill him in.

Saber-clawed insectoids were on the level of seventh-class adventurers and above. Although they were more aggressive and speedier than rockworms, they didn't have the latter's superior movement that allowed them to make sharp turns or climb walls. They were extremely territorial and would pick fights even with elite creatures, which meant most of them didn't have a very long life span. Since they had no problem cannibalizing their own species, encountering them in packs was incredibly rare.

They had low intelligence and could easily be lured or caught in traps, so despite their aptitude for combat, they weren't considered very dangerous. If an adventurer kept their wits about them and managed to get behind the creature, it could be dispatched quickly.

"Still, a couple might show up together from time to time, but you don't see a whole pack very often," the man murmured as he watched Alan and his party take down a second and third saber-clawed insectoid.

They appeared to be mainly coming from the flanks, so the high-level party had split into two and were intercepting them on both sides.

"I'm going to let them know what's happening up there," Zig said.

"It's a waste of your time. Anyway, we'll be here protecting the rear."

Zig wanted to let Siasha know what was going on, so he headed for the front of the squad. The man he had been talking with languidly waved goodbye behind him.

Siasha was in the squad deployed to the left side, the one assigned to Alan. He found her among her comrades, still blasting the rockworms with one wave of magic attacks after another.

Her black hair drifted around her as she unleashed another spell; that's when Zig noticed something.

"She seems to be holding back quite a bit?" he said to himself.

Zig was well aware of what Siasha was capable of, but the spells she was using were mediocre in both power and range. She was still superior to the magic users around her but nowhere close to her usual potency.

"Is she trying to match everyone else, or is there another reason...?" Zig wondered as he approached.

That's when Alan came into view. He had caused one of the saber-claws to lose its balance, and the magic user of his party assisted by engulfing it in flames with a spell.

He immediately rounded upon the next saber-claw, slashing off its claws with a sword combination. The creature's head toppled to the ground.

Zig happened to glimpse Alan's expression, and what he saw made him freeze.

"Hm?"

Something felt off.

Alan's swordplay was impeccable—he was working in perfect harmony with his colleague and didn't seem to be tiring at all. But Zig couldn't shake the strange feeling in his gut.

From where he stood, Zig saw Alan's face as he evaded another saber-claw's attack.

"Is he panicking...?" That was the only way Zig could describe the swordsman's expression.

Zig thought for a moment, then it finally hit him. Alan and his party had already killed many saber-clawed insectoids—monstrosities that very rarely traveled in packs.

The mercenary surveyed his surroundings once more. He hadn't realized it, but more and more protective magic was being sent Alan's way. And, as if to accommodate, the frequency and might of Siasha's spells were increasing.

"I think I need to hurry."

What he was witnessing wasn't normal.

His gears now shifted, Zig started running toward her.

Siasha saw Zig approaching out of the corner of her eye and called out to the other magic users. One of them that was resting switched places with her, giving her room to meet Zig.

He could see faint beads of sweat on her cheeks.

"Are you okay, Zig?" she asked.

"I'm fine," he said. "How are things going over here?"

"It seems like another swarm of monstrosities spawned at the same time."

Why would that have happened?

His mind swam with questions, but it wasn't the time or place for that, so he pushed them aside for the time being.

"Alan and the others are fending them off," she explained, "but they don't have enough manpower, so some of the others are lending their aid."

Siasha had been single-handedly filling in for compatriots, having the spellcasting ability to cover for several people at once.

"Zig!"

He turned at the sound of his name to see Alan as he crossed blades with yet another saber-clawed insectoid.

"How are the other squadrons doing?!" the swordsman yelled.

"The central one is unaffected, but the right squadron is dealing with the same conditions as here!" Zig shouted so Alan could hear him.

Alan grimaced as he sliced through the monstrosity.

"We've got Siasha taking charge over here," Zig continued, "so I think we'll make it work, but the other side doesn't have someone like that!"

Another insectoid charged at Alan. He dodged and slashed at its arm, sending it flying off.

"In that case, do you think you could lend them your assistance?!" he shouted.

"That's..." Zig stopped short. He wasn't an adventurer; his job was to protect Siasha. He couldn't just desert his post.

"Zig, please go," Siasha said when she saw the conflicted look on his face.

"Is that really okay?" he asked.

"I can handle this much just fine. I've still got plenty of energy left!"

"All right."

His main job was to act as her bodyguard, but if this was what his client wished, he couldn't refuse.

"Please, Zig!" Siasha called out as she returned to her place in the front row. "Let's finish this job and quickly move up in the ranks!"

He couldn't help but give her a small smile. Spending time in Halian had turned the timid witch who was nervous about joining the guild into a confident, independent woman.

It was time for him to get back to work.

Before he could leave, he heard Alan call out to him.

"Zig, I have something to ask of you. No... I have a job for you!"

"Say it. I'll consider taking it depending on what it is."

This wasn't a favor that he was about to ask. Alan didn't have any misconceptions about his and Zig's relationship. He didn't have a lot of time, but he needed to think carefully about how to say it.

Zig would refuse his request if it interfered with his current one, but he couldn't ask for something unrealistic either.

"Please protect my companions," he said. "I'll give you 500,000 dren regardless of what happens, and an extra 500,000 if you're successful."

There, that shouldn't interfere with what he was already asked to do. Alan wanted to include the rest of the adventurers too, but protecting them was his job.

Zig nodded. "Fine. I accept."

"I'll determine if you're successful based on any injuries sustained by my companions."

Zig didn't respond, already dashing away to do his task.

Alan moved to take on the next monstrosity without giving the mercenary another glance. Zig's ability was an unknown quantity. Alan knew it was far beyond that of an ordinary man, but he was just *so* unlike the rest of them.

With his values—not to mention the way he thought and worked—it was almost like he was dealing with someone who came from a foreign country.

And that gaze... He could still remember its intensity the first time they ever spoke. Zig called himself a mercenary, but Alan couldn't recall ever seeing someone in that line of work who had such an intense stare.

He had the feeling there was a critical difference between Zig and what the rest of them knew mercenaries were.

And that was why he hired him.

Alan and his companions were strong.

Working together, the four of them had enough grit to defeat even a lesser species of dragon. But every group has their weaknesses. For Alan's, it was numbers.

Each of his party members were strong in battle and could decently handle close combat even when fulfilling rear-guard duties. However, they didn't have powerful spells that covered wide areas, so when the enemy numbers were too great, some of them would manage to get close.

Basically, it meant they were excellent against strong individuals but weak against numerous average foes; and usually, it wasn't a problem. It was easy to spot large groups of enemies, so they were never taken by surprise. Even if they had the misfortune of encountering a situation they couldn't handle, retreat was always an option.

But today...that wasn't the case.

It was their job to handle the unexpected, and they couldn't just run away this time.

An arrow penetrated through one of the saber-clawed insectoids. It was a magic item, fortified with increased speed and power so that it could shatter claws trying to deflect it and pierce its target.

The situation at the left squadron was dire.

The female archer, who usually stayed behind the party, resisted the instinct to fall back and continued to fight. The saber-clawed insectoids had seemingly come out of nowhere, and more kept coming. The party's only saving grace was that they weren't a massive swarm like the rockworms, but she and her companions were quickly approaching their limit.

"Damn it! Just how many are there?!" she seethed.

The party's shield fighter, who usually took hits for his teammates, delivered a fatal blow to one of the saber-claws. Although his expertise leaned more toward protection, he was still an elite swordsman. Right now, the best protection he could give was annihilating as many insectoids as possible. Since the rest of the squadron had to focus on the enemies charging toward them, they could only provide limited assistance.

If they couldn't defeat the monstrosities with the forces they currently had, the battle lines would collapse. However, monstrosities were appearing at such a rate that they were having difficulty handling them all.

A look of panic began to spread on the archer's face as the battle continued. No matter what they did, the tides weren't turning in their favor, and she was being forced to use magic along with her arrows.

Invisible blades tore at the saber-claws' legs, crippling the creatures so that the shield fighter could decapitate them. If it weren't for her strenuous efforts of shooting an endless volley of both arrows and magic, they would already be overwhelmed.

However, both her magic items and ability to cast spells were running out fast. She was almost out of mana, and it didn't look like the assault would be ceasing anytime soon. The other squadrons likely couldn't spare any additional firepower either.

It's going to come down to my mana versus my physical strength—which one will give out first?

She shook off the troubling thought, gripping her bow and summoning her willpower to keep fighting. The archer reached into her quiver but only found air.

"Damn it...!"

All of her ammunition, including everything she had brought as a backup, was gone. In that moment of agitation, the curse escaping from her lips interrupted her casting.

Her spell fizzled out. The volley of arrows ceased.

She forced herself to keep calm and began the incantation again, but by then it was too late.

"Crap! Incoming!"

A few of the saber-claws slipped past the shield fighter, charging straight for her. Slinging her bow across her back, she grabbed the weapons she kept sheathed to her waist: a pair of hand axes with short handles.

One of the creatures swung its claws at her. She scrambled under it, slamming her axes into its knee. The crushing blow sent the monstrosity tumbling to the ground and writhing in agony.

She barely had time to deliver the finishing blow when she was forced to step back to avoid the attack of a second saber-claw. Although she somehow managed to dodge its flailing claws, she ended up losing her balance; her strength was giving out, and the mana that was magically fortifying her was running dangerously low.

The opening provided the monstrosity with an opportunity to slam her with a kick. The archer gasped, the impact so strong that it sent her flying backward. She clenched her teeth, desperately trying to hold on to consciousness.

Her injuries weren't life-threatening. Her breastplate had taken the brunt of the attack, but the impact had made her drop her weapons.

She had to stand back up. Using the momentum that had sent her reeling, she slowly rose to her feet. Her vision was blurry. She shook her head to clear it, but once the haze was gone, the monstrosity was upon her—swinging its claws at her from both sides.

So, this is how it ends, the archer thought with resignation as she stared at the murderous claws flying at her neck.

But before the claws could dig into her flesh, there was a dull thud just around her shoulders.

Confusion washed over her. "Huh?"

The monstrosity looked just as flummoxed as she was.

It kept moving its arms, trying to push them into her neck, but they wouldn't budge.

What in the world was going on?

"Get down!"

The archer jolted at the words, her body moving of its own accord before her mind could even process what was happening. The moment she ducked, a powerful kick sent her attacker tumbling to the ground.

Its chest was caved in where the blow landed, and it thrashed around in pain before being cleaved in two by a blue-tinted blade. Both halves twitched for a few moments before coming to a stop.

She looked up at her savior—a large and muscled man with a steely gaze. In his hand was a dual-bladed sword, a weapon she had never seen anyone use before.

"Are you okay?" the man asked, glancing at her.

"S-somehow..." she stammered.

Blood was pouring from both of his shoulders. Everything suddenly clicked into place.

The man had rushed up behind her and blocked the creature's claws with his gauntlets. He had saved her from certain death, but the claws had managed to pierce his shoulders. From the amount of blood, she could tell the wound wasn't too deep, but grievous enough.

What this man had done was drastic and could've killed them both...but he somehow pulled it off. He nodded at her and picked up one of her hand axes.

"I'm going to borrow this," he said and threw it.

The blade struck the head of one of saber-claws that were now surrounding the shield fighter, slicing right through it and giving him enough time to slip away.

The man held out his hand to the archer.

"Can you still move?" he asked.

"I can still fight," she replied, grabbing his hand and pulling herself back to her feet.

"I like your spunk," the man said with a smile as he handed her three new quivers.

"Where did you get these?" she asked, bewildered.

"I, um, *borrowed* these from the central squadron on the way over here. Make sure and thank them on my behalf later."

"You're a lifesaver."

She really needed to thank her lucky stars that the man had come prepared.

"Keep me covered from the rear," he called as he ran toward their foes. "I'll take care of the front, and there won't be a single one that breaks through!"

That man sure was quick! He was sprinting so fast with that bulky weapon strapped to his back that she couldn't believe her eyes. He dashed into the group of saber-claws that were trying to surround the shield fighter again.

"Get wrecked!"

He rushed forward with a blow that seemed to carry all his momentum and speed, ripping any monstrosity his blades made contact with into shreds. Pieces of the saber-claws cascaded through the air.

"Wh-what's going on?! Did another one attack?!"

The situation was so outrageous that the shield fighter thought a new type of monstrosity had joined the fray. It was only after the shower of blood had dissipated that he saw the newcomer was human.

"Who are you?" he asked.

"A mercenary," the man replied. "Alan hired me."

"Why would he hire a mercenary... No, that can wait. If we fall here, the extermination squad will be in peril. Help us protect them like your life depends on it!"

"Got it."

Having finally recovered from the shock of seeing their companions blown away in a pink mist, the remaining monstrosities pounced on the fresh meat. Zig swung his twinblade around to meet their attacks in a clash of claws and blades.

The moment the blue blade met their claws, it shattered them and tore their bodies apart. Zig's weapon, on the other hand, didn't have a single blemish.

This was an excellent first battle for him to test his new weapon out.

The impressive results made Zig smile as he slashed at the next saber-claw. He found that he could evade the monstrosity's attacks, block them with his gauntlets, and deflect them with his blade with ease.

If he put his entire weight on it, the flat of the blade could crush them entirely. The fierce blows he delivered sent more viscera scattering.

He swung his blade so fast that only a trail of blue was left in its wake. One after another, any monstrosity that entered his radius was chopped into pieces.

The archer from Alan's party continued to let loose her arrows as the scene unfolded. She saved what little mana she had left and only picked off enemies that came too close to Zig, preventing him from being surrounded.

The destructive force of that man was incredible. He was such a threat that the monstrosities were too busy with him to pay her much attention. Thanks to him, she was able to stay fixed to a single spot and keep firing.

The shield fighter went to assist Zig as soon as he saw him locked in combat. He parried their attacks with his shield, finishing off any saber-claw that took its eyes off him. The monstrosities soon became confused about which man to attack.

The shield fighter wasn't being aggressive, but if they ignored him, his fierce attacks could decimate them. At the hint of any hesitation, Zig would rush at them, breaking through their defenses and obliterating anything in his path.

"Yeah, humanoids are way easier," Zig said to himself.

He may not have had much experience when it came to fighting different types of monstrosities, but it was a completely different story if they were humanoid. It wasn't the same as facing another man, but their build and joints, movements, and behaviors when attacking were close enough.

But unlike humans, they weren't particularly cunning.

Having two veterans assisting him was also a large benefit. Their assistance in picking some off helped him exponentially, providing him with the opportunity to mow down the rest like practice dummies.

Before Zig arrived, the archer and shield fighter were barely holding back their foes, but his appearance dramatically shifted the odds. Since the two adventurers could now perform their usual roles, combat became more efficient.

Zig stole a glance in their direction as he continued to hack and slash with his sword.

"Haaah!" The archer fired three shots in one breath.

One stuck true and sunk into one of the creatures as it tried to dodge sideways. The arrow seemed to be reinforced because it shattered the monstrosity's carapace upon impact.

The archer was now holding her bow horizontally, the stance allowing her to fire more rapidly at the cost of stability. This was her true role—relying on her companions to keep the attention off her so she could keep launching a volley of shots.

Zig shifted his focus to the shield fighter.

"Taste my blade!" the man cried as he rammed his sword through the neck of a monstrosity that was stumbling from trying to parry an attack. He was also an impressive warrior, and his skill with the shield allowed him to fend off multiple attacks at once.

Despite attracting the attention of so many enemies, he still hadn't sustained anything worse than flesh wounds. Conversely, any saber-claw that left him an opening was quickly dealt with.

"Over here, you bug-brained freak!"

He turned to face a monstrosity a little farther away and pointed his shield in its direction. Small darts shot out from a contraption fitted on the inside. The darts bounced off the carapace but succeeded in grabbing the creature's attention.

Despite his brash taunting, the man understood tactics quite well. As soon as he recognized Zig was an attacker that could decimate enemies, he immediately changed to a supporting role.

Both the archer and shield fighter were far more competent than Zig thought. The only reason they were being worn down was because they were overwhelmed.

"Nnngh!" Zig ducked an insectoid swinging at him and counterattacked, slicing clean through its torso.

He gave its corpse a fierce kick, slamming its body into the monstrosity behind it. Gaining momentum by spinning the twinblade around, he slashed it down on the still-dazed creature, destroying both it and the corpse.

Pieces of flesh scattered in every direction, and blood sprayed through the air. The archer took the opportunity to pick off any saber-claws frozen in shock as they witnessed the gory sight.

The number of enemies was finally starting to dwindle.

Most monstrosities would sense that they were being culled and flee, but the nature of saber-claws propelled them to fight until the very last breath.

"Most humans aren't even half this tenacious," Zig commented.

But the battle had long been decided. The last remaining saber-clawed insectoid's body flew through the air.

Zig went around to confirm there were no survivors, finishing any off that were still twitching. It was only when he was sure that every last one of them was dead that he let himself relax.

He wiped the blood off his weapon, giving it a quick inspection. Some of his moves had included severing their claws, but there wasn't even a visible scratch on the blades. He gave the sword a couple of swings to make sure nothing felt off.

"That's how it is, huh?" he said. "Seems like the high price tag was worth it."

But what shocked him even more was remembering that his weapon was only slightly above average quality.

That thin blade Isana had on her—the katana, she called it—just how well does that thing perform?

The two members of Alan's party approached Zig.

"Wow, you sure saved our hides," the shield fighter said.

"It's fine," he replied. "Just doing what I was hired to do."

The rest of the squadron was still engaged with the rockworms, but that was the extermination squad's job.

The shield fighter put out his hand. Though he was reluctant to expose his dominant arm, Zig reciprocated the gesture, and they shook hands.

"About that—what exactly were you supposed to do?" the man said. "You mentioned our Alan was the one who made the request?"

"That's right. He wanted me to support you."

He'd been asked to protect them, but Zig chose his words carefully, not wanting to hurt their pride.

"I'm guessing that means the other side wasn't as bad?"

"Pretty much. The number of monstrosities spawning was about the same, but there's a skilled magic user over there who can do the work of several people."

"That's some good luck," the archer said. "Hey, you're injured, aren't you?"

"Hm? Oh, now that you mention it, I guess I am."

He hadn't been expecting to see one of them about to get her head sliced off when he dashed over. It was good he was able to force his way into the fight and intervene, but that had literally been cutting it too close.

Since Alan told him he would be paid for a successful job depending on the injuries sustained by his party members, he had been far too reckless.

The archer walked up to Zig as he began to try and stop the bleeding.

"Let me take a look," she said. It seemed like she was going to lend him a hand.

"Sure. Thanks."

"That's my line, you know," she said as she examined his wound.

Taking out a waterskin, she poured water over the injury to remove any dirt before covering it with her hands—apparently, she could use restorative magic as well.

The archer started chanting, and after a few moments, light covered his wound. She noticed him looking at it and began to speak again.

"Thanks for earlier," she said. "My name is Listy."

"I'm Zig," he replied. "And I don't need any thanks. Like I said, it was my job."

"That's irrelevant."

"Okay, then you healing me makes us even."

"It's not nearly enough. Let me buy you a drink."

"That's not—" he began.

"I'm buying you a drink," she insisted.

"Fine."

"Good."

The woman had basically twisted his arm into agreeing. She was a high-level adventurer; perhaps being pushy came with the territory.

The shield fighter cackled as he watched their exchange. "She sure got the best of you, Zig. The name's Lyle, by the way. Pleasure to meet you." He looked him up and down. "I thought mercenaries were just groups of thugs."

"Lyle," Listy chastised.

"Ack... Um, my bad."

Zig waved it off, silently indicating that it wasn't a problem.

"I've never seen a mercenary like you before," Listy said.

"I've heard that's common around these parts," Zig said.

"Where do you come from, Zig?"

"Somewhere far away." He avoided the question with a vague response; he thought it best to hide the fact that he'd come from across the sea lest it cause him any hassle.

Listy and Lyle were curious, but didn't probe any deeper.

"You mentioned a skilled magic user was with the other squadron," the archer continued. "By any chance, is she your companion?"

"Yeah. You've heard of her?"

"She's well-known around here. A rising star, you might say. All the clans are vying for her to join them. However, people say the scary man whose company she always keeps prevents them from approaching her."

That chilling glare he had given anyone who looked their way the first day seemed to have done the trick.

"I heard the rumors, but I didn't know you were *this* good," Lyle chimed in. "Wouldn't you make a lot more as an adventurer?"

"My current line of work suits me," Zig said. "I've been doing it for a long time now."

"That's just how it goes, eh?"

"Okay, this should be good enough for now," Listy said as she lifted her hands. Zig's injury had healed up while they were talking.

He rotated his shoulders a few times. Listy's restoration magic seemed to have done the trick.

"There shouldn't be any more trouble over here," Lyle remarked. "You can head back now."

"All right."

"Say hi to Alan for us."

"Will do."

Zig left the two to their duties as he made his way back over to Siasha. As he walked, he noticed the extermination squad had succeeded in thinning the large swarm of monstrosities.

It seemed like their work for the day would be finished even sooner than anticipated.

"Were they okay?!" Alan grilled Zig as soon as he returned—he must've been incredibly worried.

"Calm down," the mercenary said. "Neither of them sustained any major injuries."

"S-sorry," the swordsman said apologetically. "I see. That's a relief."

"How are things going over here?"

"All the saber-claws are dealt with. There are still some rock-worms left, but they should be finishing up shortly."

It seemed like nothing else out of the ordinary had occurred.

"Do things like this happen often?" Zig asked.

"It's not uncommon for monstrosities besides the ones the extermination squad is taking care of to show up," Alan said. "But having two outbreaks at once is exceedingly rare. I've never even heard of a swarm of saber-claws before."

Zig had heard stories of animals that didn't naturally form groups clustering together with other outcasts, but would it be possible for these insects to go so far against their natural instincts?

He mentioned his thoughts to Alan, who agreed.

"Something does smell fishy, doesn't it? I'll talk to everyone about it once we wrap up here and contact the guild. Depending on what happens, we may need to end this mission prematurely."

"Understood."

"Anyway, thanks again for helping my companions."

"I'm looking forward to the payment."

"As you should."

Zig parted ways with Alan and headed over to Siasha. Her squad had completed their extermination of the large swarm, but the whole area was in a terrible state. Monstrosity carcasses littered the ground as far as the eye could see, and the magic users were setting fire to them to clean up the mess.

Zig spotted Siasha among them, but she was still working, so he went looking for his belongings and waited for her to finish.

"We're finally done," she said.

"You did a good job."

There were a lot of bodies, so cleaning up had taken quite a while. Siasha looked exhausted.

"I'm beat," she complained. "The killing part was so much easier. And the smell! Oh, the smell..."

"Disposing of the remains is hard work, huh?" Zig commented. "Guess it doesn't matter if it's a monstrosity or human."

He handed her some bread and water. It was hardtack, since that was the only type of bread that kept well during travel, but some jam was sure to make it a little more palatable.

"Thank you," Siasha said gratefully. "Oh, something sweet really hits the spot..."

Meals on the battlefield affected morale, so making sure they were as delicious and filling as possible helped soldiers to persevere. Zig knew this from his own experiences, so he'd come prepared.

Siasha seemed to have recovered some strength by the time the squadron regrouped. Once everyone was accounted for and ready, they headed for the encampment.

The troops remained vigilant as they marched. Fortunately, there were no incidents, and everyone was able to reach camp safely.

Once the adventurers returned to the camp, groups split up to rest and recover. There was not much to do in the wasteland, so most ended up simply chatting and enjoying themselves as they drank and ate.

Zig finished his meal and prepared the materials to maintain his weapon while Siasha looked on.

"How was the new sword?" she asked.

"Even better than I expected," he replied. "I didn't realize how much easier it would be to not have to worry so much about wear and tear."

Siasha smiled as she watched Zig cheerfully clean and polish the blades. The campfire bathed her pale face in its soft light, giving her lips a glossy red sheen. The sight was so enchanting that the other adventurers nearby couldn't help but be enraptured.

However, Zig was too enamored with his sword to notice her or the envious glares being thrown his way.

He's probably going to enjoy *her company tonight,* the men thought, their ragged breathing becoming *very* audible as they imagined what her moans might sound like.

In complete contrast to what they were fantasizing, all Siasha and Zig were discussing was work.

"What did you think about what happened today?" he asked.

"The very nature of the saber-claws makes it impossible for them to swarm like that," Siasha mused. "There has to be another factor at play."

He trusted her knowledge. Siasha had devoured so many books, including the entirety of *The Illustrated Guide to Monstrosities*, that she was practically a walking library. Zig wasn't sure whether it was an inborn quality of being a witch or she was just talented. Either way, when it came to what she knew, she was probably already on the level of a veteran adventurer.

"An external factor, huh?" he said as he recalled their encounter with the ghost shark. "Maybe something big drove them out?"

"That still wouldn't explain why they formed a pack," Siasha said. "I think something made them go against their natural instincts, like they were being manipulated somehow."

"I didn't sense any magic coming off them, though."

"Maybe it was a drug of some kind?" she suggested. "But how would you administer it to that many at once? And what would be the benefit? Even if you wanted to experiment, there are so many other monstrosities that would be better in combat and easier to handle." Siasha groaned as she continued to brood over her thoughts.

"We've still got tomorrow," he said. "Maybe we should just call it a night for now."

"Okay. When should I wake up to go on watch?"

"You don't need to be on watch tonight."

Siasha opened her mouth to object, but after seeing his face, she sighed and nodded.

"Okay. Thanks." She made her way into the tent.

"There's always pluses and minuses to working with large groups," he murmured.

He had started to sense something dangerous swirling in the gazes the men were giving Siasha, so he bade her to go to bed. She needed to be kept hidden away—there was no knowing what would happen if he didn't keep watch.

Zig was hardly enthusiastic about the prospect. After all, it wasn't Siasha he had to worry about—it was the men. He tried to get his mind off such worries as he stood guard the entire night.

The early morning sun's rays were just beginning to color the skies when he went to wake Siasha up. Despite not being a morning person, today she roused quicker than usual. Zig handed her a small towel and a bucket of water so she could clean up and prepare for the day ahead.

"You're kind of a neat freak, aren't you, Zig?" she commented. "I never got the impression that cleanliness was something mercenaries cared about."

"Your impression isn't incorrect," he said, "but you won't be long for this world if you're unhygienic."

He had met plenty of mercenaries who lost an arm or a leg due to forgetting to clean dirty wounds sustained on the battlefield.

"Besides, keeping yourself presentable enough sometimes even leads to jobs."

There were more than a few times in the past when he was told he had been selected for escort or protection work over others because he didn't smell. Depending on the nature of the task, being suitably groomed was occasionally one of the requirements.

"Even mercenaries can't just rely on their skills with a weapon and ignore everything else."

"I see. Hm? Oopsie... Ngh!"

He could hear rustling about within the confines of the tent.

"Is everything okay?" he called.

"It's so cramped in here that I can't wash my back very well," she complained. "Zig, can you lend me a hand?"

He was at a loss for words. What a reckless thing to ask!

Zig knew Siasha didn't have much experience interacting with others, but this behavior was crossing a boundary. He really needed to do something about it before there were any misunderstandings.

It had crossed his mind several times, but he didn't know how to approach teaching her about certain etiquette.

"Ziiiig!"

"All right, all right," he groaned as he entered the tent.

Skin as white as porcelain came into view. Siasha was facing away from him with her long black hair hanging over her shoulders. Her clean scent tickled his nose.

"Please help me," she said softly, holding out the towel.

He took it and wrung it out over the bucket of water. Not sure how much pressure he should use, Zig wiped the towel over her skin very carefully so that he wouldn't do any damage.

"Is this okay?" he asked.

"I can take it a little harder, you know?"

Zig was not a celibate man.

Sex wasn't high on his list of priorities, but that didn't mean he never had carnal urges. She was having this effect on him because it had been a while...

He tried to keep his gaze unfocused, taking in her silhouette instead of her seductive exposed back. He moved the towel in sweeping strokes, acting like he was viewing his own arm from a distance.

To silence the growing desire within him, Zig utilized the "observer's eye"—a martial arts technique he learned in his home continent. Through it, he could rely on using the heart rather than the eyes to see and somehow quiet the lust that was bubbling up within him.

Siasha's back was just a back. Nothing more, nothing less.

Holding on to that like a lifeline, he slowly composed himself.

"I'm done," he finally said.

"Thank you!"

Zig handed the towel back to Siasha before quickly exiting the tent. Taking a few breaths to calm himself down, he called out to her in the most casual tone he could muster.

"Siasha, you know you shouldn't go around asking men to do that kind of stuff."

"I know!" Her cheerful reply made him feel even more uneasy.

Because of who Siasha was to the guild, no sane man would ever think he could get close to her. But he couldn't help but worry that her behavior toward him would lead to unnecessary trouble.

Once Siasha was ready, they had breakfast together. Gathering with the rest of the squadron, they listened to the information Alan and his party had to share.

"Thank you everyone for your hard work yesterday!" the swordsman said. "You all did an excellent job. Despite the unforeseen circumstances, no one suffered any serious injuries."

The adventurers cheered. They knew that due to the tireless efforts of Alan and his colleagues, they were able to prevent the swarm of saber-claws from reaching the extermination squad. If the squad members had to deal with additional attacks from their flanks, they likely would have been trampled by the charging rockworms.

"When I reported this irregularity to the guild," Alan continued, "they decided that we've thinned enough of their numbers for now and asked us to come back, but we first need to conduct a reconnaissance mission of the vicinity. We'll pull out after we've completed investigating the same area as yesterday."

Murmurs swept through the adventurers. Were yesterday's unexpected incidents that big of a deal?

"We'll also be collecting some monstrosity carcasses as part of a separate inquiry. I'll announce the collection squad shortly. In addition..."

Alan took a few more minutes detailing the day's instructions. Once he wrapped things up, it was time to move out.

Everyone was on high alert as they made their way down the same road as the day before, but they managed to make it back to the battlefield without any trouble.

Alan, his party, and a group of about ten others broke away from the squad to select some monstrosity carcasses that were still in relatively good condition to bring back to the guild. Most of the ones Zig had killed were so mangled that it was hard to tell what the creature originally looked like, rendering them useless for the inquiry.

The rest of the adventurers combed the vicinity, searching for any remaining members of the swarm. Zig went with Siasha and kept a watchful eye on the perimeter.

They soon came across the body of one of the saber-claws. Siasha crouched to examine it.

"I don't detect any traces of magic being used," she said. "There doesn't seem to be anything out of the ordinary that I can... Hm? Oh, this must be it."

"Did you find something?" Zig crouched beside her.

He followed her gaze and noticed something that seemed to be growing from the back of the creature's head. It looked like a cluster of black-colored berries dangling from the tip of a small protrusion.

"What do you suppose that is?" Siasha asked.

"No clue," he said. "It doesn't look like it was originally part of its anatomy."

"Did you notice something like that when you were fighting them yesterday?"

"I can't recall. Don't touch it; it might be poisonous."

"Okay."

There was no time to observe his foes carefully in the heat of battle. Even if he noticed a bulge of some sort, it was unlikely he would remember.

Siasha seemed adamant on finding an answer, however, so they went to examine some of the other bodies. After checking out a few more, they discovered that each one had the same protrusion.

"What the hell?" Zig said. "This definitely isn't normal."

"Considering where and how it's sticking out of their carapaces... it doesn't look like a natural feature. It's possible this is what's behind their abnormal behavior."

"That does seem likely, doesn't it?"

"Let's tell Alan."

It didn't take long to find Alan and his group, who were busy wrapping up some of the bodies in cloth, and inform him of their discovery. After listening to Siasha, the swordsman ordered his group to check the bodies they currently had bundled.

Sure enough, they also had the same protrusions. Alan immediately issued a warning to the rest of the adventurers.

"Do not, under any circumstances, touch the bumps on their head! Anyone carrying bodies needs to keep their eyes, nose, and mouth covered, and make sure they don't come in direct contact."

The members of the body collection squad didn't look too pleased with the additional layer of instructions but followed them all the same. They all tried to cover any exposed parts of their skin as much as possible as they started hauling away the carcasses. While they felt a twinge of guilt for the group that had to adhere to the additional safety measures, Zig and Siasha were relieved they weren't one of them.

"Looks like the situation took quite a turn," Zig said.

"But it also got much more fun!" she chirped.

"You really think so?"

The additional chaos seemed to excite her. Ever since she became an adventurer, trouble always seemed to lead to something favorable in the end. On the other hand, Zig was ready for all the extraordinary occurrences to stop.

Fortunately, they found no further oddities, and the entire extermination squad was able to return home. Alan and his party were ushered to the back offices for a debriefing while the rest of the adventurers formed a long line in front of the reception desk.

With such a large crowd and Alan's party in a meeting with the guild staff, they doubted the process was going to be handled smoothly and resigned themselves for a long wait. To their surprise, the receptionist made sure to keep the reports and postprocessing brief so everyone could be free to leave as soon as they finished.

Siasha fiddled with her money bag, filled with her commission reward, as they walked home.

"Since everyone was tired and only a few people had injuries," she explained, "they said we can make our full report at a later date. It didn't seem like that luxury applied to Alan and his party, though."

"Yeah," Zig agreed, watching how her black hair rippled behind her as she walked.

Siasha was an exception, but the squad was mostly made up of magic users who weren't as physically robust as sword fighters and the like. It made sense that using that much mana exhausted them.

Even Siasha and Zig felt fairly drained, so they decided to just buy some food at the stalls on the way home and eat at their lodgings.

Zig and Siasha returned to the inn and ate together while discussing what they needed to do the next day. They both decided to turn in early so they wouldn't have to worry about any lingering fatigue.

Zig noticed something out of the corner of his eye the moment he opened the door to his room.

"Hm?"

"Is something the matter, Zig?" Siasha asked, peering over with her hand on her own doorknob.

"No, it must've just been in my head," he said. "Night."

"Okay, good night!" she giggled.

It was just a simple bedtime pleasantry, but her tone made it seem like it was the finest regards she could give.

Watching Siasha close the door behind her, Zig stepped into his room.

Witch and Mercenary

CHAPTER 5

PAST AND PRESENT

Later that night, Zig sat up and looked out the window. Everything was still, and the moon shone brightly in the sky. He got out of bed and put on all his gear before leaving the room.

He paused for a moment in front of Siasha's room. Hearing no disturbances, he turned and made his way out of the inn.

The mercenary walked slowly, like he had no particular purpose in mind. Anyone watching would just see a man taking a midnight stroll. The town was quiet and there were no signs of anyone else out and about; he only passed the occasional drunkard toppled over on the side of the road, still clutching a bottle of booze.

Zig made his way past the downtown area, taking the back roads to the outskirts. Finally, he stopped.

"Around here should be fine, right?"

No one else was nearby, and his voice was the only thing that broke the silence.

Then a set of footsteps emerged from the shadows of a storehouse, and out stepped a man. He was handsome, with a mop of semi-long brown hair. Although he wasn't as well-built as Zig, his physique was by no means inferior.

Despite the man's youthful appearance, he was actually around ten years Zig's senior—something that Zig had never quite been able to accept.

"The moon looks beautiful tonight," he commented. "Long time no see, Zig."

"Ryell," Zig returned.

The man—Ryell—smiled wryly at Zig's ever-grumpy demeanor. They had once both been members of the same mercenary brigade. Ryell was even the fledgling mercenary who was responsible for looking after Zig when he was first taken in.

"I was surprised to learn you were on the investigation team too," Zig said.

"I came with the vanguard unit," Ryell said with a shrug. "You saw it, right? That hellscape. I barely escaped with my life."

Zig said nothing and began to rummage through his pockets until he found the familiar insignia with the motif of a hawk.

Ryell eyed the token. "Oh yeah. I did drop that."

Zig held out the badge, but the man waved him off.

"Did you quit the brigade?" the mercenary asked.

"It's not that..." Ryell said as he wistfully looked at the moon. "But it's not like I'm ever going to make it back."

He had a point. Zig didn't know how far the ship-building technologies of this continent had progressed, but it was probably impossible to build one that could make it across that sea teeming with monsters.

"So what do you want?" he asked.

Zig had been aware someone was looking for him. If he hadn't found the note wedged in the door of his room, he would have never come to this meeting.

Ryell turned his gaze away from the moon, his brown eyes—the same color as his hair—locking with Zig's.

He's not the same man I knew, Zig thought.

He could sense something had changed. Ryell had always been cheerful, someone whose smile never faded even in the face of hardship—he had none of that exuberance now. Zig could see the man's cheeks were sunken in and his eyes were clouded with fatigue.

"What the hell is this place?" It sounded more like Ryell was talking to himself than asking Zig. "Everyone and their mother can use magic like it's nothing. They don't even question it. They're creating things like fire and ice out of nowhere, you know? Don't you think it's bizarre?"

"Well, when you put it that way, yes."

The questions Ryell brought up were completely reasonable—Zig had felt the same way when he first arrived. But at some point—he couldn't quite say when—he just stopped caring.

Was it because I was always in the company of a witch? he asked himself. *Or maybe I've just been so busy that there's no free time to dwell on such things anymore?*

He had no answer.

"And the pièce de résistance is those monstrosities," Ryell went on. "When I found out monsters were just strolling around like they owned the place... I'm embarrassed to admit it, but I burst into tears. We just made it to land and those giant worm things burst up out of nowhere. I still can't forget the looks on my friends' faces as they were being dragged into the ground..."

He put up a hand to cover his face, his stare vacant.

"When I realized you were here too...well, to be honest, I thought I was saved. You were one of the stronger ones in the brigade, despite starting out as some punk kid who was being handled by his sword more than he could handle it. I thought that maybe if it was the two of us, we could deal with things even over here," Ryell said, but the look in his eyes was hardly one of hope.

"I was planning to meet you as soon as I found out you were here too. You stick out like a sore thumb, so it wasn't hard to find information on your comings and goings. But when I found out things were going well for you, even in a messed-up place like this... I was jealous."

Ryell chuckled softly, but his expression grew dark.

"However, I changed my mind when I saw the woman you were with. What the *hell* did you bring here?!"

It was less a question and more an accusation. Zig remembered the intense gaze he felt on the way home the day they bought his new weapon.

He said nothing in response to Ryell's biting inquiry.

That was enough of an answer for Ryell, who looked at him like he was putting Zig's sanity into question.

"I could tell just with one look at her eyes. She's a witch, isn't she?"

Just as Zig could tell Siasha was unusual at a glance, Ryell was able to do the same. Maybe it was because they also had mana, but humans in this continent didn't seem to notice those kinds of things. Zig was starting to realize just how much people like him and Ryell were biologically different from those that lived here.

"How are you okay being around *that*?" Ryell spat.

"She's my client."

Ryell's eyes nearly bulged out of his head. He brought one hand to his forehead like he was trying to stave off a headache.

"Didn't I teach you to choose your jobs wisely?" he groaned. "Why would you accept... No, more importantly...how did you even *meet* a witch?"

Zig's reply was curt as he played with the insignia in his hand. "You're also the one who taught me not to share details about a job with anyone."

Ryell had been charged with teaching Zig the skills needed for their job. At the time, he was also fairly new himself, so teaching Zig became a way for him to confirm with himself that he knew the tips and tricks of the trade.

But Zig's attitude seemed to give Ryell the impression that he was in circumstances he was unable to discuss.

"Is she threatening you?" Ryell demanded. "I can help you to get away from—"

"That's not it," Zig said, remembering how Ryell would scold him. "That's not how it is at all, Ryell. She asked me to help her, so I did."

The other man must've been worried for his tone to sound that indignant.

"I accepted her request freely," Zig said. "That's all there is to it."

Silence fell over the two men.

After a few moments, Ryell slowly squatted down as he heaved a great sigh. "So, that's how it is."

"You're not willing to accept her, no matter what?" Zig asked.

"My family was stolen from me by a witch." Ryell's voice was strained, his face a mix of both grief and rage. "You know that, and yet you still have the *balls* to ask that question?!"

"It's not like she was the one who did it."

"That doesn't matter!" Ryell shouted. "Witches are dangerous monsters! Why can't you understand that?"

Zig remembered the story Ryell once told him about the sinister deeds of a witch. When Ryell was still a boy, he and some of his friends left the village to play. Ignoring their parents' advice, they went to climb a nearby hill. Around dinner time, they were start-ing to get hungry and were making their way back when the earth began to rumble, accompanied by the roar of water.

Running back to their village, they found it swept away by a flash flood, leaving only the wreckage behind. The waters of the river had suddenly risen, even though it had been sunny without a cloud in the sky.

Everything, buildings and people alike, was taken by nature's fury.

With their families and homes taken from them, the children fell into despair. Ryell wandered around until he was found by a band of mercenaries.

At least, that was the story a drunken Ryell had shared with him.

"There's no doubt about it," he had said. *"That had to be the work of a witch."*

He had no proof, but the wounds were so deep that he was blind to all other explanation. He wasn't alone either—similar stories were common all over their home continent.

Ryell's expression was dark. "So, have you really lost your judg-ment to the point that you'd willingly associate with a monster?"

Ryell unsheathed his longsword, pointing the blade at his former companion. Zig sighed and stared at the weapon.

"A monster, huh," he said. "Both you and I have seen plenty of those on the battlefield, and you also should know humans don't need a reason to become one. Can't you ignore a witch who's come here to escape it all?"

"Can predators live among their prey?" Ryell asked. "I knew it, something's off. When did *you* of all people become so unrealistic? Are you sure that witch didn't do something to you?"

Ryell moved into a fighting stance and slowly began to walk toward him. He seemed to be utterly convinced that Zig was being manipulated by a witch.

"I guess it falls to me to open the eyes of the boy I considered to be my little brother to the fact that he's under a witch's spell."

Zig silently unsheathed the twinblade and pointed it at his former comrade-in-arms.

"Removing an arm should do the trick," Ryell continued. "Don't worry, I've heard they've got the ability to reattach them over here."

"Oh yeah?"

If this man knew Siasha's true identity and was intending her harm, there was only one thing Zig could do. He had tried his best to talk some sense into Ryell, but the man's hatred was clouding his judgment.

"I see." He tightened his grip on the twinblade.

He knew what he should do, but...

Even if a mercenary's enemies changed with each day, it was rare for members of the same brigade to turn on each other—especially a mentor and his protégé.

"I guess...you leave me no other choice," Zig said softly.

However, he was long past the stage where those sentiments could've stayed his sword arm. The man before him was no longer his former comrade. Ryell had threatened his client, and for that he had to die.

"How long has it been since we last crossed swords?" Ryell mused.

He kept the longsword at his shoulder, one hand under the guard and the other loosely at the pommel. It was a basic stance taught by the mercenary brigade—one Zig was intimately familiar with.

"Who knows?" he replied.

The nostalgia almost made him smile.

Moonlight shone down on Zig and Ryell as they took stock of each other.

The moment a cloud blocked the moon, shrouding the area with darkness, their two shadows crossed.

They only made one pass. It was a decisive battle to the death. They had no need to exchange words. They had the implicit understanding between two people with a long history.

The moon shone again.

A high-pitched clang rang out as shattered pieces of metal glittered in the moonlight, and Zig found himself bathed in crimson.

"Ha..." Ryell's voice was but a croak.

Zig's twinblade had cut through Ryell's iron blade like a piece of drywood, taking most of his abdomen along with it.

"Haha... Ha... Ha. You've...gotten...stronger, Zig..."

The tribute of the defeated party was paid in his own blood.

"Yeah." Zig nodded. He didn't even bother to try to avoid the spray of blood.

Ryell's feet gave out from under him, and he fell to the ground as he struggled to breathe. "I always figured...I'd die a dog's death. But...for it to be in this forsaken land...of all places..."

He tried to laugh, only to cough up flecks of blood instead. No matter how advanced recovery magic was on this continent, nothing would be able to save him.

"What do you want written on your grave?" Zig asked softly, noticing the light fading from the man's eyes.

Ryell's breathing was labored, but he managed a weak smile as he peered into Zig's bloodstained face.

"I don't need a grave," he said. "Dying alone...and forgotten...is befitting of a mercenary."

"Is that so?"

"Even...ahh...here...the stars...ngh...are...beau..." Ryell looked up at the sky. Zig was no longer reflected in his eyes. "Oh...I just wanna...go home..."

There were no more words after.

Zig closed Ryell's eyes and put his longsword in his hands.

"What a stupid thing to do."

Ryell had known from the start that he didn't stand a chance.

Zig had surpassed him long ago, back when they were both still in the mercenary brigade. He couldn't remember when, but one day Zig was given a different partner to spar with.

Neither of them said anything about it, but they both knew. And yet he still challenged Zig.

Was there some meaning behind it? Zig would never know what his real goal was.

"Still..."

Zig stood back up. He was about to walk away, but something sparked his memory. He took the mercenary insignia out of his pocket and placed it on Ryell's chest.

"I've passed through the door you've opened."

Even if they were past comrades, Zig didn't hesitate. He wiped Ryell's blood off his cheek. He stared down at his bloodstained hand, clenching and opening it as if what he had done had yet to sink in.

Zig stepped over the corpse and out of the moonlight, disappearing into the dark of night without looking back.

The next day, Zig and Siasha stopped by the guild so she could pick up a bonus based on her report and achievements from the previous day. Zig sat down, watching the adventurers mill around the reception area. There seemed to be more than usual today.

Last night didn't shake him. It was a loose end that was now tied up.

His focus was on the future.

The extermination quest would probably be enough to promote Siasha to eighth class. She still had a long way to go as an adventurer, but she was rising through the ranks quite quickly.

"My part in all this is going to get tricky," he mused.

Since Siasha was traveling with a non-adventurer, she would have a hard time finding a party to accept her. Zig was her bodyguard; he would always prioritize her safety. He couldn't imagine other party members being thrilled having someone they couldn't rely on since they weren't her.

He was still wondering what to do when he sensed a presence. Raising his head, he saw a familiar white-haired woman dressed in the unique garment that concealed the easy gait of her feet.

"I heard what happened," she said. "Sounds like there was some trouble again."

Without even asking his permission, Isana Gayhone slid into the seat in front of him. Zig didn't bother to suppress a drawn-out sigh. Trouble seemed to have found him once again.

"Hey, what's up with you?!" she cried. "Sighing as soon as you see someone's face... Is something wrong?"

"It's nothing," he said coldly. "What do you want?"

Isana's lips pressed into a pout. "Am I not allowed to talk to you unless I have a reason?"

"You're a royal pain, you know. Do you ever plan on growing up?"

Isana winced at his cutting words but quickly regained her composure and flashed him a fearless smile. "Are you sure that's the

attitude you should be taking with me?" she said. "After I specifically came to you with some information that I'm sure that you'll
want?"

"What? About the monstrosity swarm? I don't really care about
that; I can just ask Alan to tell me what he knows later."

The swordswoman blinked in surprise. "You also associate with
Alan and his party? You're surprisingly well-connected..."

"If you're not planning on telling me what you've got to say, can
you just go take a hike?"

Spending time with Isana would only bring more negative attention, and that was what he wanted to avoid. He could already feel
the stares of other adventurers.

"Fine," she sighed. "According to the investigation committee,
it was a type of mushroom."

"A mushroom?" Zig looked surprised; that wasn't what he was
expecting to hear. "It didn't look like one at all."

"There are many species of mushrooms in the world, and they
come in a wide variety of colors, shapes, and sizes. There are probably types that haven't even been discovered yet."

Zig had done his own research on mushrooms in the past, thinking they might be a viable food source in emergency situations.
The conclusion he'd reached was: Only eat them if they'll prevent
you from starving to death.

The more he researched, the more he learned that many of
them were poisonous—and a surprising number of them bore an
uncanny resemblance to the edible ones. Even veteran hunters lost
their lives to eating them by mistake.

There was perhaps more information, but studying that much
demanded time he didn't have, so the only lesson he took from it
was to stay clear of wild mushrooms as much as possible.

"Those mushrooms use the body of an insect as an incubator for their spores," Isana continued, "and they can exert some level of control over the actions of their host."

She further explained that insects parasitized by the mushroom sought out places where many of their own kind gathered. When the host died, the parasitic mushroom broke through its body, discharging the spores at the tip, which then attached themselves to the body of the next host. Thus, the life cycle began again.

For whatever reason, the insect hosts didn't attack their own kind. Aside from that peculiar behavior, they acted normally and so were likely to reproduce and hunt.

"Hey, are we okay?" Zig sputtered. "Is the team in charge of cleanup infected?"

"It seems they don't parasitize humans. And apparently, not all insects are fair game either—the only ones that can be new hosts need to be a similar type to the original."

Despite sounding terrifying, the mushroom's unique ability seemed to be rather limited.

"I see. So that's why there was such a big pack of them."

"Guess it wasn't your lucky day," Isana chortled.

That's rich coming from someone who was so unlucky the other day that she almost died.

"Is that all?" Zig said curtly. "Okay, you can go now."

"Why are you being so cold?" she complained. "I gave you some pertinent information, so at least keep me company for a bit."

It looked like Isana wasn't going to give him any other choice. Finding out those mushrooms didn't pose a threat to humans was a handy piece of knowledge, though.

He would just have to deal with her presence until Siasha got back.

"So, is your fighting style self-taught?" Isana asked as she snacked on some nuts.

She even ordered a drink—she was planning to stick around for a while.

"I adapted it into my own style after accumulating enough experience, but it was originally based on spear techniques from some country's military."

"You used to be in the military?!" Isana was so surprised she lurched forward in her seat.

"Not me," Zig said, "the leader of the mercenary brigade I once belonged to. He was the one who taught me the basics of handling a weapon when I was just starting out."

"Ah, gotcha. Was this mentor of yours...strong?"

Zig thought for a moment, squinting a little as if he was imagining the man standing before him.

"Yes," he said. "I'm probably now at the point where I could stand my ground against him."

"Excuse me?"

"But he was also an elite tactician, smart with excellent insight. Taking those skills into account, there's no way I'd be able to best him in a fight."

"You're...kidding, right?"

Isana was a capable fighter herself, and she was reasonably proud of those skills. But hearing all this had her looking at the ceiling in disbelief.

As Zig watched her slight panic, his thoughts drifted to his former mentor. His capabilities and knowledge were far beyond that of a common soldier... Perhaps he was formerly the general of some major power's military.

But there was no way of knowing now.

"As my body grew and I gained more strength, I changed my preferred weapon type," he went on. "I went from spears, to halberds, and finally the twinblade."

"Interesting."

Now it was his turn to ask *her* a question.

He gestured at one of Isana's elongated ears. "Tell me about these things."

"What do you want to know?" She didn't look exactly pleased at the question. But since she was the one who had started asking personal questions, it would be rather rude to refuse.

"I know you've got good hearing, but just how much can you hear?" he asked.

"Well..."

Isana glanced around the reception hall before pointing. Zig looked over to see three men, all who appeared to be melee fighters, observing Siasha as they also waited in line.

Isana's ears twitched forward ever so slightly.

"We're finally going to get promoted with this."

"It sure took a long time. We really need to find us a magic user."

"Say, why don't we ask her if she's up for it?"

The men were standing so far away, and the hall was filled with so much noise. Eavesdropping should have been impossible, but Isana was repeating their conversation word for word.

"Not only is she easy on the eyes, but she's apparently got a lot of promise."

"That'd be real nice, but isn't she the one who's always got that guy attached at her hip?"

"We don't need any more obnoxious men hanging around. I wonder if there's a way we can get just her to join us."

"Don't even try it. The old man warned us not to mess with that guy."

"What the hell? What's so special about him?"

"It's just gossip, but apparently, he's made some powerful connections. I've seen him talking with Alan before, and there are even rumors of him associating with Isana."

"Wait. Isn't that him?"

One of the men turned his head toward Zig. The man's two companions also glanced over and saw him sitting with Isana.

"They're seriously together?!"

"Don't make eye contact, idiot! Even with those pointy ears, she shouldn't be able to hear us from all the way over there!"

"Our clan is going to kick us to the curb if we end up on the wrong side of the Princess of White Lightning!"

Isana was quite the performer. She put on a good show, changing her tone to match the men's emotions. The men quickly turned away and didn't even glance at Siasha anymore.

"That's about what I can do," she said.

"I'm impressed. Not only do you have good hearing, but you can distinguish between sounds too."

"It's taken years of practice to get to that point," Isana boasted.

While she wasn't enthusiastic with being asked about her ears, she was practically preening at his praise. However, Zig could tell from the look on Isana's face when she repeated the phrase "pointy ears" that it was likely a derogatory term.

Maybe they hadn't meant it that way, but it seemed like she had taken it as a slight.

"Still, Isana, they seem really scared of you," Zig commented. "What did you do to them?"

"Excuse you!" she huffed. "Do you really think I go around attacking people willy-nilly? You were just a rare exception."

"Maybe so, but wasn't that a fairly extreme reaction?"

"That's..." Isana averted her eyes.

Her face told him she didn't feel awkward because of what happened, but actual regret.

"Let's just leave it at that," he said. "At least you're helpful for keeping the small fry at bay."

"I'd rather you not use me as a living pest repellent, thank you very much."

Although it didn't spark any conflicts, discrimination against foreigners seemed to be the same in any country. The tensions may even be worse on this continent because factions weren't able to openly fight, causing the hatred to simmer.

"You're not planning to do anything about that?" Isana asked.

Zig guessed she was referring to the men's conversation.

"My job is just to protect her," he said. "They may have an ulterior motive for asking her to join them, but as long as they mean her no harm, the decision is up to her. If they start to become a problem... Well, then it's a different story."

"Oh? Is she interested in joining a party?"

"Not just yet, but in the future it's hard to imagine we'll be able to get by with just the two of us. I've been thinking about it a lot lately."

Isana shifted awkwardly in her seat, realizing she touched on one of Zig's worries.

"Yeah, I can see how that might be off-putting," she said, "to party up with someone who comes along with bodyguard baggage."

"I was thinking maybe I could follow them at a distance and rush in if necessary..." he murmured.

"Don't. You'll definitely be reported to the guards."

"You're right. Any ideas?"

Isana was silent for a few moments.

"You could just try joining as supporters?" she suggested.

"What does that mean?" he asked.

The swordswoman then began to explain.

There were usually two types of parties. The first type was people looking for a long-time partnership. This was the most common option, with clans formed by multiple parties of this type coming together. The other type was one that was temporarily formed by a group of people who had a common goal at the time. These were the supporters.

These included parties needing a replacement for an injured companion or the temporary assistance of a magic user. The benefits were that it was no strings attached, and any rewards were clearly outlined so there would be no in-party squabbling.

However, it only worked for the short term. Supporters often didn't hold back when it came to their capabilities and beliefs, which could lead to personality clashes.

"I usually work on my own," Isana said, "but there are times I'll work with others to go after a big prize."

If anyone needed someone quick, there were advantages to temporarily teaming up with someone like Isana.

"It kind of sounds like the adventurers' version of mercenaries."

Zig didn't know such a system existed. Giving it a try might not be a bad idea—in fact, it was probably a good chance to practice working in tandem with others.

"That's just the advice you'd expect from a veteran adventurer," he said.

"Exactly!" She beamed. "You should show me more respect.

I don't mean to toot my own horn, but I'm a second-class adventurer, and that's pretty damn good."

"So I've been led to believe. Not that it has anything to do with me, though."

They then spotted Siasha walking toward them.

"Hello, Isana," she greeted.

"Hey there. Looks like things went well."

Siasha's grin was wide. "Uh-huh! I just received a promotion to eighth-class adventurer."

"That was quick," Isana said. "Just make sure not to misjudge your opponents, even if you're shooting up in the ranks. Of course, you do have some insurance, so you'll probably be okay."

The swordswoman glanced at Zig. He silently shrugged in return.

"I'll be careful," Siasha replied. "Oh, Zig, I spoke to Alan. He invited us to eat together. He wants to pay you your reward and mentioned something about you promising them they could treat you to a drink?"

"Oh, right. That."

The archer woman, Listy, did mention something along those lines back during the extermination request. Apparently, she was a woman of her word.

Zig got up from his seat.

"I think I'm going to head out as well," Isana said. "Take care out there."

The hem of her robe fluttered as she walked away. Siasha noticed Zig seemed to be staring at her legs as she departed.

"Is that what you prefer, Zig?" she asked.

Zig shook his head. "It took a little while because of the outfit, but I finally have a feel for her stride. She has surprisingly long legs."

"Her...stride?"

"Right. There's no guarantee we'll never cross blades again."

"You think she'll betray us?" Siasha was about to tell Zig she didn't think that would be the case when he continued to speak.

"There are plenty of reasons beyond breaking your word that could lead to two people fighting."

Even if they shared drinks, even if he carried someone on his back across the battlefield, that didn't mean he would never raise his sword to them again.

"Does that include me?" Siasha asked.

She already knew the answer, but she felt compelled to ask anyway. She had changed; that had to count for something.

"My job is to protect you."

Just like him to give her an answer that also wasn't an answer. Still, she couldn't help but wonder...how would the Zig of the past have responded?

He had also changed.

For now, just knowing that was enough.

Witch and Mercenary

THE RECEPTIONIST'S CONCERNS

I T WAS JUST ANOTHER DAY AT THE GUILD.

Cautiously, a young man pushed open the double doors. This young man and his four companions were startled by the clamor that greeted them, but they soon regrouped themselves and headed straight for the reception desk. Many appraising gazes watched them along the way, but the group was too preoccupied with themselves to take notice.

"Hello. How can I help you?"

"Umm...we've come to register as adventurers."

An attractive receptionist with brown hair who was busy with paperwork lifted her head when one of them gathered enough courage to speak up. The sight of her was a relief to the young men, who felt overwhelmed by the atmosphere of the guild.

"All right. Please start by filling out the required sections of these forms."

"S-sure."

The guild's receptionist—Sian—was wearing her usual customer-service smile as she watched the young men clumsily fill in their names and other information.

After Sian pointed out some details they'd omitted and conducted a short interview and briefing, the men's registration was complete.

"You are now tenth-class adventurers. We look forward to seeing your future accomplishments."

"Yeah! We're gonna climb through the ranks real quick!" the young men responded emphatically before turning to leave. No trace remained of the frazzled nerves they'd arrived with as they held their shoulders back and confidently walked away from her; they were probably headed straight to the armory.

"They'll be getting a reality check soon enough," Sian muttered under her breath as she glanced down at their paperwork.

These men—more like boys—were all second or third sons from farming families between the ages of fourteen and sixteen and had confidence in their physical strength. Although they had no formal training in swordplay, they'd practiced with wooden swords for a long time before coming to the guild to register.

After taking in the information they had scrawled onto their registration forms, Sian examined the papers that had been marked with a drop of blood from each adventurer. This was a special kind of paper that reacted to the presence of mana by changing color. You could approximate the amount of mana one possessed by observing the color that formed around the blood droplet, which varied depending on how concentrated it was in the blood. But it's not like this "reading" was a precise assessment. It didn't provide much information beyond determining whether the response was strong or weak. At most, it could suggest that a new recruit might be suited to becoming a magic user.

"No contacts, no money. Only self-proclaimed skills and no mana levels worth mentioning..."

Sian didn't see much hope of a bright future for them, but that was just their lot in life. She'd attempted to mention other career paths as an option, but they dismissed her suggestions outright. Well, if they were as good with their swords as they said and had some other special talent, maybe they'd slowly make progress?

No way, that's impossible, she thought. Dismissing the what-if from her mind, she turned back to her paperwork.

"Hey! Watch where you're going!"

It sounded like someone had bumped into another person. Sian recognized the voice: It was one she'd just heard. Her expression stiffened as she looked up and glanced in the direction it had come from.

One of the boys had fallen flat on his butt. He was rubbing it as he yelled at the enormous figure silently towering above him.

The man stood at least two meters tall. His well-toned physique had a breadth that matched his considerable height. His gaze was sharp; even Sian, who was used to dealing with adventurers and other rough types, didn't feel comfortable meeting his eyes. On top of all that, he carried a massive weapon—a sword with blades attached at both ends—making him the very picture of a seasoned warrior.

"Hello! I'm talking to you!"

These boys had chosen the wrong person to pick a fight with. But the advantage in numbers seemed to be imbuing them with confidence because they were verbally trying to press his buttons.

"For crying out loud!" she muttered in an exasperated tone.

This was definitely a scene she couldn't afford to ignore. Sian hurried away from the reception counter, making her way to the group. She glanced over at the usual crowd of adventurers who'd been watching on in amusement, but they just shrugged their shoulders like they didn't want to get involved—it was unlikely she'd get any help from them.

"What's going on here?!"

The boys, who'd been getting visibly upset, regained a bit of their composure at her sudden arrival. "Th-this man, he bumped into us..."

"No fighting allowed inside the guild. I believe I *just* told you that. If you're unwilling to obey the rules, there will be consequences."

Sian may have been petite, but her life experience was leagues ahead of these country bumpkins. Her intimidating demeanor unnerved the boys, throwing them into a panic as they glanced anxiously at each other.

"Th-that's not it...! Come on, let's get out of here."

Given this lady's status as a guild employee, they'd be in hot water if they got on her bad side. Finally realizing the precariousness of their situation, the young adventurers awkwardly averted their eyes and hurried out of the guild.

"This is why dealing with kids is such a pain," Sian groaned.

The boys were dispersing like skittering spiders. Sian drew herself up to her full height, her hands pressed firmly on her hips as she watched them flee. No sooner had a small sigh escaped her lips when words descended upon her from above.

"Apologies for the inconvenience."

She sighed again, deeper this time, as she looked up in the direction of the heavy, resonant voice. "And you... Now, I'm not saying you need to fight back, but what kind of man just stands there and takes it?!"

"That's easier said than done..." the man replied, scratching his head with an indeterminable expression.

There was a newcomer causing quite a stir in the guild as of late... and *he* was her bodyguard.

This was Zig Crane, the man who referred to himself as a mercenary.

On this continent, where wars had long ceased to exist, there was no such thing as a "mercenary for hire." However, the job title remained, even if the people here who operated under this title were a far cry from the original definition. These self-proclaimed mercenaries were just ruffians who couldn't quite make it as members of the mafia or adventurers. Society saw them as nothing but nuisances.

At least, that's how it usually was, but...

"Doesn't it bother you to be talked down to like that?"

"People who underestimate their enemies die quickly. It's fine to leave them to their own devices."

This response, right here.

Members of the mafia, adventurers, and anyone involved in chaotic work despised being looked down upon. If you were seen as someone unlikely to retaliate after being taken advantage of, you might be vulnerable to exploitation in business dealings and negotiations. It could even lead to unnecessary conflicts. Preserving one's reputation was crucial both for the sake of work and avoiding disputes.

And yet, this man didn't seem to care about any of that. It was almost like he'd come from a completely different culture.

...What if a place really existed where his line of thought was the norm? In other words, somewhere where human-on-human violence was that common.

Success is measured by results. Honor and prestige serve no purpose.

Those values only worked in extreme situations where human lives were constantly being consumed. An environment that demanded unwavering competence. A land of perpetual strife where the weak were eliminated daily.

"Well, whatever, I guess…"

As long as this man doesn't cause any trouble, it's no skin off my back.

The most important thing was for her workday to end peacefully. She'd attempted to wrap up the conversation on that note, but Zig seemed to have something on his mind.

"Still, I've got to admit, I was a little impressed."

Sian's eyes widened in surprise. That was the last thing she'd expected him to say.

"I mean, I look how I look, right? It was oddly satisfying to have a rookie test his luck with me. The guys over here sure have some balls."

Zig nodded almost appreciatively as Sian's shoulders sagged in resignation.

That take completely missed the mark. But explaining why seemed like too much of a hassle, so she decided to just leave it at that. It would be a pain to rehash the same thing again since she had already explained it once to his client.

"Well? What brings you here today?"

There was a slight brusqueness to her attitude. Zig wasn't an adventurer, but it was because of him that his client, a newcomer with great potential, continued to work on her own without joining a party.

"I don't have any business with the guild. I'm here to talk about a job."

Zig waved her off with a final, "Sorry for all the trouble," before heading toward the attached dining hall.

It seemed this client of his was an adventurer. She could make out the other party giving Zig a quick bow before handing him some money.

"Now he's working for another adventurer…"

In addition to being a bodyguard, he seemed to take on a lot of side jobs on his days off. As expected from his appearance, he specialized in violent work, and since he didn't seem picky about his clients, adventurers also came to him with requests.

Sian had done some investigating because she was concerned he might be trouble, but his reputation among the adventurers was overwhelmingly positive. In any case, he was hardworking and would readily accept even dangerous jobs so long as the money was good. And while she hadn't witnessed them firsthand, she'd heard his skills were quite impressive.

"It's a little scary how steadily he's building a network, though..."

Despite not being the type to lay all his cards on the table, business was going well for him. It was very difficult to find a dependable and efficient hired arm who would take on even troublesome jobs, and it probably didn't hurt that hiring him rather than another adventurer meant one could save on paying the guild's brokerage fee.

"I've got to keep an eye on that one...!"

Sian Ebreiz had been working at the guild as a receptionist for three years. She enjoyed her job, and always kept a watchful eye on suspicious individuals. Her words were a declaration of determination from a woman fueled by a sense of purpose.

Witch and Mercenary

AFTERWORD

I

T'S MY HONOR TO GREET EVERYONE WHO PURCHASED A copy of this book. This is Chohokiteki Kaeru, the author. Did you enjoy reading *Witch and Mercenary*?

There weren't any major events in my life that prompted me to start writing it. I was just reading various works and began to think, *I would've written it this way,* or *The story could've been so much more interesting if this had happened.* It wasn't much more than daydreaming until a change in my work situation finally gave me the time to write, and I started to put those thoughts into action.

This isn't a tale of invincible characters, nor is it a satisfying revenge drama. The hero isn't surrounded by girls who worship him. It's a somewhat unrefined and matter-of-fact story, but maybe that's just what entices those who pick up the book into purchasing it.

Light fantasy stories are enjoyable, but at times, we have a desire to consume something grittier. It's easy to shy away from hardcore fantasy stories that often have complicated settings and circumstances.

I'm writing this afterword in the hopes that this book will satisfy the needs of the people I've described above.

With its occasional comedic scenes and less complicated setting, *Witch and Mercenary* can't really be called a hardcore fantasy novel, but the dark and coarse aspects are too frequent to consider it light fantasy either.

I suppose you could call it an "in-between" fantasy.

I tried to emphasize readability when creating this story (although my ability as a writer was surely lacking in that department). I was hoping to keep long-winded descriptions down to a minimum so that newcomers to the genre could read it without getting overwhelmed.

Due to that restraint, I let myself loose during action scenes. I'm actually worried they might feel a little cloying. I'm a huge fan of action video games, so you'll have to forgive my tendency to describe all the fight scenes in detail.

The fighting styles aren't entirely grounded in real swordplay and are more of a "knockoff combat style." I tried to depict them in easy-to-comprehend imagery since I figured that keeping the fighting too realistic might not be as interesting to the reader.

The main character, Zig—a man who's willing to take the lives of others for money—is hardly someone the average person can project themselves onto. Empathizing with and understanding his thoughts and actions is difficult and forces the reader to observe the story from a third-person perspective.

If you found him appealing as a character, it may have been his way of life that attracted you.

Readers can look forward to seeing how Zig's encounter with the witch and the journey they set off on together changes him and his beliefs.

This story ignores all the latest trends, templates, and writing styles. To be honest, I never planned for it to be read by many people, so even now it's still hard for me to believe it's being released as a novel.

This book came together thanks to the constant support of my readers, my editors who worked tirelessly through the novelization process, and the wonderful illustrations of Kanase Bench.

I offer my biggest thanks to all of you!